Thirty Days to Home

Thirty Days to Home

A Novel

CATHRYN RAKICH

SHE WRITES PRESS

Published in 2026 by
She Writes Press, an imprint of The Stable Book Group

1569 Solano Ave #546
Berkeley, CA 94707
https://shewritespress.com
Library of Congress Control Number: 2026904389
ISBN: 979-8-89636-304-0
eISBN: 979-8-89636-305-7

Interior Designer: Tabitha Lahr

Printed in the United States

To my husband, Mark, for his unwavering support
of me and our crazy clan of rescue animals.

“Bless the beasts and the children
For in this world they have no voice
They have no choice.”

—BARRY DEVORZON & PERRY BOTKIN, JR.

Chapter One

"One in a million chance," the police detective said, "of hitting your head on an object just exactly right to kill a person."

Eighteen-year-old Franklin May, son to Marli and Nick May, was dead. He fell in a freak accident. A police investigation determined he was on the top step of a ladder hanging ornaments on his Christmas tree—the first holiday in his new apartment. Family and a few friends were coming for Christmas Eve, only a week away. He wanted the place to look "festive," he told his mom. The police report stated that the victim had lost his footing. He reached just a little too far, probably focused on filling that one open spot at the back of the tree. Too fixated to move the stepladder just a bit closer. Just a little more. Then it was over. His head met the edge of the wrought iron and glass coffee table.

Marli twisted uncomfortably in her seat. She hated flying. She felt trapped like a feral cat in a steel cage. Nick, her husband of twenty years, sat stoically next to her, glued to another spy novel on his Nook.

"What are you reading?" she asked.

"You wouldn't know the author," Nick replied without looking up.

Marli stared out the airplane's dual-paned plexiglass window, its surface crazed with hairline cracks and smudged from previous passengers. Nothing to see but vastness. She finally achieved a semi-comfortable position, slouched down, her slim legs bent to a 90-degree angle, feet wedged between the seat in front of her and the side of the aircraft. They were halfway to their first stop of Mexico City. Another four hours to go. Then, thankfully, a quick ninety-minute jump to their final destination of Puerto Escondido.

"I was just trying to make conversation," she whispered.

This was Marli's first trip since Franklin had died two years earlier. But there was not enough time to erase the pain. The ache was always there. It consumed her. It dominated her daily activities. It threatened her career and marriage. She stopped getting dressed in the morning, choosing to remain in her baggy sweatpants and the white, cotton T-shirt she slept in. Makeup was an unnecessary amenity. It only forced her to look at herself in the mirror, to see her anguish. If she never ventured beyond the shelter of her private cocoon, never came in contact with well-meaning acquaintances and unaware strangers, she had no need to be presentable. A clean blouse and a layer of mascara were useless to her.

Marli's editor at South Bay Accent was sympathetic. He found someone else to temporarily cover arts and entertainment for the San Jose–based magazine, providing his senior writer with the space and time to grieve. But, when she attempted to write again, too many missed deadlines, careless fact-checking, and poor prose led to a more permanent departure.

"It's just too soon, Marli," he told her. "Come back when you're ready."

Marli knew Nick was also overwhelmed with grief, but he confronted Franklin's death with distractions. Work was his escape—escape from the sadness that saturated their walls, escape from a wife who could not bear to be touched, escape from the guilt of not being able to help their son.

The pilot brought the 130-seat B737 into the small coastal town of Puerto Escondido at 4:30 p.m. A south-of-the-border burn greeted Marli as she stepped from the frigid interior of the aircraft. Passengers disembarked the plane directly onto the heat-radiating tarmac and the searing humidity dripped over Marli's body like steam trapped under the lid on a pot of boiling water.

"Keep up, will you?" Nick pleaded as they fell into line with the other passengers heading toward the terminal.

A layer of perspiration grew heavy under Marli's cool-weather clothing, sweat pooling under her arms and slowly winding down her back. She juggled her bright chartreuse carry-on bag from one arm to the other as she peeled off her black-and-purple Baja hoodie and tried to keep pace with her less-than-chivalrous husband.

"I don't want to be last in line at customs," Nick said, as they entered through the large automatic glass doors that soundlessly slid open to a mercifully air-conditioned terminal.

Marli embraced the cool relief, wiping away the dampness that had formed at the back of her neck. A heavily armed Mexican federale, dressed in black fatigues and combat boots, stood statue-like nearby.

Marli had become accustomed to Nick's terse attitude and his curt commands. He was becoming increasingly impatient each day without Franklin, each night without Marli—her body next to him in bed, but her mind hopelessly lost in heartache.

The customs check went smoothly, and the couple found their weary luggage stuck in a repetitive loop on the single baggage-claim carrousel, only a handful of travelers still mingling around. Marli cringed as she inspected the oily, black scuff marks on her favorite travel bags.

"Ready?" Nick asked, grabbing his black carry-on and checked suitcase.

Back outside in the insistent heat and humidity, they found their way curbside and to a waiting shuttle van. Nick and Marli climbed in and took their spots in the two seats directly behind the baseball-capped driver. Icy air blasted from the vents, scattering the smell of exhaust fumes and sunscreen lotion throughout the shuttle. A line of statuesque palms sprouted from the asphalt parking lot. Overhead, an A320 Airbus thundered past.

"We meet again," announced a suntanned gentleman situated in the right-hand corner of the back row of the van.

Marli twisted around to find the same friendly twosome with whom she and Nick had just shared the short aerial hop from Mexico City to Puerto Escondido.

"We were not formally introduced before. I'm John. This is my wife, Annie," the man said, wiping away a trickle of sweat from his bronzed forehead with an ecru handkerchief.

Marli introduced herself and Nick as she dug for the seat belt buried between the off-white vinyl van cushions.

The well-kept shuttle bus rambled down a paved path to the airport exit and took a hard left onto Mexican Federal Highway 200. Cold air continued to pulse from the vents, and Marli contemplated pulling her hoodie back on, its sleeves now wrapped around her slim waist like the arms of an awkward teenage boy.

The two-lane road, more in line with a simple city street than a designated federal highway, meandered past small shops and family-owned restaurants, some open for business, others boarded up with wide wooden slats across the doors and windows. Broken cement sidewalks and brick paths came to abrupt stops, dropping off into dirt and gravel and resurrecting themselves a half a block later. Children stood silently in front of store entrances, often barefoot, watching vehicles speed past as if there was nothing better to do.

"What brings you to Puerto Escondido?" John asked.

"Work retreat," Nick responded, pushing his thinning brown hair off his forehead. "My wife is along for the ride."

Marli, engrossed in the passing sights, tried to take her mind to a different place, a place far from Franklin, far from grief. But something always pulled her back. *Why don't you just tell people our son died and we are trying to escape our misery, our wretched despair?* she wanted to scream. Because that would break all the rules of social correctness. *Don't burden others with your pain. Keep it to yourself.*

"What do you do?" Annie asked.

"Pharmaceutical sales," Nick replied.

"Well, you could not have chosen a more beautiful place for a retreat," Annie said, removing her demure sun hat and smoothing down her curly, gray hair, now unruly from the lingering mugginess. "We decided to buy a condo in Puerto Escondido about a year ago after spending just about every winter here for the past—"

"Watch out!" Marli shouted as the van abruptly swerved, throwing its startled passengers swiftly to the right and then to the left, while the driver applied the brakes to slow down but did not stop. There was a thump under one of the van wheels. A small tan object, an animal, sprinted from the left side of the bus, across the road paved with oncoming traffic, and through a thick hedge of oleanders dotted with crimson blooms.

"I think you hit a dog!" Marli shouted, pressing her face into the passenger-side window as the scenery rushed past her.

The driver, relaxed and low in his sunken bucket seat, waved his suntanned hand in the air, rattled off something in Spanish, and kept driving.

"Stop!" Marli screamed. "Why won't you stop?"

"He won't stop for a dog," John replied, looking at Marli as if to beg her forgiveness. "They get hit all the time. There are hundreds of street dogs in Mexico."

"But what if he's really hurt?"

"What are we supposed to do about it?" Nick chimed in, barely looking up from his cell phone as he fumbled to punch in a text. "Damn autocorrect! Listen Marli, I'm sure he belongs to someone. They'll take care of him. Just forget about it."

"How am I supposed to forget about it?" Marli mumbled with no expectation of a response. Their first hour of vacation in the picturesque coast-side town of Puerto Escondido, Mexico, was off to a rocky start.

Marli slumped disheartened into the Naugahyde seat and stared out the window. Nick and the other van occupants exchanged a few unpleasantries about "street dogs" and what a shame there were so many. Their garbled voices were inconsequential background noise as Marli relived the thump under the bus wheel over and over again in her gut.

Her mind wandered without direction. She thought about her mother back home in California and recalled a story she had told Marli years ago during a long journey across the United States, Ford station wagon loaded down with most of their belongings when Marli's parents moved from New York to the West Coast almost fifty years earlier.

Alice and Allan Stewart, recently married, young and adventurous, stopped at every state and national park they could fit into their tight schedule and even tighter budget, taking advantage of the numerous hiking trails carefully carved throughout America's landscape. During one backcountry trek along a secluded stream just outside of Yellowstone National Park, the backpack-clad couple came across a litter of six puppies drowned in the clear shallow water, their small lifeless bodies tied up in a plastic mesh bag weighed down with river rocks beneath the cold surface.

"It ruined the trip," Alice had shared with her daughter years later.

"Are you OK?" Nick asked, turning to his wife.

"I'll be fine."

As the van drew closer to the core of Puerto Escondido, Marli began to take note of what seemed masked before—more and more stray dogs. Like runaway children sleeping in dark alleys, the wayward canines started to appear everywhere. They slept curled up so close to the roads and side streets that it was no wonder so many were killed or injured by indifferent drivers. They meandered the broken cement sidewalks and unpaved pathways from one block to the next. They stood guard in front of shops and cafes, amiably stepping aside as customers entered and exited. They were invisible creatures sniffing the ground for anything that might be edible.

The majority of vagrant mutts were medium to large in size with short fur coats draped across bony ribs and protruding hip bones. The smattering of long-haired dogs were severely matted, tight wads of scruffy twisted coats hanging down in clumps along their skinny torsos.

Bulging testicles conspicuously hung down from some of the mongrels. Females with swollen nipples swinging low were a certain indication that there was a brood of puppies somewhere waiting for their mother's return. It was impossible to determine if any of the indigent dogs had owners. None wore collars. Most appeared malnourished.

"Our first stop is coming up, *mis amigos*," announced the driver as the shuttle continued along Highway 200.

Corner shops and intimate eateries gave way to sprawling new housing developments, some still under construction with mechanical caterpillars and long-necked cranes serving as temporary garden art. Some were gated. Most were two-story, white stucco condos with terra-cotta roofs and climbing trellises laden with colorful tropical flowers and foliage.

Puerto Escondido, situated between the Sierra Madre del Sur mountain range and the Pacific Ocean, was built around an idyllic bay surrounded by massive rock formations that lurched from the sea. In recent years, the once-obscure fishing port, located in the state of Oaxaca at the southern end of Mexico, had become popular with tourists and expatriates searching for unspoiled beaches, spectacular surfing, and minimal commercialism. The residents were unpretentious, friendly, and easygoing.

The van took a right on Camino Carrizalillo stretching toward the ocean, then a left into a residential courtyard, and finally came to a stop in front of a dual-level casita painted over by a magenta bougainvillea and brassy trumpet vines in full bloom.

"This is our stop," announced John as he and Annie maneuvered their way from the back of the shuttle bus to the side door, which the driver had already yanked open.

A burst of heat slapped Marli across the face like an open hand.

"You will get used to the street dogs," John whispered to Marli as he exited. "You won't even notice them after a while."

The van pulled back onto the highway for several more miles and then turned left on Del Morro Street, coming to a halt in front of Hotel Santa Fe, its impressive, colonial-style, white structures and lush sprawling grounds dominating the street. Marli grabbed the driver's outstretched hand and eased out of the vehicle onto the cracked pavers that led to the hotel entrance. An older woman, her face and hands creviced with ancient wrinkles, sat hand stitching a piece of ivory cloth in front of the massive, wooden entry gate.

"*Hola*," Marli nodded, employing one of the few Spanish words she knew.

The elderly woman smiled back, waving her hand across stacks of neatly folded blouses and shawls displayed on a wool blanket covering the ground. "Please, look."

Cotton and crocheted dresses draped from wire hangers on a nearby fence caught the warm breeze so the graceful fabrics fluttered and fell like an uncomplicated ballet.

"*Gracias*," Marli replied, momentarily forgetting her sorrow. "Shopping right outside our hotel. Such beautiful things," she said, peering down the sidewalk to two more vendors, one with hundreds of brightly colored textiles piled high on two long folding tables, the other offering row after row of handmade jewelry.

"You can shop later," Nick said as he led Marli through the carved gate into the hotel's main courtyard and to the registration area, a mere three-sided room barely big enough for more than one visiting couple or vacationing family to check in at a time. A large, sun-faded map of Puerto Escondido, undoubtedly out-of-date, was casually taped to the right wall. A display of one-pound bags of coffee beans sat for sale to the left of the counter.

"Enjoy your stay," the young woman said from behind the counter, handing Nick two room keys—the old-fashioned, metal kind. An eager bellhop led the way down a stone path wallpapered on both sides with plush exotic plants. Hibiscus, purple morning glory, pineapple sage, and Mexican honeysuckle splashed across the courtyard like a child's finger painting. The lane twisted past an outdoor bamboo bar with a palm-thatched roof just gearing up for the evening's happy hour and ended at a steep set of tiled Talavera steps that led to their hotel room. Two unfinished pine rocking chairs kept company to the left of the door.

"Nice," Marli said, stepping inside the spacious yet modest room. A layer of perspiration grew heavy under her clothes, sweat pooling at the nape of her neck and slowly winding down her back. A bulky ceiling fan with white-washed wicker blades whirled above their heads. A wall-mounted air conditioner clicked tirelessly away in one corner.

She tossed her bag onto the king-size bed adorned with a vibrant red quilt and framed by a carved headboard of Mexican cedar. "I love the terra-cotta floors."

"Too rustic," responded Nick, dropping his luggage on the bed and quickly turning to a white security safe on the closet floor to stash a small envelope of cash. Nick preferred a formal decor that conveyed an air of financial success. In their twenty years of marriage, Marli had learned to live with the stodgy furnishings and ornate embellishments that adorned their overpriced Bay Area home.

A small, wooden writing desk held a water pitcher covered with clear plastic wrap and two drinking glasses alongside a glossy tourist pamphlet titled, "Discover Puerto Escondido." Marli sat on the edge of the desk chair as Nick strategically moved his belongings from his luggage to a well-worn wooden dresser. He preferred to take all his travel clothes out of his suitcase, place the socks and underwear into drawers, and carefully hang up his shirts and pants in the closet, commandeering most of the hangers. Marli chose to leave her travel attire, with the exception of a nice blouse or dress that she wanted wrinkle-free, in her luggage. Depositing her clothes into an unfamiliar set of hotel room drawers, especially for as brief as one week, just did not suit her. Casual, even free-spirited, described Marli's way of managing her world.

As she watched her husband unpack, Marli's thoughts turned to the street dog struck by their shuttle van, and where he must be now—dead or worse, suffering.

"Is this going to ruin our trip?" Nick asked as he lined up his socks in the order he planned to wear them during their week in Puerto Escondido. "You have to let this go. Dogs probably get hit here all the time. There are so many. I am sure someone will find him and take him to a vet."

"What vet?" Marli asked. "I didn't see a vet, did you? No one is going to help that dog. Not even a well-meaning tourist," she added, quietly referring to herself.

"Listen, Marli. You wanted to tag along on this trip. I told you I didn't think it was a good idea, but you insisted. So don't drag me down about a dumb animal. You don't even like dogs."

"That's not true. I like dogs. I like all animals. Franklin always wanted a dog, but you wouldn't let him have one."

"I can't believe you would say that to me," Nick responded.

Marli sat silent, staring into nothing. "I'm sorry," she finally said. "I didn't mean it the way it sounded. It's just so hard. When will it get easier?"

"I don't know," Nick replied. "Probably never." He finished unpacking his suitcase. "I'm going to take a shower."

Sitting on the corner of the bed, Nick carefully slid one loafer off at a time and placed the shoes on the cedar-planked floor of the closet. He removed his creased khaki slacks and light-pink polo shirt and hung them on the hotel's wooden hangers, gliding his hand down the pants to press out any wrinkles from the day's travels.

Looking at Nick, his muscular thighs against the tight, white briefs, Marli remembered what initially attracted her to him. She loved the thick, coarse, black hair that twisted and curled across his wide chest. His stomach was not as toned as it was when they first met, but she still found his masculine physique desirable. Hailing from a Mediterranean descent, he was graced with olive-toned skin that easily tanned. His solid arms and legs were a rich coffee color that stopped abruptly at the ankle where his socks began, reminding Marli of how Nick had futilely promised she would not become a golf widow after they married.

As Nick picked up his black, leather toiletry bag, Marli thought back on a time when he would have invited her into the shower with him, something that was second nature when they first started dating, when making love was easy and frequent. Marli would catch herself thinking about Nick in the middle of the day, a tickling sensation surging up within her when she visualized his strong body on top of hers, his warm skin, and his determined touch.

The first few months are the best time in a relationship, Marli mused, *when everything is fresh and untarnished, when two people are still discovering each other, when bad habits remain hidden, when an uncontrollable energy takes over the body and mind, and makes one crazy with hunger, desire, and what feels like love . . . before there are memories, before there are complications, before there is grief.*

"I won't be long," Nick said, bringing Marli back to the present. "Then we can walk down to the beach and scope out a place for dinner."

Chapter Two

Marli opened her chartreuse suitcase, cursing the oily scuff marks from the airport baggage belt again, and pulled out a pair of black, cotton shorts and a red, sleeveless top that were better suited to the steamy weather than her travel clothes. She released her excessively curly ponytail from the elastic hair tie that imprisoned it, stopping to carefully untangle the fragile, blond strands tangled around the stretchy pink band. Her rebellious ringlets, set free by the unrelenting humidity, danced and dangled around Marli's pretty, soft-featured face.

Still waiting for Nick to emerge from the bathroom after his solo shower, Marli stepped out onto the room's tiled terrace and up to the wrought iron railing adorned with decorative metal sunflowers reaching for the early evening sky. The long day was coming to an end, and Marli breathed it in—and then, looking down, she saw another street dog.

This vagrant mutt was slightly larger than the one Marli had glimpsed as it darted out from beneath the airport shuttle van. This one was lying on his side across the road from the hotel at the outer edge of a cement sidewalk that took pedestrians past beachfront restaurants and trendy outside bars. Slick, charcoal fur ran from his head all the way down his back to the tip of his tail accompanied by small patches of burnt cream under his legs and upper chest. The dog was positioned uncomfortably close to the high-traffic road. If he stretched out even a few inches more, he risked being struck by a vehicle with a driver who was not paying enough attention to stay in the middle of the lane. Cars and trucks sped past him. He was invisible to walkers and bicyclists.

She monitored the dog from the hotel room balcony for several more seconds trying to assess if the reason for his peculiar posturing was because he was perhaps injured or ill. He lay so still, his eyes closed as the world went on around him. A tall, tanned, young man brushed past the motionless mongrel on a skateboard plastered with colorful logo stickers. A middle-aged couple, talking back and forth with emphatic hand gestures, almost tripped over the reposing canine, too distracted to notice him. An overweight woman, wearing a bright-yellow T-shirt stretched tightly across her substantial middle, escorted two boisterous toddlers, one in each hand, without even a glance down in the dog's direction.

Finally, the misplaced mutt lifted his furry head, followed by his long lean body, and took a deep satisfying stretch with two paws pushed out in front, his rear in the air. When he came to a full stance, adeptly balancing on three legs, his back left limb dangled lifelessly from the hip socket.

Marli stretched over the railing for a better look. The dog was injured. And she was not going to walk away twice.

A steady stream of water continued to pound the walls of the shower stall. "Nick," Marli spoke in an elevated voice through the slightly ajar bathroom door. "I'm going to walk around the hotel grounds. I'll be right back," she said over the ongoing pulse of the water.

Without waiting for Nick to respond, Marli stuffed her room key in the front pocket of her shorts and pushed through the door to the outside. She hurried along the cobblestone path, past one of the two hotel swimming pools, through the reception area littered with arriving guests, and out the large, carved double doors where the elderly Mexican woman still crouched with her needlepoint in hand.

Marli paused for a battered, off-white truck to move past her and out of the way and then darted across the street before several more oncoming vehicles could deter her. By the time she reached the curve in the road where she had eyed the compromised dog from her hotel room balcony, he was gone. Disappointment swept over her. Marli's face flushed with anxiety as she scanned the vacant cement from the left to the right.

The sidewalk where the handicapped hound had lain was steps away from the beach and a few feet from a stone staircase that led up to a lookout over the Pacific Ocean. The dog could have gone in any direction—toward the beach, up the steps, down the sidewalk—anywhere. Which way should she go in search of him? If she found the dog, what would she do with him? Standing in the exact spot where she saw the mutt resting, on his own terms and without a bother to anyone, Marli opted to return to the hotel room and hoped Nick did not take issue with her absence.

There are hundreds of street dogs, she reminded herself. *You cannot help them all. Try to save yourself first.* The warm air of the day was beginning to settle into a comfortable coolness as a light breeze flowed from the ocean over the sand and up into the town.

"Where have you been?" Nick asked without looking up from his cell phone when Marli rushed into the room.

"Just wandering around the grounds. Are you ready?"

Del Morro Street was a milelong expanse that awakened from its daytime siesta as soon as the sun hit the ocean. College students, surfers, retired expats, and vacationers descended on the strip every night like it was an endless frat party. Restaurants, one right after the other with an occasional tourist shop stuck in between, varied in size and formality from small, family-run diners with plastic red tablecloths and handwritten chalkboard menus to large chain-like establishments with tequila bars and live music. One thing they all had in common was that they faced the ocean, opening wide onto Del Morro Street only steps away from where the asphalt met the sand.

"Where should we eat?" Marli asked, struggling to keep pace with Nick as he impatiently weaved around an obstacle course of slow pedestrians and awkwardly placed building posts, passing outdoor vendors with flimsy folding tables displaying handmade jewelry and artwork.

"I'll know it when I see it," Nick said as if he already had a specific restaurant in mind. "Here, this one looks good," he said, stopping at La Hosteria, a small open-air eatery that specialized in handmade, wood-fired pizzas. The aroma of sizzling Italian pies emerged from an adobe oven that dominated one corner just left of the entrance.

"Italian?" Marli asked. "OK. I guess there will be lots of opportunities for Mexican food later."

The lively restaurant was almost at capacity with only two open tables, a positive sign that the food would be good when several of the other cafes along the boulevard were void of customers. A lanky, suntanned man in his early thirties wearing beige surfer shorts and an untucked, button-down Hawaiian shirt greeted Nick and Marli as they stepped inside. The spicy smell of fresh oregano- and basil-infused sauce floated past them. An employee in a white, tomato-stained apron stood between the pizza oven and a long, bar-height countertop scattered with coarse cornmeal. Undistracted by his intimate audience, he kneaded, stretched, and coerced the dough into delicate submission.

"How is this?" asked the welcoming host as he waved Marli and Nick to a small, round table for two situated next to a tiki-style bar occupied by two women in their early thirties. One was dressed in tight skinny jeans resting so far down on her curvaceous hips that a tiny butterfly tattoo fluttered into view just above her left rear cheek. The other woman wore a tasteful skirt in a floral burgundy print that casually brushed her tight calves. They both had on fitted blouses that accentuated their breasts. From the ample amount of shimmery eyeliner and shiny lip gloss, it was evident they were hoping for a long, productive, and entertaining evening. The woman in skinny jeans exchanged a momentary glance with Nick as he pulled out his chair to sit.

"Do you speak English?" Nick asked the young waiter, who shook his head no. Nick pointed to the red wine listing on the menu and held up two fingers. "Two glasses, *por favor*."

"This is nice," Marli said, twisting from side to side to get a better look around the compact room. A glass-front refrigerator, humming in place behind the cash register, lit up from the inside, showcasing amber beer bottles of Modelo, Tecate, and Corona keeping company with the red-and-white cans of Coca-Cola de Mexico. A set of stairs precariously void of a banister led to more seating on a second level, and a herd of hurried waiters, busboys, and bartenders shuffled back and forth from the kitchen to the dining room.

All of the tables were full now, and a line of anxious customers was beginning to form at the entrance and stretch out onto the sidewalk. Dusk officially gave way to nightfall, and the crowds outside were growing increasingly enthusiastic.

"Yes, it seems fine," replied Nick as he emptied his wine glass and waved the waiter over for a second.

"Listen, Nick," Marli said, lowering her voice. "I know you didn't want me to come on this trip. You think I'll be a burden. You think you will have to worry about me. But you won't. I promise. I'm trying really hard to get back to normal. I love you, and I think you still love me."

"Marli," Nick replied, taking a long, deep sip from his replenished wine glass. "I have to use the restroom," he said, abruptly pushing back his chair. "I'll be right back."

Marli looked up to see the skinny-jeans woman at the adjacent bar also retreat to the back of the restaurant and down a short hall stacked with plastic crates of iceberg lettuce and tiny green Mexican limes.

Ten minutes later Nick returned, pushing back strands of disheveled hair from his flushed face.

"You were gone so long. The salads came and I was so hungry I started without you," Marli said, putting down her fork. "Why do you look so flushed?"

"Sorry. I got a call from a coworker reminding me of the retreat's start time tomorrow, and then we got to talking about some work-related thing that has me on edge. But it's nothing I want to talk about." Nick tossed back the rest of his wine in one quick shot and tried to spear an uncooperative cherry tomato.

Setting her empty salad plate to the side, Marli caught a glimpse of something shooting through the jumbled line of waiting patrons at the entrance of the restaurant. A medium-sized dog with short, oak-brown fur and a dirty white chest dashed between the barricade of human legs like they were slats in a fence. The canine's slim muscular body darted under dining tables and in between chairs as he circled the room in a random dance of exhilaration, his pink nose glued to the scarred-wood floor as he voraciously vacuumed up every stray crumb in his path in his food-driven mission.

"Oh my god!" screeched the skinny-jeans, butterfly-butt woman, who had returned to her seat at the bar. "Get him out of here! Get him out of here!" she shouted as she pulled her knees to her cleavage, balancing her shapely rear on the barstool and lifting her designer stilettos off the ground as far as possible. The harmless hound took the hysterical woman's exuberance as a sign of encouragement and made his way toward her with determination and glee, while a well-intentioned waiter tried to intercept the dog and shoo him in the direction of the exit.

"Stay away! I hate dogs! Get away from me!" the woman continued to scream while her friend lifted her icy margarita glass in indifference.

"What is she getting so upset about?" Marli whispered to Nick.

"Well, she should be upset. They shouldn't allow dogs in here," Nick said, shoving his empty salad plate away.

"I'm sure they don't allow dogs in here," she replied, this time her voice amplified in annoyance. "He just snuck in. Can't you see they're trying to get him out? But what is the big deal? Poor guy is probably just hungry."

"There you go again, whining about a stray dog. I don't blame her for being so upset."

"Seriously? She's behaving like a child. The dog is harmless."

Marli watched as the flustered waiter finally corralled the spirited canine and guided him out the front entrance and onto the street. Seconds later, the copper-toned host in his tropical attire placed a crusty cheese pizza, its edges charred to exactness, in front of the quarrelling couple.

"I apologize for the commotion," the man said.

"No worries," Marli replied, now taking note that the man's shirt was patterned with motorcycle-riding cats wearing Hawaiian leis. "I can't believe that woman reacted the way she did. The dog didn't bother us. Has he come to visit before?"

"Yup, he's my buddy. I give him scraps of food. He's harmless. I try to keep him out of the restaurant, but he can be persistent, as you saw."

"Yeah, quite persistent. And disruptive," Nick said as he negotiated a piece of pizza, the melted mozzarella cobwebbing across the table.

"Why don't you take him home with you?" Marli asked optimistically.

Grinning as though it was not the first time he had encountered that very same question, the man replied, "I just can't now. I live in a small apartment. Maybe someday when I have a bigger place."

"That's too bad," Marli said with an uncomfortable smile. "I hope he hangs around long enough to see 'someday.'"

Marli heard the familiar ping of her cell phone, nestled within her small travel purse. The screen lit up with a text message from her best friend Tammy, the one woman she trusted maybe even more than her own mother.

"Are you really going to answer that?" Nick asked, irritated. "We're trying to have a nice dinner here."

"It's Tammy. Just let me check to see if it's about Mom. There might be something wrong."

"There is always something wrong with your Mom. Let it go."

Marli opened the text message with a stroke of her forefinger and looked down at the smudged screen.

Hey, Marli, the text read. *Cómo estás? Just checking in to make sure all is bueno south of the border. I am missing our workout sessions already. Down a tequila shot for me and stay safe, good friend.*

"Sorry, Nick," Marli said, dropping the phone back into her bag. "It was nothing. I'll text her back later. How's the pizza?"

Before Nick could respond, Marli's cell phone pinged again.

"Seriously?" Nick said. "Tell her to give us a break."

"I'm really sorry. I'll turn off the phone." Marli reached back into her purse, glancing at the screen before attempting to shut it down. But this time, it was not Tammy. An unfamiliar number and three lines of text glared up at her.

It's been too long. You need to know. Franklin's death was not an accident.

Chapter Three

"What?" Marli said, staring down at the text message. "What is this?"

"Keep your voice down," Nick said. "What's wrong?"

"This text message. It says Franklin's death was not an accident! Is this some kind of sick joke?" Marli handed the phone to her husband. Nick swiped the glass to bring the black screen back to life.

"What the hell?" he shouted. "Who sent this?"

"I don't know! I don't recognize the number."

Nick angrily tapped on the screen and the message swooshed into space.

"What did you say?" Marli probed in a helpless panic.

"I asked, 'Who is this?' What idiot would send that? It has to be a bad joke."

"Who would do something like that?"

The phone pinged again. Nick read the message aloud. "It's not important who I am. You just needed to know."

Nick's face swelled with anger. "Idiot! What a ridiculous thing to say. It must be some kind of nutcase. Some asshole who read about Franklin in the newspaper and wanted to play a sick game on us. Just ignore it."

"Ignore it?" Marli responded in an emphatic whisper. "I can't ignore it. What if it's true?"

"It's not true. Don't be ridiculous. Marli, this is just going to upset you again. First the dog, now this. You don't need this. I don't need this."

"I just don't understand why someone would send this message." Marli's heart twisted in her chest.

"I don't, either. Listen, as soon as we get home, I will try to track down the number. See if I can figure out who sent it. I will even make some phone calls from the retreat tomorrow. OK? But for now, let's forget it. There is nothing we can do about it now, anyway."

"Everything all right here?" the restaurant host asked as he cleared away the salad dishes.

"Yes, fine," Nick replied, pushing his dinner plate away. "We just need the check."

Marli woke at 6:00 a.m. the next morning to find an empty space next to her in bed. Nick had left early. She walked barefoot out the front door and peered over the banister and down at the hotel pool just outside their room. Nick was squeezing in a swim, which he often did at home, before heading to his retreat. The courtyard surrounding the pool was tranquil. Only faint chatter and the rattling of kitchen pans drifted over from the hotel's open-air restaurant as employees prepared for the breakfast throng. The untarnished morning, still cool from the night before, hinted of white jasmine blooming on an overhead vine.

Marli made her way back into the room and into bed, faking slumber when Nick returned. He quickly showered, dressed, and was about to silently slip out the door when Marli stretched and sat up.

"Have a good day," she managed to utter.

"Thanks. You, too." And Nick was gone.

Marli sat on the edge of the bed. She picked up her cell phone, still attached to the charger cord, tapped open "Messages," and read the stranger's text from the night before over and over again. *Franklin's death was not an accident.* So many hours, so many days spent agonizing over how her son could have died so needlessly. She had made herself sick, weeping uncontrollably until her head pounded. For months, she refused to accept what the police and the coroner had told her—that Franklin's death occurred by "accidental fall."

Nick had pleaded with Marli. "There is no evidence of foul play," he endlessly repeated to her, sometimes calmly, sometimes in a rage, until she finally gave in and stopped questioning, at least out loud, the reason for her only child's demise.

Marli walked out onto the room balcony. Stretching out over the railing, filling her lungs with the fresh sea air, she saw him again—the same street dog, still favoring his back left leg, in the spot on the cracked pavement where she had spied him the night before. What was it about this poor pathetic pup that gripped Marli by the heart and would not let go? Who was he? Why did he affect her so? It was too late to help the mutt struck by the airport shuttle. She could not go back in time and alter the path that led up to that moment. There were too many things in her life she could not change. But this time, she had to try.

"*Buenos días*," Marli said, stepping up to the long oak countertop in the hotel reception area. "Do you speak English?" she asked a young lady folding a pile of light-blue pool towels.

"No English," she replied, shaking her head. "Rosa!" the employee shouted over her shoulder.

Marli saw Rosa Perez, the concierge at Hotel Santa Fe, appear at the door of an adjacent office.

"How can I help you?" Rosa inquired as she stepped into the reception area. She wore a traditional Mexican peasant dress, embroidered in a colorful floral pattern, with a lava-red belt that gathered the folds of the fabric tight around her slight waist. Her long, jet-black hair was braided to the side so the ponytail hung over her left shoulder and down her breast.

"Hola. I'm Marli May. My husband and I checked in yesterday."

"Sí, of course. Is everything to your satisfaction?" Rosa asked. She was an attractive woman in her early forties, with a gentle demeanor that seemed well-suited for meeting the needs of hotel guests.

"Yes, the room is lovely. Everything is fine. But I have an unusual request—something I hope you can help me with. There is a dog—*el perro*—down on the street."

"Oh yes, we have many street dogs. They won't hurt you. They are harmless. They stay to themselves."

"No, I'm not worried about me. I am worried about the dog. He has an injury to his back leg," Marli said, pointing to her own leg as if the gesture would make Rosa better understand.

"Oh yes, I know the dog you are referring to. He has been around for a while."

"Do you know what happened to his leg?"

"No, no, I do not know."

"Is there a veterinarian in the area?"

"*Veterinario? Sí*, there is one in town."

"Do you think he is open today? How far away is he?"

"Not far. Ten minutes driving. I can call him."

"Yes, please. That would be great. Can you call him and find out if he can see the dog today? I will pay. I have money." Marli reached into her purse for a white envelope—the one she grabbed before leaving the room from the safe where Nick had deposited it the day before.

"That can wait," Rosa said as she retreated back into her office, closing the door partially behind her. Marli paced the reception area as the other female employee continued to fold the blue, cotton pool towels. Anxiety welled up in Marli's gut. Perspiration swelled under her armpits and hovered over her upper lip. She silently commanded Rosa to expedite the call; the unwitting canine might disappear again.

After several eternal minutes, Rosa reappeared. "The veterinario cannot come here but he can see the dog if you take him there," she said, placing a sympathetic hand on Marli's shoulder.

"Yes, of course," Marli replied in relief. "Thank you. How should I do this? Can you call a taxi for me? And I will need something—food—something to get the dog into the car. Can I get some food from the restaurant?" Marli feared Rosa would grow tired of the foolish American tourist who wanted to help a stray street dog.

"I will call the restaurant," Rosa said. "Ivan is the restaurant manager. He will give you something. And I will call a taxi and tell him where to take you. Go to the restaurant now and then come back."

"Thank you, Rosa. I'll just be a minute."

Marli dashed down the stone-paved path, past the hotel swimming pool, and up a slight incline to the entrance of the restaurant. Round Equipale bistro tables were set with candle votives and classic, blue-glass, Mexican stemware. Shiny terra-cotta tiles flowed across the floor like shimmery water over red clay. The time was nearing 8:00 a.m.

Marli maneuvered around several hotel guests waiting to be seated for breakfast. Finding the hostess preoccupied, Marli pushed through the swinging employees-only double doors into the commercial kitchen, momentarily caught off guard by the surge of heat from the numerous industrial ovens. Several apron-clad staff scurried about.

An older gentleman stood at a long stainless-steel worktable, a professional butcher knife in hand. Wispy, gray strands of hair were flattened against his shiny scalp by a black nylon hairnet. His stiff, white chef's coat, already stained with the day's menu, draped past his stocky shoulders and hovered over his rotund abdomen.

"Come in!" Ivan Lupe called out to Marli, waving the thick blade through the air like a steel flag. "Rosa called. You want food? For a dog?"

"Sí, for a street dog," Marli replied in a hurried tone. She knew the courteous thing to do would be to explain why she needed food for a homeless street mutt, but she was in too much of a rush. If the dog had not already, he would soon find his way down another road, away from the hotel and away from Marli. There was no time for politeness.

"I have bread, but I think the dog would prefer a delicious piece of albacore, don't you?" Ivan said in his loud, jovial voice.

"Tuna? OK, tuna should be fine," Marli said, remembering that the restaurant offered a strictly seafood and vegetarian menu.

"Bueno! Freshly roasted albacore, it is. Today's lunch special! No bones. Bones are bad for dogs, sí ?"

Ivan unfurled a long piece of foil across his worktable and carefully placed several slabs of the moist fish into the center of the aluminum. The pungent smell of garlic and exotic spices twirled up from a large pot of mole sauce and mingled with the sticky kitchen air. Bringing the sides of the foil together in the middle, Ivan folded the silver wrapping paper into a neat package.

"A gift for your amigo, a dog!" He laughed.

Marli thanked Ivan and darted through the gardens and back to Rosa waiting at the front gate of the hotel.

"The taxi is right across the street," Rosa said as she walked Marli to the curb outside the hotel entrance and pointed toward a small, four-door sedan, dented and dinged with its windows cranked wide open. The smiling driver stood on the sidewalk next to the bruised vehicle. Rosa waved to him and he gestured back, flapping his arm above the roof of the car.

Marli scanned the walkway to the left of the taxi searching for her furry mission-of-the-moment. On first glance, she did not see the dog and her heart lay flat and defeated in her chest. But, with another visual cast farther along the beach, Marli spotted her charge. The unsuspecting mutt lay motionless in a nest of smooth sand, his face resting on his two front paws, one crossed over the other. Foil package in hand, its gourmet contents still warm from the oven, Marli dashed across the road in the direction of the dog, dodging a slew of oncoming vehicles, Rosa right behind her, heading toward the taxi driver.

Questioning the sanity of the entire endeavor but realizing it was too late to turn back, Marli quickly reviewed the three possible outcomes as she cautiously approached the prone pup. One, the dog would simply stand up and run away. Even with an injured back leg, he was quite capable of a speedy retreat on just three limbs. Two, the mongrel would turn out to be less than friendly or simply unwilling to be wrangled into a taxicab. Three, the hound would cooperate with the strange American woman, seduced by food superior to his normal daily scavenging, and jump into the waiting vehicle.

"Hi, sweet boy. What happened to your leg?" Marli cooed, subconsciously hoping the dog would actually respond. She held out the back of her hand so the cautious canine could sniff her skin, fragrant with mango-scented lotion. Mildly interested, the dog pushed himself up into a standing position and gazed up at Marli as if to say, "What do you have to eat?"

He was a medium-size pooch, maybe thirty or forty pounds—a muddled mix of terrier and Labrador retriever. Marli felt his black nose, faintly wet as it brushed against her hand, before the dog quickly pulled back and made a half circle away from the stranger. From behind, she could see his trim frame and mature testicles. A steady river of disinterested pedestrians moved along the pathway without a glance in their direction.

Marli unwrapped the foil container, the curious canine now at full attention. Staring intently at the fragrant offering—several pieces of warm roasted albacore, the fish pulled fresh from the Pacific that morning—the unsuspecting pooch looked up at her with that undeniably cute head tilt that is so effective in television commercials. Marli placed a chunk of the edible bribe on the cement sidewalk and watched as the mutt eagerly took the tuna into his mouth, scarcely chewing before swallowing.

"Good boy. Want some more?" she said.

Step by step, the intrigued dog inched his way toward Marli on his three good legs as she slowly backed up, doling out the tempting treat in small, strategic portions until the duo reached the waiting taxi. The driver held the back door open as Marli wiggled in rear first. Rosa stood by quietly, careful not to make a quick move that would startle the canine into a fast retreat.

"Come along, little guy," Marli said, holding out the last of the albacore from the backseat of the cab. "Come on, we're going for a ride."

The dog's wet black nose twitched and strained for the scent of the seafood as he drew closer to the interior of the vehicle.

"Come on," Marli repeated, this time slapping the seat cushion with her free hand. "Come on, you can do it."

With one quick bound, the trusting street mutt was in the cab, enjoying his rightful reward. The taxi driver quickly closed the car door behind him.

Chapter Four

The taxi pulled up to a small building adjacent to a family-owned grocery store skirted with vibrant piñatas swinging from a faded red awning. Large wooden bins were mounded with colorful melons, papayas, and bananas warmed by the ever-present heat. The exterior of the vet clinic was painted a welcoming orange. A small, wood-framed window to the right of the entrance desperately needed a good washing. The rustic front door held an open sign that dangled directly below the word "Veterinario," hand-stenciled in white lettering.

Gripping the dog tightly to her chest for fear he would bolt when the car door opened, Marli waited for the taxi driver to circle around and help her out of the vehicle.

"I think I'll call you Puerto," she told the calm and cooperative canine, who had settled in nicely for the quick ride from the hotel to the vet's office. "It has a nice ring, yes? It means 'port' in English . . . where ships take refuge from a storm." The name seemed appropriate for a lost pooch that needed shelter from life on the streets.

Marli pondered over how old Puerto might be. She had read somewhere that the most effective way to determine the age of an animal was to examine his teeth for signs of tartar or decay. But Puerto was a stray street dog, after all, an unknown and unpredictable commodity. An unwelcome inspection into his physical well-being might provoke a bite, which was an outcome Marli was uninterested in risking. But something about the dog's quiet demeanor, his gentle tail wagging, and his willingness to trust gave Marli the impression that he was an older soul, if not chronologically, then certainly spiritually. Perhaps years of surviving on the run had aged him in many diverse and unimaginable ways.

"Gracias, gracias. You don't need to wait," Marli told the cabbie, handing him a hundred-peso note for the twenty-peso fare.

Inside, the office was void of people and pets. The room was dusty, lit by filtered sunlight through the dirt-covered window and a fluorescent tube dangling overhead. The air was hot—clearly no air-conditioning—and smelled of wet animal fur. A makeshift receptionist's desk stood vacant.

"Hola! Is anyone here?"

"I'll be right there." A male voice drifted from behind a chipped stucco wall that separated the rear of the vet office from the front reception area.

"Thank goodness he speaks English," Marli whispered to the dog cradled in her arms. Within moments, a somewhat disheveled man appeared. About six feet tall with walnut-brown hair and skin a shade lighter, he had an easygoing, friendly face that gave Marli reason to relax.

"Rosa from Hotel Santa Fe called about this dog," she said, struggling as the deadweight of the pup grew heavier and heavier the longer she held him. Puerto shot his round, brown eyes, pupils dilated, at Marli and then to the man.

"Come on back," he said, leading the way through a white veneered door smeared with greasy fingerprints and into another room to the right, seemingly unaware of Marli's increasingly weighty burden.

"Let's take a look at you, old boy," he said, gesturing to Marli to set the dog down on the worn, gray linoleum that curled up around the edges where it was supposed to touch the wall. A metal exam table protruded into the middle of the room. Medicine bottles, cotton balls, and a plastic container of dog treats shared space on the Formica countertop near a small, stainless-steel sink.

"So you decided to help a street dog?" the man said, looking up at Marli now from the dog's perspective.

"Well, yes. I mean, how could I leave him? He needs help."

"They all need help," the man stated matter-of-factly, now focused on the bewildered mutt before him. Puerto lowered his head and raised his bony rear in pleasurable submission as the man scratched that unreachable spot at the base of his skinny tail.

"Yes, I know," Marli replied with a hint of resentment for having to agree to the obvious. "But he seems to be injured. He does not put weight on his back left leg. And you can see how thin he is. Excuse me, but are you the vet?"

Grinning from the absurdity of the question, as if he could afford to pay staff to triage patients first, the man introduced himself as Dr. Rosado. "But you can call me Ben."

"Nice to meet you. I'm Marli May."

"I don't really have the budget to hire a vet tech like veterinarians do in your country. It's just me," he added, with a cynical lift to his voice.

Ben continued to run his hands over the dog's sparse, muddy-black fur, carefully separating the fine hair as he came to each scab and patch of dry crusty skin in search of fleas and other blood-sucking creatures. Despite Puerto's compromised back left leg, he did not have difficulty standing. Ben gently extended the injured limb while monitoring the cooperative mutt for signs of pain or discomfort. Puerto wiggled and pulled away when the leg reached its stretch limit and then turned to affectionately lick the vet's comforting hand.

"It's an old injury," Ben announced, rising from the floor to meet Marli face-to-face. "Maybe hit by a car a while ago. He does not seem to be in pain and has learned to compensate for the handicap with his other three legs. But he has fleas. Might be allergic to them. One bite will send an allergic dog into a scratching and biting frenzy, and then he will develop these skin irritations."

Marli was familiar with flea allergies. Her mother's now-deceased terrier mix had received monthly doses of a topical flea treatment in San Jose. Without the medication, the nine-pound dog would scratch and bite until his skin was raw. The entire ordeal made her husband, Nick, crazy—that and the endless shedding, the incessant barking, the relentless licking, not to mention the requisite defecating and urinating. Nick's only use for animals was grilled, roasted, or barbequed.

"I can give him a pill that will kill the fleas immediately, and a topical dose of flea treatment to help relieve some of the itching, but it only lasts four weeks, so unfortunately the fleas will return," Ben said. "And I will treat him for tapeworms, too—if he has fleas, he has worms. Do you want me to give him a shot to relieve the itching and an antibiotic in case there is any underlining infection?"

"Yes, please. That's all good. But are you sure you can't do anything to help the leg? You don't think he's in pain? I mean, he doesn't put weight on it." Marli offered her own amateur analysis. "I have money. I can pay."

Ben smiled. "It would be a waste of your money. Whatever pain he endured when the injury first occurred is long gone. He may be stiff, but these street dogs are resilient.

They are survivors." After a momentary pause, he asked, "So what are you going to do with the dog now?"

That was the big unanswered question—the same query Nick would have asked. But Marli acted on emotion. Help the dog now and figure out the rest later.

"Well, I don't know. Can you keep him?" she asked in all seriousness.

"Miss, there are thousands of stray street dogs in Mexico. We cannot help them all. I can offer some relief from pain or discomfort, but I cannot give them all a home."

"I suppose I knew that," Marli said. "It's just hard to believe there are so many on the streets without homes, fending for themselves."

Switching her focus from Puerto to Ben, Marli now took note of the veterinarian's large, sentimental eyes, strangely not unlike the dog's. Ben's brown hair was pushed back by a red and yellow hairband that kept the curls from falling in his eyes. How practical. How feminine. How handsome.

"I can't take him to my hotel, either," Marli sighed. "My husband would kill me. He doesn't even know I'm here."

Reaching down to stroke Puerto's head, as though to assure the dog that they were not talking behind his back, Ben added, "My suggestion would be to take him back to where you found him. He is obviously finding food and water somewhere. He's not dehydrated. He is skinny but not starving. You have done a good thing. The flea treatment, the steroid, and the antibiotic will give him some relief. You can feel good about that."

"Why are there so many street dogs?" Marli asked. "Why doesn't anyone do anything about them?"

"It is a different mindset here," Ben replied. "There is a lot of poverty. People cannot afford to take care of themselves and their families, let alone a pet. Stray dogs are just part of the landscape. They are not owned by anyone, so no one takes responsibility for them. And people who do take dogs into their homes cannot afford to alter them or they don't believe in it. So the dogs—and the cats—just keep reproducing. The strong ones live and the weak ones die. It's just the way it is."

Marli gave Ben the go-ahead to give Puerto a steroid shot to relieve his itching, an antibiotic to knock out any infection, a pill to kill the tapeworms lurking in his intestines, a topical ointment to eliminate the insidious fleas, and a vaccination for rabies. Ben charged her 1,125 pesos—75 US dollars. Marli pulled the bills out of the white envelope and handed them to the kind doctor.

"Do you have a ride back to the hotel?" Ben asked.

"I'll have to catch a taxi."

"I can drive you. I have errands to run."

"That's really nice of you. I accept."

"Just give me a minute," Ben said, as he slipped out the exam room door. When he returned, he had a blue plastic lead, which he lassoed over Puerto's head. "We can go out the back," Ben said, flipping off the lights.

Ben escorted Marli to his truck, a rusty, red, 1968 crew cab Chevy with a large dent in the front passenger side door that impeded its ability to open properly.

"I've never bothered to get it fixed," Ben said. "Sorry, but you have to get in from the driver's side."

Marli hoisted herself up and slid across the bench seat's well-worn upholstery to the passenger side.

"Come on, boy," Ben said slapping the driver's seat. Despite his useless back leg, Puerto made the jump in one sturdy leap. "Not bad for a dog with a bum leg."

Marli detected a grin, the first smile she noticed from the doctor since meeting him.

Puerto settled into a comfortable place between Ben and Marli, sitting upright and eager as he watched the road stretch out before him. His pink tongue flapped from side to side as the warm wind whipped through the truck's open windows.

"Thank you for taking us back to the hotel," Marli said to Ben, pushing back stray strands of hair that had escaped from her disorderly ponytail. She pressed her face into the breeze to calm the perspiration that glazed her skin. "It's going to be hard to let him go."

Ben was silent with no relevant response, his eyes on the road.

"How long have you been a vet?" Marli asked in another attempt to make conversation.

"Five years here in Puerto Escondido. Before that, thirteen in California where I went to vet school before moving back to Mexico."

"California? UC Davis?"

"That's the one," Ben said, still focused beyond the front windshield.

"Go Aggies," Marli said with a smile, hoping for a positive reaction from the stoic doctor. "I went to grad school at Davis."

"When?"

"Graduated in 1995. You?"

"2000," Ben responded. Marli quickly did the math in her head. The good veterinarian must be about forty. She was five years his senior.

"No wonder your English is so good." She paused and then asked, "What brought you back to Mexico?"

"I was born in Oaxaca. My parents still live here," Ben replied, adjusting his rearview mirror. "I wanted to be near them as they grow older. I also wanted to help the animals where I grew up."

Puerto lost interest in watching the pavement roll beneath the truck and lay down between the two humans, his muzzle resting on Marli's lap.

"There's another one! And another one!" Marli shouted emphatically, pointing through the passenger-side window at two more vagabond dogs traveling nowhere along the side of the road. "How can you stand it?"

"I can't," Ben said softly, this time looking over at Marli.

Without warning, Marli's angst turned to regret. Regret that she sounded so harsh toward the good doctor, as though he was not doing enough to help the destitute creatures. Regret that she was a spoiled American who would go back home to her perfect pet-less life. Her perfect, uncomplicated, tragic, pet-less, childless life.

"One American couple moved here to retire, not knowing about the street dogs," Ben added. "When they became aware of the extent of the problem, the woman came to me for help. She told me that she either had to do something or leave Mexico. Now we are holding spay and neuter clinics when we can. And I have talked to the local government about opening an animal shelter, but we need land and money and volunteers. It's no easy task."

"Nothing is easy," Marli whispered, turning her gaze out the passenger-side window to follow the passing buildings, each one blurring into the next. She had lost herself in a crazy space in time. Her focus had blurred and then sharpened again. A wayward mutt had taken her away from the insistent pain, if only for a few brief moments. He had helped her forget the confusion and anxiety that haunted her from the text message she received the night before. Back into focus now, she swiped open her cell phone, checking for a text from Nick saying he found out who sent the foreboding message about their son's death. But there was nothing.

"Everything OK?" asked Ben.

"Yes, fine. Just seeing if my husband was trying to contact me."

Ben pulled his truck up to Hotel Santa Fe. The three new acquaintances tumbled out of the driver's side door onto the cobblestone driveway. It was late morning and the heat and humidity was picking up. Marli gestured across the roadway to the sand and cement corner where she had kidnapped the unsuspecting mutt an hour earlier, and they hurried across the street, Puerto still on a lead and happy to oblige.

"Well, this is it," Marli said, squatting down next to Puerto, taking his face between her hands and kissing him above his shiny black nose. Never in a million years did Marli think she could ever put her bare lips to a stray dog's furry forehead, but it seemed so natural at the moment that she puckered up without hesitation. Puerto licked Marli's right cheek in return.

"You take care of yourself, little guy."

Ben slid the lead off over Puerto's sleek, charcoal-colored head. "OK, boy. You are on your own again," he said. But instead of bolting to his newfound freedom, Puerto sat on his compromised back leg and looked up at the two of them.

Chapter Five

"It's OK, boy. Go," Ben urged, waving his hand to shoo the dog along. Puerto looked to the left and then to the right, stood up, and was gone. Marli reluctantly watched the vagrant mutt prance down the sidewalk on his three good legs, away from the hectic beachfront, and disappear down the main road that led to the center of town.

"He'll be back," Ben said. "He knows the area. You may even see him again before you leave," he added, looking in the direction of Puerto's escape route and not at Marli. "When are you leaving?"

"This Friday. Only four more days."

"Well, it was nice meeting you. Enjoy Puerto Escondido."

Marli took Ben's outstretched hand, holding it a couple of seconds longer than a customary handshake. She looked up at the imposing veterinarian standing at least six inches taller than her. She took a moment to venture into his dark eyes and appreciate his smooth face and gentle features. Marli was struck by his composed and calm demeanor. He was quite handsome, but his attractiveness was somehow masked by a sense of sadness, by the way he spoke, and by the way he gestured. Marli wondered if the kind animal doctor was married or perhaps had a girlfriend.

Ben Rosado had one more stop to make before heading back to his veterinary clinic and an afternoon of appointments. He pulled his truck onto Highway 200, then right onto Oaxaca Avenue, passing through the heart of Puerto Escondido until he reached the central cemetery.

"Ben!" called out an older man, garden clippers in hand. "How are you, amigo?"

"Very good. And you, José?"

"Bueno. Beautiful day, isn't it?" the man added, gesturing to the flawless turquoise sky.

"Sí, beautiful," Ben replied, stopping in front of one of the house-like crypts scattered across the graveyard. Elaborately adorned altars, each resembling a miniature home with walls, a roof, and an arched entrance, were lined side by side within inches of each other. Many were painted white, while others stood out in varying pastels of blue, pink, green, and yellow. Some were paved with colorful floor tiles or decorated with hand-painted bouquets. All had a cross perched above the door or balanced on the rooftop. Offerings of candy, flowers, photographs, and other gifts for the afterlife littered the front of each altar.

Ben kneeled down in front of the crypt and brushed away a few golden leaves that had fallen from a nearby citrus tree. The home, a place of rest for the departed, was painted a soft shade of creamsicle orange. A small terra-cotta pot of bright marigolds bloomed on each side of the structure. A modest wooden cross hung above the entryway.

"Your wife was a lovely woman," José sighed, placing his hardened hand on Ben's shoulder.

"Sí," Ben agreed.

"The marigolds like it here. They represent the fragility of life."

"Funny thing about the marigolds," Ben said. "They were Lucy's favorite flower. But she could never have them in her garden because snails would devour them. And she refused to put out snail bait. She refused to harm anything. She would say, 'This is their garden, too.' In life, she lived without. Now, finally, she has her marigolds."

José made the sign of the cross across his chest and pulled a tattered white handkerchief from the hip pocket of his threadbare jeans. "Heat of the day," he said wiping the perspiration from the back of his neck. "I better get back to work. Take care, amigo."

"José," Ben called out. "I brought these wedding cookies for Lucy. But you take them. Lucy would prefer for you to have them instead of the ants." Ben lifted a small bag, sweet butter seeping through the brown paper and staining its sides.

"No, no. You must leave them to welcome her soul into the home."

"I know, I know. But I will come back with more gifts later. You take these. It would make Lucy happy."

Marli spent the rest of the day mindlessly shopping the large open-air market in the center of town that housed hundreds of vendors showcasing an abundance of local treasures—brilliant textiles, hand-crafted jewelry, colorful folk art, and stall after stall of fresh produce and regional cuisine.

She checked her phone every half hour or so, anxiously waiting for Nick to call or text about what he found out regarding the message Marli received the night before.

Franklin's death was not an accident. Marli read the words over and over again on her cell. Was it a sick joke? Or was it true? What did Nick find out, if anything?

By the time Marli chose one of the many eateries for lunch and circled the market several times, stopping often to browse the endless array of goods, it was close to 5:00 p.m. Nick finally texted that he was back from his work retreat and would be waiting for her at the hotel's outdoor bar by the upper-level swimming pool. She quickly replied that she was on her way. Hopefully Nick had news about who sent the mysterious message. But before heading to the hotel bar to meet her husband, Marli made a quick stop in their room to freshen up and replace the small white envelope, now a few bills lighter, back in the closet safe.

Guests, as if summoned by a solar deity, were already gathering on Hotel Santa Fe's second-story terrace to witness the famous Oaxacan sunset. Tonight, the sky and sea would merge at 6:37. By twilight, the sun was kissing the ocean and slipping seductively into her depths. The scattering of refracted rays created a sensuous glow that illuminated the atmosphere and lingered erotically on the horizon.

Marli spotted Nick balancing on a barstool, oblivious to the nightly gathering of lovers and others being seduced by the view of the mesmerizing sunset only steps away. As Marli pulled up a second barstool to join him, she took note of a half-empty bottle of Mexican liquor.

"Where have you been?" Nick asked, his speech distorted just enough for Marli to determine that the shot glass in his hand was not her husband's first libation of the evening.

"Just shopping. How was the retreat?"

"Boring. Bunch of corporate garbage on team building and crap like that," Nick said.

"I'm sorry. Well, only one more day of the retreat, right?"

Nick was silent, looking down at the golden liquid in his glass.

"What are you drinking?" Marli asked.

"It's called mescal. Remember that shit we used to drink in college with the worm in it?"

Marli looked alarmed.

"Well, maybe you never drank it. Anyway, it's the thing to drink in Oaxaca. Here, try it. You'll hate it." Nick pushed his glass toward her.

Marli took an ever-so-tiny sip, her face wincing from the toxicity. "Tastes like turpentine. You're right, I hate it. Can we get another glass?" she said with a grin. "When in Oaxaca . . ."

The bartender had slipped away for more ice, so Nick teetered on the footrest of his stool, reached over the counter, and grabbed a shot glass himself. He poured Marli a half glass and filled his own to the rim again.

"Too bad," Nick said. "Most mescals don't contain the worm anymore. Or I should say, the larva of a moth, as I was just informed by my buddy, the barkeep."

"We have an old saying in Mexico," said the young Mexican bartender, who had returned to his patrons under the palm-thatched hut. "For everything bad, mescal, and for all good, too!"

"Did you have a chance to figure out who sent that text message to me last night about Frankie?" Marli asked, frustrated that Nick did not voluntarily come forward with the information himself.

"No," he said. "I didn't have time."

"Don't you want to know? Isn't it bothering you?"

"It's been two years since he died. The police said it was an accident. There is no need to give some crackpot any attention, any of our energy. He probably wants money. Trying to blackmail us with some made-up story. He's praying on our pain. Just let it go. There are a lot of sick people out there. Just let it go, Marli." Nick filled his shot glass again.

"OK," Marli replied reluctantly. "Maybe you're right." Nick was too intoxicated to argue with him.

"I did something crazy today," Marli said in an attempt to change the subject.

"We should get something to eat."

"Let's get some appetizers. So anyway, I had just gotten up this morning and—"

"Look at all these people. I don't know what all the fuss is about a stupid sunset. You've seen one, you've seen them all," Nick said.

"You always do that. You always interrupt me when I'm trying to tell you something."

"OK, what? You went shopping today?" Nick asked.

"Yes, but before shopping. I saw that street dog again, the one with the injured back leg."

"What street dog?" Nick lobbed back.

"I guess I didn't tell you about him. I saw this dog when we first got to our room yesterday. Down on the street. He was holding up his back leg like he was hurt. So anyway, I saw him again today."

"OK, sooooo?"

"I spoke to the concierge and she helped me get some food for the dog. And then we got him in a taxi and I took him to a vet in town."

Nick's eyes focused. The mescal high drained from his face. "You did what?"

"I know it sounds crazy, but I was trying to help the little guy."

"Are you out of your mind? What if the dog bit you? What were you going to do with the dog? What *did* you do with the dog?" Nick's voice began to elevate in anger. Several of the sunset watchers turned their way.

"Shhh. You don't have to yell. People are looking."

"I'm not yelling," Nick said, lowering his voice.

"As it turned out, the dog had an old injury that could not be helped." Marli had lost her enthusiasm. Nick had annihilated her story. He had lifted a shotgun to his shoulder, aimed, and fired at her words until they lay dead on the ground. "I just brought him back and let him go." Marli was delusional to think Nick would care about a helpless street dog. She purposely avoided mentioning the handsome animal doctor.

"I can't believe you did that. That is such classic Marli," Nick said, lowering his lecture to a whisper. "Think you can save the world. Act without thinking. Never taking into consideration anyone but yourself."

"What are you talking about? How was this a selfish act? Why are you mad at me?"

"Look, we need to talk." Nick looked around the pool area to see who was in earshot. But all the other hotel guests were still preoccupied with the lingering sunset, a water-color of gold, crimson, and rust bleeding across the horizon.

Marli's irritation, anger, and frustration with her husband abruptly turned to anxiety. Was it about Frankie? Did he know something but was afraid to tell her before?

The shot of mescal was taking effect, making Marli's head float in a shapeless fog. Her heartbeat doubled to a manic thump in her chest. The sweat forming under her armpits and welling up along her upper lip was not from the warm evening air, but from the angst and anguish deep within her.

"I'm just going to say it," Nick mumbled in a quivering, irrational voice. "I'm seeing someone else. She is here in Oaxaca now. I work with her. She came to the retreat. I want to spend my time here with her. I've been seeing her for quite a while now. I want to be with her. I want a divorce."

Chapter Six

Marli wondered if other women imagined their husbands telling them one day that they want a divorce or that they are seeing someone else. In her twenty years of marriage to Nick, Marli had rolled it over in her mind more than once. That one night he was late coming home from work with no credible explanation. The time he had to run an errand and was gone all afternoon. The cell phone pinging over and over with text messages from within his coat pocket. She was sure it was just her paranoid imagination, but what if it was true? What would she do? How would she react? Would she be bitter and angry? Would she get violent? Would she cry? Would she scream? Or would she be calm and levelheaded? Would she want a divorce, too? Would she thank him for telling her the truth instead of letting the affair go on behind her back? But in reality, she never really thought it would happen.

"Wow. I did not see that coming," Marli said to a seemingly remorseful Nick. The sun had finally faded into the horizon and the hotel guests were turning their attention from the seductive solar show to the next endeavor of the evening. An attractive young couple, perhaps newlyweds by their unapologetic display of affection, meandered up to the bar to order two frozen margaritas, while others began to congregate at the outdoor tables surrounding the swimming pool. Several strings of little white lights dangled from each patio umbrella and encircled the trunks of nearby palm trees. The air temperature had dropped at least 10 degrees as a salty breeze swept up from the ocean, rolled across the terra-cotta tiles, and gently kissed Marli on her flushed cheeks. "I'm not sure what to say."

"Don't say anything," Nick whispered, looking around at an audience now in earshot. "I'm sorry. I don't mean to hurt you. You know things have not been good between us for a long time, ever since Franklin died. I'm sorry you are stuck here with me now. I did not expect it to all happen here in Mexico. It is just the way it turned out."

"So, this other woman? She is here now? You spent today with her?" Marli quizzed her fretful husband, not attempting to minimize the pitch of her voice.

"Yes, at the retreat. But it was work. It just seems wrong to let you go on thinking everything is OK and to try to have a good time here . . . now . . . like this . . . when I want to be with her."

"And not me?"

"Yes," Nick mumbled, too embarrassed to look his wife in the eyes. "What will you do? You can have the hotel room for the rest of the week. It is paid for by the company. I will stay with Lisa."

"Lisa? Is that her name?"

"And we will work everything out when we get home."

Marli had met Nick when she was twenty-two years old, living in Davis, a college town approximately one hour from the Bay Area, and attending grad school at the University of California. It was a Thursday evening with nothing better to do when Tammy, Marli's then-roommate, suggested they go see an alternative rock band from England called The The. The concert was at the Crest Theatre in downtown Sacramento, a short drive east of Davis.

"The band's name is The The?" asked Marli from her comfortable corner on the apartment's only sofa, textbook open to the week's assigned reading.

"Yeah, I know, weird," Tammy replied. "It's some punk group from the UK. But I heard they are pretty good. Come on, please let's go. As The Animals would say, 'We gotta get out of this place!'"

Marli and Tammy found parking in a nearby garage and walked a short two blocks to the historic theater. The word "Crest" pulsed vertically in a brilliant neon sign above the marquee. A golden, glassed-in ticket box sat just outside the heavy double doors that led into the building. There was just enough time for one cocktail before the concert at the theater's full bar, a round, sunken area three steps down off the main lobby. The wall-to-wall carpeting's intricate swirls of burgundy and royal blue were stained nearly black from years of foot traffic and too many spilled drinks. A slight musty smell of alcohol saturated the air. While Tammy pushed her way through the concert crowd toward an overworked bartender, Marli surveyed the room. The majority of people were approximately the same age as Marli and her roommate. They were mostly in their early twenties, but some as young at eighteen, with significantly more body piercings, visible tattoos, and revealing clothing.

Then she saw Nick. He was easy to spot across the expanse of other bodies because he stood about six inches taller than everyone else in the room. And he was handsome

. . . very handsome. He had thick, maple-brown hair that swept across his forehead and lingered over his ears. His face was approachable, his smile inviting. He was holding a Heineken in his right hand and waving both arms through the air as he spoke nonstop to another shorter man who stood just far enough away to avoid being hit by the weaving beer bottle. Nick was wearing faded 501 jeans that framed his slim hips and a tucked-in, basic, white, short-sleeved T-shirt with printing on the front and an image of a man holding his hands over his mouth.

"They only had one kind of white wine," Tammy said, handing Marli a glass of chardonnay.

"Check this guy out," Marli said. "Straight ahead. Tall. What does his T-shirt say? 'Lensorship is Un-American'? Lensorship? What does *that* mean?"

"No idea. He's cute. Let's go ask him."

Marli could always count on Tammy to lead the way and make the first move when it came to meeting men. The double margaritas they enjoyed at dinner before the show did not hurt to lower her inhibitions, either.

The two single, motivated women weaved their way through the crowd until they were almost on top of their male target. Now standing awkwardly close, Marli stared at the white T-shirt, still trying to decipher its mysterious message.

"Can I help you?" asked the tall, good-looking man with the Heineken.

"What does your T-shirt say?" Tammy asked with purpose.

"Censorship is Un-American," he responded, using the neck of his green-glass beer bottle to underline the words printed across his chest.

"'Censorship'! Not 'Lensorship'!" Marli exclaimed followed by an intoxicated giggle. "The C looks like an L!"

"Lensorship? What the hell does that mean?" the man asked in bewilderment.

"I thought it might be a play on words. Like maybe it meant Lenny Bruce . . . Lenny . . . Lensorship. You know, how he stood up against censorship . . . you know, the comedian Lenny Bruce," Marli said rambling, starting to feel a little embarrassed but inebriated just enough not to care.

"Yes, I know who Lenny Bruce is," the man shot back with an amused laugh. "Hi, I'm Nick," he said, holding out his hand.

Marli knew she was coming off as slightly irritating, but hoped Nick would be impressed with her knowledge of Lenny Bruce, the stand-up comic from the 1960s, famous for his stinging political satire and controversial obscenity conviction.

"This is my friend, Scott," Nick added.

"Hi. I'm Marli. This is Tammy."

Tammy took Nick's extended hand. Marli shook Scott's.

"So you like The The?" Scott asked Marli.

"Never heard of them. My girlfriend talked me into coming," Marli answered, fully aware that she was now engaged in a polite conversation with the short friend of the tall handsome man, who was now in a focused discussion with Tammy. "Does your friend have a girlfriend?" Marli asked, casually dropping her voice and hoping not to sound rude or hurtful to Scott, whom she had absolutely no interest in.

"No, not really. He just broke up with someone."

"Is he gay?" asked Marli.

"No!" replied Scott with a laugh. "Why would you think that?"

"Well, he is talking a lot . . . like nonstop. Most straight men don't talk that much," Marli added. "I hope that didn't sound bad. I have nothing against gay people." Marli wondered if the alcohol was starting to make her say really stupid things.

The house lights flickered on and off several times. The four new acquaintances finished their drinks and moved toward the auditorium doors. The historic hall glimmered from the art deco lighting fixtures and ornate gold scrollwork adorning the walls and ceiling.

The show was general seating, and Marli hoped Nick and Scott would stick close so they would not lose each other in the crowd. She wanted a chance to get to know Nick better. The theater seats quickly filled, and the foursome was forced to find a spot in the standing-room-only section just left of the stage. Nick squeezed in directly behind Marli, where he remained for the duration of the concert.

Marli never heard a note or a lyric. She would remember nothing of the music, nothing of the band. All she could think about was the tall attractive man standing so close behind her that she could sense his body swaying, feel him moving as she moved to each pulsing beat. Every other song or so, Marli would swing her head slightly to the left to catch a glimpse of the opinionated, white T-shirt just to make sure Nick was still there. And he was. He had not left her . . . yet.

The concert ended, and Nick and Scott followed Marli and Tammy into the lobby.

"Do you girls want to smoke some weed with us?" Nick smiled, his teeth straight and white.

"Yes!" Tammy said without hesitation.

"No!" Marli said. "We have classes early tomorrow morning. This *is* a Thursday, remember?"

"Then may I have your number?" Nick asked Marli. "Maybe we can get a drink sometime."

"Yes, that would be great," she nonchalantly responded, while doing backflips in her brain.

Nick grabbed two paper cocktail napkins from the now-empty bar, while Marli dug into her small purse for a pen.

"Here you go." Nick smiled, handing Marli the ink-smeared square. "You should always ask for the guy's number too," he added, handing Marli the second napkin.

"OK," Marli said, trying not to tear the tissue-thin paper with the tip of her pen.

On the drive back to Davis, Marli was still in a daze over meeting Nick. "He never would have asked me for my phone number if he wasn't interested," Marli said, looking for agreement from Tammy, who was behind the wheel for the ride home.

Almost two agonizing weeks later, when Nick never called, Marli finally made the first move.

"Men just don't get it," Tammy reassured her frustrated friend.

Marli sat alone in her tastefully appointed room at the Hotel Santa Fe in Puerto Escondido, Oaxaca, Mexico, two thousand miles away from home. Nick, her husband of twenty years, had just left her.

Nick had taken his neatly hung pants and pressed shirts out of the hotel closet and packed them back into his nondescript black luggage, along with his scuff-free shoes, folded socks, and monogrammed underwear. He had put his soft toothbrush back in its sanitary plastic holder and placed it in his brown leather travel bag with the dental floss and special whitening toothpaste he carefully squeezed from the bottom of the tube. His expensive aftershave was gone from the tiled bathroom counter, along with the musk-scented shampoo from the shower stall. The room's security safe, its door left ajar, was now empty of the small white envelope stuffed with extra spending money. There was no trace that Nick May had ever been there.

Marli slipped off her sandals and eased her fully clothed body under the covers on her side of the bed, the side she had slept on the previous night next to the man she thought loved her, before he left her for a woman named Lisa.

Chapter Seven

Marli woke the next morning with an intense headache. Her mouth was rancid from the extra shots of mescal she downed the night before to help her cope with the fact that her husband had left her alone on their dream-turned-nightmare vacation to be with his coworker lover. She sat up and draped her legs over the edge of the bed. What was she going to do? Should she stay in Mexico for the remainder of the week and give herself time to process what had happened, think about what it all meant and how she would handle the pending divorce? Or should she go home now, home to her best friend, Tammy, and her mother, Alice, who would both help her sort it all out? A long, hot shower and a cup of strong black coffee were necessary before she could make any decisions.

The hot water was divine as it flowed through Marli's soft, blond hair and down her back, taking the foamy soapsuds to the drain below. She lingered several extra minutes under the showerhead, letting the steam envelop her like the welcome touch of an old lover. Reluctantly turning off the water, she reached for the hotel towel. A small green lizard scurried from beneath the cotton bath sheet, over the tile bathroom countertop, and across the plaster wall.

Normally, this unexpected visitor would have sent Marli into a minor hysterical frenzy, but now, still numb from the evening before, her only hope was that the harmless reptile made its way safely back outside.

After drying her hair and digging a pair of wrinkled shorts and a blouse from her luggage, she headed down toward the beachfront in search of caffeine. She wanted to call Tammy back home and scream into the phone that Nick was sleeping with someone else and had left her, but Marli, still in shock, was finding it difficult to grasp the reality of what had happened, let alone put it into words. It was still early. A cool, soft, morning wind whipped off the water and breezed past Marli, sending a chill through her small frame. She was glad she brought along her warm hoodie.

The coffeehouse was three blocks from the hotel. Two oversized, wood-framed windows, wide open to invite in the fresh sea air, accented each side of a small set of stairs leading inside. High countertops under each window allowed guests to sit and look out toward the ocean. Crazed tribal masks hung on the brightly painted walls. Carved benches surrounded a free-form, Mexican cedar table on one side of the room, while a scattering of two-tops offered more seating on the other side. An affectionate orange tabby demanded attention, weaving in and out of Marli's legs as she scanned the chalkboard menu that hung over the cash register. Just strong black coffee would do.

The friendly feline followed Marli out onto the sidewalk but would go no farther than a few steps past the entrance of the coffeehouse. Marli waited for a large, municipal garbage truck to ramble past her, then took her paper cup filled with caffeine across the asphalt road to the beach. It was just past seven in the morning now, only twelve hours since her husband had abandoned her in this foreign country, and the sky was a glorious glow of magenta and gold. She slipped off her sandals and let the smooth sand wrap in between her toes and around her feet as she walked toward the water. She found a spot void of rocks and seaweed, just out of reach of the fluctuating surf, and sat down, bringing her knees up to her chest. The coffee was still steaming, and she cupped it within her bare hands to help take off the morning chill. The world was a strange and different place now.

Looking out over the Pacific, Marli was humbled and insignificant. The strength and vastness of the powerful sea helped her put things into perspective. She had been alone and single before; she could do it again. If Nick did not love her any longer, she could not force him to. He had made a choice to sleep with another woman, even while still sharing a bed with Marli. Whatever they had as a married couple was gone. Perhaps their love for each other had vanished months or even years prior. Maybe when Frankie died. And Marli just did not notice or maybe did not care. Regardless, the ocean, the sun, the earth lay before her with no pretenses, no lies, no sorrow. What was important yesterday was no longer important today.

Marli finished her coffee and stood up, wiping away the fine sand that clung to her shorts and bare legs. The few people who had shared the early morning with her had now grown into several dozen. Vacationing couples walked hand in hand along the shore, Mexican families spread colorful, wool blankets out onto the sand, and eager screaming children chased the waves back into the ocean. Five or six homeless dogs weaved in and out of the humans and between the battered, wave-weary rocks in search of food. Marli turned to head back up to the street and then to the hotel where she would find a quiet place to call her best friend and mother. She decided she would tell them that she was returning home as soon as she could get a flight out of Puerto Escondido.

When she reached the sidewalk, Marli braced herself on the cement seawall, brushing the silky sand from between her toes before slipping her sandals back on. When she looked up, she saw Puerto. Even though he was in the distance, at least a block up the road, Marli knew immediately it was her stray friend.

Puerto came back just like the thoughtful veterinarian said he would. Marli quickened her pace toward the wayward mutt, who had his nose to the pavement, seemingly oblivious to the pedestrians inches away from him. Marli knelt down on the sidewalk and called him, disregarding that the dog didn't really know he had a name.

"Puerto! Puerto! Hey, Puerto!"

In a second, Puerto looked up. He recognized Marli's voice. He seemed to remember the kind human who had given him roasted albacore, scratched him behind his ears, and rubbed his itchy back. Puerto bounded toward Marli on all three paws.

"Hey, big boy! How are you?"

Puerto sniffed his new friend's outstretched hands as if to say, "What do you have to eat?" and pushed affectionately against her body, knocking Marli off balance and onto her rear.

"Hey! It's good to see you, too."

The homeless hound circled frantically a few times in unabashed excitement like he was welcoming his owner home after a long day at work. Marli could not help but laugh. For a moment, her heart was healed. Puerto was like a ray of light in the middle of a blackout. A gift from an old friend for a birthday family forgot. A bouquet of sweet alyssum blossoming up through a crack in the cement.

The timing of their reunion was the commandment of an unknown force, a directive from above or below or wherever goodness perpetuates.

"Rosa! Look who's back!" Marli called out to the kind concierge who had helped secure food for the stray dog and a taxicab to take him into town to see a vet just the day prior.

"Muy bueno," Rosa said, maneuvering her way out from behind the hotel reception desk.

"I honestly thought I would never see him again," Marli said, pressing her thumb and index finger above her nose and into the corners of her eyes to stop the tears. "But he remembers me. He trusts me."

Marli sat on a long wooden bench across from the reception area and allowed the tears to escape at will, something she had denied herself from the time Nick announced he was leaving her until just that moment. She wept openly without regard to the other hotel guests as they walked past in their flower-themed shorts and bathing suits. The gardener pretended not to notice the weeping woman while he pruned the hibiscus bushes on the adjacent lawn. A maintenance worker looked the other way as he replaced a burned-out lightbulb in the open-air bar to the left, while the Mexican housekeepers continued to fold freshly laundered pool towels. Rosa and Puerto stood by, helplessly watching.

"What is it, mi *amiga*?" asked Rosa, sitting beside Marli and wrapping one arm around her shaking shoulders. Puerto nuzzled up next to Marli's legs and rested his head on her knee. His dust-laden fur felt soft and easy on her bare skin.

But there was nothing Marli could say that Rosa would understand. Marli was not even sure she understood why her emotions were kicking in at that exact moment. Was she crying because of her failed marriage? Because she was alone two thousand miles away from home? Because of a stray dog she could not adequately help? Because of her dead son?

Something within her snapped. She would not try to reason with it or direct it elsewhere. She would not try to understand it. She would embrace whatever it was—fear, loneliness, helplessness, grief. She would welcome it and let it guide her to the next stop on her journey.

Tammy picked up the disposable cell phone she had purchased with cash at Walmart. She tapped on "messages," looking for a second response to the text she sent Marli anonymously the night before. Nothing. Why wasn't Marli more outraged? Why wasn't she demanding to know the truth? Should Tammy send another text, one with more information? But how much was Tammy willing to expose about Franklin's death? What was she trying to prove? And why now, two years later? Haunted by her own relentless guilt and the inconsolable grief of her best friend, Tammy dropped the phone back into her purse and hoped it would all go away.

Chapter Eight

"Hi, Mom," Marli said over her cell phone from poolside at Hotel Santa Fe.

"Marli? Is that you?" Alice Stewart asked. "Where are you?"

"I'm still in Mexico. I've decided to stay a while longer. Maybe another week or two."

"Oh really? You must be enjoying yourself! I'm so glad. How is Nick?"

"He is going home as planned. But I'm staying."

"Is everything all right?"

"Yes, I will tell you more when I get home. Is Aunt Abbey there?"

"Yes, honey. Hold on."

"Hello, Marli! Don't you worry about us. We are doing just great!" said Abbey, a fun, vivacious woman who greeted everyone with a smile, laughed without apology, and always had a humorous story to tell. "We sit outside on the patio and enjoy the flowers and the birds. We are just relaxing and talking. Don't worry about a thing! I am taking good care of your mother."

Aunt Abbey was about ten years younger than Alice and a godsend to Marli, especially as Alice grew ever more dependent on her daughter. With no siblings, Marli was her mother's sole caregiver, chauffeur, and personal shopper. Doctors' appointments were almost weekly, and Alice had been hospitalized twice in the past few months for maladies related to cancerous tumors that could not be surgically removed on her aging kidneys and lungs.

"Never grow old," Alice would whisper to her daughter as they waited endlessly in exam rooms holding firmly to each other's hands. Fortunately, Marli's Aunt Abbey from Southern California had agreed to an extended visit with Alice while Marli and Nick were in Mexico so the couple could enjoy their trip free from worry.

Tammy was next on Marli's list to contact, but she would be more forthcoming with her best friend than she was with her mother. Tammy answered on the first ring.

"Marli? Hola amiga! Are you still in Mexico?"

"Yup."

"Hey, I miss you! Are you having a fabulous time?"

"Nick left me," Marli casually replied.

"What? Nick left you?"

"Don't tell Mom. I haven't told her yet."

"Oh my god! He left you in Mexico?"

"Yup, for another woman. A coworker. She's here in Mexico, too." Saying it out loud made the whole scenario seem absurd.

"You can't be serious!"

"Yeah, I know. Crazy, huh? Well, anyway, I'm going to stay in Puerto Escondido a little while longer. I found a dog."

Tammy was silent for a moment.

"Marli? Are you OK?" Tammy asked. "What do you mean you found a dog?"

"Well, I didn't actually find him. He's not lost. He's a street dog. There are hundreds of them here. You wouldn't believe it. They are everywhere. It's heart-wrenching. Our shuttle van even hit one on the way from the airport to the hotel." Marli rattled on. "I feel so helpless. No one cares. No one wants to help. Nick didn't want to help, either, but I met this really nice vet. He wants to help, but he has no one to help him help. Did I mention he was really nice? And actually quite handsome. He—"

"Stop!" Tammy yelled. "You are losing it, Marli. You have to come home."

"No, I'm fine. Really. At first I thought I was going to lose it. But I'm fine now. I need to stay here and figure things out. At least for another week or until my money runs out. I mean Nick's money runs out. Really, I'm fine. But don't tell my mom."

"I'm coming to Mexico," Tammy said.

"What? You would do that? That would be great! You can meet Puerto. I named the dog Puerto. Did you know that means 'port,' like where ships dock—not like port, the sweet after-dinner wine?" Marli continued to ramble. "When can you get here?"

"By this coming weekend, I think. I will let you know the day and time as soon as I book my flight. Don't do anything crazy before I get there!"

A year earlier, Tammy had walked away from a high-paying job with an employer-matching retirement plan, full health and dental coverage, generous vacation time and sick leave, a private office with a sprawling view of downtown Los Gatos, friendly coworkers, and a flexible work schedule. She had started as a nonexempt assistant and earned her way up to exempt status, accompanied by a slew of respected titles from manager to director to vice president, over a span of twenty years.

Then late on a Friday afternoon, only an hour from the official start of the weekend, Tammy found herself in the wrong place at the wrong moment. She had stopped by her supervisor's office to drop off a report, innocently unaware of her employer's particularly wicked mood after a long, stressful week. What previously had been a congenial employer/employee relationship took a negative turn when Tammy attempted to mitigate her boss's unexpected bad attitude.

"Why are you giving me this report now?" Tammy's supervisor yelled at her.

"I thought you would want it for the weekend," Tammy innocently responded. "You seem stressed. Maybe you should take a deep breath and sit down."

Two decades of outstanding performance reviews and well-deserved accolades were negated in the course of five minutes. Nothing between Tammy and her employer was the same after the encounter.

Tammy found herself purposefully left out of meetings, overlooked on new projects, and given unrealistic assignments. The ultimate insult came when a coworker Tammy had hired to be her assistant ten years prior was promoted to be Tammy's new supervisor. With the blessing of her devoted husband, who was gainfully employed, Tammy packed up her personal belongings and walked out the office door to a new life she would fully embrace. At only forty-five, she would work again if she had to, but right now she was free. And that included the freedom to drop everything and fly to Mexico to help a friend.

"Oh, and another thing," Marli added before hanging up. "I got a text message from someone about Frankie."

Tammy paused. "Really? What did it say?"

"It said 'Franklin's death was not an accident.'"

"What? Do you know who sent it?"

"No. I don't recognize the number."

"Did you tell Nick?"

"He says it's just a sick joke. I should ignore it."

"Let's talk more when I get there."

Defiant over her emotions, Marli would not let her grief—first over losing her son and now over losing her husband—define who she was. She would see past her sorrow and find a new reason to love and to nurture, and to be loved and respected and adored. She ached to know her son's love again. His silly sweetness as a child who giggled in delight when in the comfort of her arms and wailed with fear when he knew she was not nearby. As a teenager who was too busy, too old, too embarrassed for outward affection toward his mother. But it did not matter; she knew it intuitively. And as a young adult, now past the rebellious years of middle and high school, when he could let down his guard and give his mom all the love and value she deserved.

Then the tragedy. The heartbreak. The end of her life. Now just Marli and her husband, a companion, another person who understood their specific anguish. Days into weeks, weeks into months. Morning goodbyes. Empty afternoons. Silent dinners. Solitary nights. But at least she was not alone. Until now.

Love had found her, embraced her, teased her, promised her, and then abandoned her.

Marli would stay in Puerto Escondido for at least another week, due in great part to Puerto, the mysterious mutt who made his way into her overturned life just when she was searching for something to keep her upright. Were they both abandoned, alone, and unloved? Perhaps Marli needed Puerto as much as the homeless hound needed her.

Over the next few days, Puerto became Marli's new male companion, following her from shop to shop, restaurant to restaurant, down to the beach and back up to the hotel. Ivan Lupe, the restaurant manager, brought Puerto leftovers of the nightly dinner special. Rosa, who was extremely strict when it came to the hotel's no-pet policy, allowed Puerto to visit Marli in her room. But the wayward canine never stayed the entire night. He became restless after dark and scratched at the door until Marli let him out and watched his crippled form disappear into the darkness of the hotel gardens. Where did he go? Would he come back?

In the mornings, Marli would find Puerto good naturedly waiting across the road from the hotel, sitting quietly on the pavement where Marli had first spied him from her room balcony. Unlike Nick, Puerto never complained, never criticized, and was always pleased to see her.

Marli woke up early on Friday, six days after she and Nick had arrived in Puerto Escondido and five days from when Nick had left her. Tammy would arrive tomorrow and the two friends would be young again in each other's company, far from home and everything that complicated their lives. But today, Marli and Puerto were on their own.

"Good morning, Puerto," Marli said, sitting down on the cement curb next to the mutt. "So, how was your night, huh? Where did you go? What did you do? Were you out with your buddies? Drinking whiskey and smoking cigars?" Puerto lifted his head so Marli could get a better angle for scratching under his chin. "No, I suppose not. Me neither. I had a quiet night."

Puerto shook his head, ears flopping from one side to the other, followed by a deep, satisfying yawn. "I know you don't understand this, but it's kind of lonely when you leave. I miss you when you are not around. I worry about you. I worry that something will happen and there is nothing I can do to help." Puerto sat back on his good leg and leaned into her.

"You know, my soon-to-be ex-husband wasn't always such an asshole. We had some good times. Especially when Frankie was alive. He was a good dad. He just became a shitty husband. So why did I stay in the marriage, you ask? I guess I was not the greatest wife, either. Grief does that to a person. Everything just becomes too hard. Too hard to stay. Too hard to leave. And way too hard to fake anything.

"You would make a good therapist, Puerto," Marli added, pushing herself up and draping her small handbag across her chest. "Enough talk. Let's go see what we can find today."

Leading Puerto along on an invisible leash, Marli meandered along the beach, Playa Principal, passing dozens of small fishing boats and water taxis that littered the shore. Weary fishermen, who had arrived before dawn, were selling their morning catch to restaurant owners and locals. Crowds gathered around the vessels to see what was available. A young Mexican boy stood barefoot, clutching four large yellowfin tuna just below their tails, two in each hand. He struggled to keep a good grasp on the slippery, weighty fish.

Eager water taxi drivers took tourists to secluded beaches, inaccessible by land, or in search of porpoises, manta rays, and marine turtles cavorting just off the coastline. Mexican mothers set up picnics of warm watermelon, fried corn tortillas, and grilled rock shrimp, while their boisterous children played soccer in the sand.

Marli and her canine friend continued down the beach, weaving in and out of row after row of lounge chairs draped in flashy beach towels and shaded by large, colorful umbrellas, until they came to a cliffside walkway called *Andador Escéncico*.

"In English, the name of this walkway means scenic walker," Marli told Puerto. "That's us! Are you ready? It doesn't look too bad," she said, peering up at the uneven stone and cement path that curved and straightened and twisted again, gripping the side of the cragged cliff. Marli and Puerto navigated the irregular rock stairs and crooked foot bridges, carefully maneuvering over the gaping spaces between the wood planks. Cacti and manzanita bushes decorated the trail, clinging to the ragged rock walls above and below the footpath. A small black bird with a magenta chest hopped from cactus to cactus, while Puerto anxiously sniffed at every dusty corner for a scrap of something edible. Brown pelicans gathered on an outcrop below, taking turns to circle out to the restless water and dive below the sea's surface, searching for breakfast.

It was late morning and the day was already beginning to wield its warmth. "OK, it's hot!" Marli moaned, peeling off the long-sleeve shirt she had layered over a tank top and wrapping it around her slender waist. The two crossed paths with several couples heading back toward the beach, and Marli nodded to each of them, thinking they were smart to get an early start while the air was still cool and kindhearted.

Marli and Puerto passed a towering white lighthouse, keeping watch over them from the jagged cliff above. As they continued the twisting upward climb toward the lookout, Marli marveled at the scope and beauty of the scenery surrounding them. The same vast Pacific she knew only minutes from her Bay Area home in California was a familiar friend two thousand miles away in Oaxaca, guiding her along with an assurance that whatever lay ahead would be better than what she left behind.

"Puerto," Marli said to the uninterested dog. "I read that Andador Escéncico was built by the wealthy landowner who wanted to make these remarkable views accessible to everyone. He didn't want to keep them all to himself. Pretty cool, huh? It took him and two hundred workers three months to build."

Puerto bounded up ahead, did a quick about-face, and returned to Marli's side. The trail offered little shade, but an agreeable breeze skipped up from the rocky ocean below.

"The Oaxacan government told the landowner that constructing this path and the lookout was impossible," Marli continued to explain to her canine companion. "As a tribute to them, the landowner supposedly put up a plaque that reads, '*Un sueño posible*.' Did I pronounce that right? It means 'a possible dream.' But you probably knew that already. You speak Spanish, right?"

When they finally reached their destination, Marli stopped to look around and stabilized her breath. The last dozen steep steps to the lookout left her lightheaded. Three camera-carrying tourists were just exiting. Marli and Puerto were alone.

The platform was encased by a simple cement wall painted a burnt-yellow and edged in white. There were two arches in the wall at the right framing a small bench inlaid with bright-blue Mexican tiles. Decorative planter boxes on each side of the lookout showcased dramatic greenery dotted with tiny red flowers. The space was well-kept and litter-free. Puerto would find no scrap of discarded food there, although he would still try. Out past the lookout to the left were several multistory white condos teetering on the edge of the precipice. The paved floor inched toward the ocean and dipped down to allow visitors the full view of infinity. The endless sky and water collided, each in its own shade of competing blue. The landowner's cast-metal plaque stood guard. Marli breathed in the saltwater air and smiled.

"The landowner was right, Puerto. This is a possible dream."

Marli and Puerto made their way back along the winding pathway—grateful that the trek down was quicker and easier than the hike up—to the beach in search of lunch. They took a detour along the Adoquin, a sightseer-friendly street where rows of side-by-side vendors sold everything from cheap T-shirts and beach gear to locally made crafts and jewelry. Interspersed among the tourist shops were family-owned eateries, small liquor and grocery stores, and money-exchange stands. Finally, back on the hotel's main road, Marli stopped when she came to Black Velvet Fish Taco & Beer.

Black Velvet was one of the most popular and lively restaurants in Puerto Escondido, especially late in the evening, among surfers, bohemians, and tattooed rockers. Now, at approximately two in the afternoon, the atmosphere was quiet and low-key. Two beat-up cedar tables at the front of the diner were always in high demand for their straight-on view of the ocean. On the wall near the entrance was a large black sign with Black Velvet Fish Taco & Beer hand-painted in white capital letters. The small establishment was decorated with kitschy lamps studded with seashells, hanging mobiles, and a flat-screen television playing an endless loop of surfing videos. A rustic bar took up the back wall and additional long wooden tables forced group seating, which was popular after sunset with young crowds looking to eat, drink, and socialize. The small claustrophobic restaurant was startlingly dark in comparison to the bright, sunlit exterior. As Marli's eyes adjusted to the sudden blackness, she spotted Ben Rosado sitting alone at a corner table.

Marli hesitated to disturb the kind veterinarian who had helped Puerto, who was patiently waiting outside on the sidewalk for his human companion. Her first instinct was to pretend she did not see him—he may want to be alone, to eat in peace. Maybe he does not want a pesky tourist invading his space. But her eagerness to inform Ben that Puerto had indeed come back overcame her initial shy hesitation.

"Hello," Marli said, approaching Ben's table.

"Well, hello. Ms. May, correct?" Ben asked, putting down his large glass mug with an "Indio" beer logo printed on the side. The restaurant air hinted of hops and fried food.

"Marli, please," she replied. "I don't mean to interrupt you, but I wanted to thank you again for helping the street dog, and to let you know that he did return just as you said he would. In fact, he is right outside. We have become good friends. He follows me everywhere."

"Well, that's great," Ben said in all sincerity. "Just be careful. Don't let him become too dependent on you. Remember you will be leaving him behind when you go."

Marli had already considered the fact that she was becoming attached to Puerto and she could not imagine just "leaving him behind," as Dr. Rosado so matter-of-factly put it. Now that Nick was not a consideration, why couldn't she bring her newfound companion home to California with her?

"What if I wanted to take Puerto home with me? How would I do it?"

Ben looked up at Marli and took a long sip of his dark Mexican beer. "Sit down. Are you here for lunch?"

"Oh, I don't want to intrude."

"It's OK. I hate to eat alone."

"Me too," Marli quickly replied. "But Puerto is outside. Do you think they would mind if we snagged one of those tables at the front so Puerto can see us?"

"Suzanne," Ben called to a young waitress standing by the bar. "OK if we change to a front table?"

Suzanne waved toward the long, wooden table on the left at the front of the restaurant. Her long, black hair was tied in a tight ponytail and exaggerated tattoos wrapped both arms from her slight shoulders to her tiny wrists.

Ben picked up his beer mug and motioned for Marli to follow ahead of him. Before sitting, Marli stopped to summon Puerto, who was lazily stretched out at the bottom of the entrance steps with his furry, coal-black head resting on his front paws.

"Look who I found, Puerto!" she said, rubbing the top of his head and behind his ears.

"Hey, amigo," Ben said, putting his beer down on the table. "Looks like you got it made."

Puerto rubbed up against Ben's dark brown legs and sniffed his beat-up sneakers. Marli noted the veterinarian's strong muscular calves exposed below his loose-fitting, long, tan shorts. Ben wore a faded yellow polo shirt untucked and his signature woven hairband that held back his curly walnut hair.

Marli slid onto the table bench facing the ocean and Ben took a seat opposite her. Puerto crawled under the table, belly against the cool cement floor, and lay directly between Marli's and Ben's feet.

"It's so beautiful here," Marli said, looking past Ben's head out to the palm-studded beach and the silver-plated waves rolling into the shore.

"What can I get you to drink?" Suzanne asked, seemingly oblivious to the homeless hound hiding under the table.

"Bottled water, por favor," Marli replied.

"How about something to eat?" Ben asked.

"I heard the veggie tacos are good."

"They are my favorite," Ben said. "Suzanne, two veggie tacos, please."

"I thought this place was famous for its fish tacos," Marli said, smiling at Ben across the table.

"It is. I'm sure they are great. But I don't eat anything with a face or a mother."

Marli grinned with a slight flirtatious giggle. The doctor was handsome, educated, and kind.

"Now you want to take the mutt home with you," Ben said, glancing down at Puerto, who had changed positions and was now sprawled out on his side, head resting on Marli's foot. "What about, 'My husband would kill me'?"

"He left me."

"He left you?" Ben repeated. "Left you or left Mexico?"

"Left me."

Ben hesitated, taking another sip from his beer mug. "I'm sorry. I hope I didn't sound flip," Ben said.

The two new friends sat without speaking for an agonizing awkward moment.

"So anyway," Marli finally said, "it appears I'm a free agent. I can do whatever I please. And I cannot imagine leaving Puerto behind when I go home. What do I need to do to take him home with me? Vaccinations? Permission from the government? How does this work?"

Suzanne returned with two white paper plates, each piled high with a mixture of shredded carrots, pickled cabbage, raw onions, and red bell peppers, topped with chunks of cotija cheese and avocado, and dressed with a creamy cilantro sauce covering a layer of seasoned black beans on two soft corn tortillas. She set the plates down in front of Marli and Ben, then reached into her apron pocket, pulled out a scrap of cooked chicken, and tossed it to the secret guest hiding under the table. Ben and Suzanne exchanged winks.

"Gracias," Ben said, picking up a plastic squirt bottle that resembled the ketchup and mustard containers at a

'50s diner and drenching his two tacos with its creamy, light-orange contents.

"What is it? Is it hot?" Marli asked of the mysterious sauce.

"No, not hot. I have no idea what's in it. It's their special recipe. Try it." Ben smiled.

Marli hesitantly turned the plastic bottle upside down and squirted one small spot of the top-secret liquid onto her plate.

"This looks delicious," she said, watching Ben dive in with both hands. Marli elected to take advantage of the knives and forks conveniently provided in a tin can on the table along with extra paper napkins.

"Who eats tacos with a knife and fork?" Ben asked jokingly.

Marli offered a shy shoulder shrug in return.

"To take a dog out of Mexico and into the United States, he must be certified as healthy by a vet and vaccinated against rabies, which you have done already," Ben said. "But if the dog has never been vaccinated for rabies before, you have to wait at least thirty days before he leaves Mexico."

"Thirty days? But I can't stay in Mexico another thirty days," Marli said.

"Well, we gave him a rabies vaccination on Monday when you came to my office. That was five days ago. Now you only have twenty-five days to go," Ben said with a casual grin as he took another bite of his taco, then wiped away a dollop of the secret orange sauce from his chin.

Marli put down her fork and looked at Ben. She was not sure if he was being mean or just messing with her. His dry sense of humor was attractive yet irritating at the same time.

"Twenty-five days," she sighed. "I'm only staying another week . . . to clear my head and figure out my life . . . and what I'm going to do. But I really need to get home."

"Why?" Ben asked.

Why? Good question, Marli thought. Her soon-to-be ex-husband, Nick, was no longer a consideration or an influence. Any arrangements regarding the divorce that they needed to work out could wait. She was still on leave from the magazine so there was no risk of losing a job if she stayed. She did not have pets or other similar obligations. The only complicating factor was her mother. However, even if Aunt Abbey could not stay with Alice for more than another week, her mom would survive on her own. She was not an invalid, she just did not like to be alone. Marli could ask Aunt Abbey to stock the refrigerator before she headed back to San Diego. And when Tammy returned home from Mexico, she could check on Alice, maybe take her to lunch or the movies a few times. It all seemed so simple, so clear, so doable.

"Well, why not? Maybe I could manage it," Marli said. "But I would have to borrow money from my mom. Nick is not going to subsidize my extended vacation, especially for a dog. He may have even cancelled our joint credit cards already. I would need to find a less expensive hotel. I can't ask my mom for that much money."

"I have a vacant rental unit behind my house," Ben said. "The tenants just moved out. You could stay at no charge if you help me at my vet clinic while you're here."

At that moment, the universe opened up and tenderly took Marli up into its arms, hushing her doubts, calming her fears, cradling her weary body, and comforting her fragile mind.

Good things happen to good people, the universe whispered. *Everything will be OK*.

Chapter Nine

Ben Rosado lived about two miles into the central town of Puerto Escondido, away from the tourist-driven beachfront in a quiet, modest, residential neighborhood. He turned his red Chevy truck down a wide, paved road with a grass median strip separating the opposing lanes of traffic. Many of the dwellings along the lane were side by side, exterior walls touching with no separation, and the doorways were only a few feet from the road with virtually no front yards. Parked cars were scattered from house to house. Errant tree branches hovered above their own shade. Erratic power lines were strung helter-skelter across the sky. In the distance, the level street gave way to the legendary Sierra Madre mountain range with its lush emerald hills curving like the female form.

Ben pulled his truck up to an unassuming tan building sharing its right wall with a neighboring house painted amethyst purple with a bold turquoise trim. Several wooden produce crates and empty straw baskets lingered on Ben's front porch. The fronds of a towering banana tree canopied the ground below.

Marli and Puerto scooted across the front seat and jumped down from the driver's side of the Chevy.

"My dog's name is Escondido," Ben said. "He's friendly."

"You have a dog? Well, of course you have a dog. Just one?"

"Yes, just one. I only have room for one. But I'm working on getting a larger place," Ben said as he inserted his house key into the main lock and a second key into the deadbolt. He pushed open the front door to a small living space almost bare of belongings.

"Come in," he instructed his two- and four-legged guests.

Puerto eased into the house with some hesitation and then, snout to the floor, began sniffing every corner, roaming from room to room in canine curiosity.

"Don't you lift your leg on anything," Ben said to the inquisitive mutt.

"Oh my god, he did that the first time I let him into my hotel room," Marli laughed. "I did not tell Rosa."

"He has no concept of what it means to be housebroken. You will have your work cut out for you when you get home."

Marli stepped into the main living area. A well-used, tobacco-brown couch draped with a traditional Mexican Falsa blanket was positioned on one side of the room, accompanied by a rustic cedar coffee table with a simple wrought iron base. The wooden finish sported a series of water rings that resembled the Olympic logo. A stack of hardback books teetered on the edge. An old kiva ladder made of Latilla sticks rested against the wall to the right of the sofa. A simple pine chair and a Southwestern Zapotec rug on the worn, hardwood floor made up the remainder of the room. The home reflected the taste and lifestyle of a quiet single man who preferred to live simply in a world where so many—people and animals—have so little.

"There's my boy," Ben said, pushing open the back screen door to greet Escondido, a quivering, squirming, whirlwind of fur that whipped through the house with uncontrollable elation to have his best friend return to him again. Puerto abruptly stopped his domicile investigation to come nose to nose with Escondido. Tails waving in unison, the two mutts circled each other twice, and then turned to their respective people for attention.

"Hey, Escondido. You're a big boy," Marli said, bending down to meet the large dog eye to eye. "I read somewhere that dog names should only be two syllables."

"Well, his nickname is Mr. Big Guy," Ben said, "Or, I guess, just Big Guy. Two syllables." Ben smiled.

Escondido, at nearly eighty pounds, was almost twice the size of Puerto, and looked to be part Irish wolfhound and who knew what else. He had a rose-colored nose, long, bony legs, and thin, creamy hair in pin curls around his torso.

"Why do you call him Escondido?" Marli asked.

"Escondido means 'hidden' in Spanish. When I found him, he was hiding beneath a pile of lumber and rubble from a building that had been torn down. It took me three days to coax him out with scraps of raw meat. He was so malnourished he could barely walk."

"Oh my god, you poor thing. Well, you have it made now, Escondido. You found the right guy to take care of you," Marli said with affection and guarded admiration for the compassionate veterinarian she was gradually getting to know.

"Puerto and Escondido?" Ben said. "Funny."

"Yes, they go together, don't they?" Marli paused. "Why don't you take him to work with you?"

"I usually do. It depends on how busy my day will be."

Ben's vacant unit was behind the house only steps away from his back door. He had converted a small, detached garage into rental property for extra money. The space, which was even smaller than a basic studio apartment in the United States, comprised two rooms—a living area with a twin bed, a half-size refrigerator, an electric stove, and a sink, and a bathroom with a toilet and shower stall. Similar to the main home's interior, the space was sparse, simple, and clean.

"I think this will work," Marli said. "I'm just worried about Puerto. He won't stay the night with me at the hotel. When I bring him in the room, he gets restless and paws at the door to go out. So I let him go. But he always comes back in the morning."

"He is a street dog. He has never lived inside. He may feel too confined, too vulnerable. Or he goes back to where he came from, maybe home?"

"I'm his home now," Marli said, stroking the pup's head. "What if he won't stay with me here, either? What if he wants to leave?"

"Let's see what happens. Maybe he will just want to sleep outside where he does not feel trapped. If he does leave, I'm sure he will find his way back." Ben knelt down to reassure Puerto on his own level that everything would be OK. Puerto rolled over on his back, exposing his gritty white chest, three paws stretched to the ceiling while his left back leg remained in its permanent bend. The temperature in the small, closed-in space was ten degrees warmer than the outside air. Ben wiped away perspiration from his forehead as he scratched Puerto's pink belly. Escondido nuzzled in for attention, too.

"What do you say we give you a bath before Marli takes you back to the hotel?" Ben asked the unassuming Puerto.

"That would be great," Marli immediately said. "He is in desperate need."

"Not a problem. Hopefully he won't be afraid of the hose," Ben said. "So will my rental unit work for you?"

"My girlfriend, Tammy, is joining me here tomorrow," Marli answered, stooping down to clutch Puerto around his neck while Ben grabbed a bottle of dog shampoo stored in a green plastic crate on the back porch. "I rented the hotel room for one more week and then she leaves. So can I stay here beginning next Saturday? Then it will be only seventeen days until Puerto goes home to America."

On the drive back into downtown, Ben shared more with Marli about the plight of homeless street dogs in Mexico. During the ten-minute route to Hotel Santa Fe, they counted more than twenty wayward mutts traveling along the side of the highway, laying in dirt ditches and sniffing gravel driveways.

"In Davis . . . Yolo County . . . I was a large animal vet. Lots of agriculture. And Mexican farmworkers with animals. Pigs, cows, horses. It helped that I spoke Spanish." Ben reached across Puerto, stopping to scratch behind the dog's floppy ears, and wrestled with the truck's uncooperative glove compartment until it finally popped open, revealing a single pair of men's sunglasses.

"Can I help?" Marli asked.

"I got it," Ben replied. "I finally broke down and bought prescription sunglasses."

"What made you switch from large animals to small animals?"

"A little dog named Jett."

"Jett? Great name."

"I would donate my time to help the county animal shelter with minor surgeries like spays and neuters and dentals. Anything I could do to help the animals get adopted. One time, I was about to perform a dental on a small dog when I found a large tumor growing right above her back molar. I had seen these tumors before. I knew it wasn't malignant.

But if I removed it, it would probably grow back. If the tumor got too large, it would affect the dog's ability to eat and chew. And it could be extremely uncomfortable.

"So, I called my contact, Kelly, at the shelter. I told her that whoever adopted the dog would have to keep an eye on it and have it removed again down the road.

"I distinctly remember, she said, 'Damn. We probably won't put her up for adoption then.' The shelter was 'busting at the seams,' as she put it, with dogs that didn't have any issues. And this little dog was older, too. Not a puppy, which is what everyone wants.

"Kelly said, 'Since she is under anesthesia now, can you just euthanize her?'"

"What did you do?" Marli asked with hesitation.

"I removed the tumor, performed the dental, spayed her, and named her Jett after Joan Jett. 'I Love Rock 'n' Roll' was playing on the radio during the surgery. That little girl was a fighter. She lived five more years. I took her everywhere with me."

Marli gave Ben an affirmative smile.

"I had a minor epiphany with Jett," Ben said. "I never understood the extent of the animal overpopulation problem until they asked me to euthanize Jett, a perfectly good dog who had only one insignificant medical issue. That's when I decided to become a small animal vet and eventually moved back to Mexico . . . where I could help homeless animals here."

Marli held Puerto, still slightly damp from his bath, tight against her chest, one arm wrapped around his neck as he balanced on her lap, leaning his head out the open truck window, tongue flapping in the wind.

"Millions of stray dogs live on the streets and beaches of Mexico—some say there are three million in Mexico

City alone," Ben said, slowly losing his usual reserve as he became more comfortable in Marli's company. "Some international organizations estimate there are as many as six hundred million stray dogs worldwide. Because they lack nutrition, shelter, and basic care, most will succumb to disease and injury." Ben sighed. "Starvation, dehydration, exposure. Cruelty.

"I see dogs with their nails growing into their paws. Their fur is so matted it pulls away from their skin. Then their skin gets raw and infected. They are covered with fleas and ticks. Many have mange. I won't even tell you about the cruelty I've seen," Ben said emphatically. "And nothing can be done. Anti-cruelty laws are ambiguous. Authorities don't prosecute offenders anyway. And despite all this, their biggest challenge is apathy and ignorance. People just don't care."

"What can we do?" Marli asked sympathetically.

"Stop . . . or at least curb the population, the breeding," Ben said, turning toward Marli for a brief second to catch her eye. "That's where I need you. That's how you can help me while you're here in Mexico." Ben turned off Highway 200 toward the beach and Hotel Santa Fe. "I am working with several expats to hold a spay clinic next Saturday. We have several vets and vet students from Mexico City who are donating their time."

"I'm in." Marli smiled. "What do you need me to do?"

"Spaying and neutering is not widely accepted in Mexico yet. Many Mexican men still have a macho attitude. They don't believe in neutering because they think it will 'ruin' their dogs," Ben mocked. "Religion is also a factor. Catholics don't believe in abortion or birth control, not even in animals. And then of course there is the cost of surgery. Many Mexican families can barely afford to feed and care for their own children. Dogs are not a priority. But the cost per dog will be minimal. We got donations to pay for the meds and equipment. And the labor is all volunteer. Now we just have to reach out to the community and convince them that spaying and neutering is the right thing to do."

"How do we do that?"

"We need help taking flyers around to all the businesses and homes to promote the clinic. Just talk to people. Not all Mexicans hate or are indifferent to the street dogs. Some families keep them as pets. We just need to make sure they are spayed and neutered. And convince others to bring in the street dogs they are feeding. Or dogs they know of—just hanging around. We will even waive the fee, if necessary."

"My girlfriend, Tammy, will help, too, while she is here."

"Excellent. Thank you. Speaking of your friend . . . would you like to do something tomorrow night? It's our annual Carnaval."

"Did you send Marli a text message about Franklin?" Nick hissed into the cell phone.

"What if I did?" Tammy curtly responded.

"Are you crazy? What are you trying to do?"

"I am just tired of the lies, the deceit. She's my best friend. She deserves to know the truth."

"And what about me?"

"What about you? Are you kidding me? You are such a selfish shit. And on top of everything, you leave Marli in Mexico for another woman? You really don't care about anyone or anything . . . or who you hurt, do you?"

Chapter Ten

Marli watched Ben as he turned his truck around in the hotel's driveway and pulled onto the main road that led back up to the highway. She would see him again in only twenty-four hours when he picked her and Tammy up for Carnaval.

"Carnaval is a Catholic tradition celebrated each year on the weekend before Lent begins on Ash Wednesday," Ben had explained.

Puerto followed Marli past the Mexican lady selling her hand-embroidered garments at the entrance of Hotel Santa Fe. Instead of going straight to her room, Marli headed to the poolside balcony where several other guests had already gathered to welcome the day's end and to embrace the flawless sun as it teased the ocean in its perfect descent. It had been a very long time since Marli had a sense of purpose. This man, Ben Rosado, was giving her something to care about, something meaningful, a way to give back, and perhaps a reason to live again.

"I'm in love!" shouted Marli as soon as she rushed to embrace Tammy emerging from customs at the Puerto Escondido International Airport.

"What?" Tammy exclaimed, grabbing Marli's shoulders with both hands and pulling her girlfriend in for an all-encompassing hug.

"With a dog! The dog I told you about! Puerto!"

"Oh right. Yes, I want to hear all about the dog. Right after my fifth margarita! We have a lot to talk about. You are clearly still in shock over Nick."

"Nick!" Marli screeched.

"Yes, Nick. Your soon-to-be ex-husband."

"No, it's Nick! He is right over there with a woman! Oh my god. She must be *the* woman. The one he left me for."

"Well look at that," Tammy said, lowering her sunglasses to get a better view. "You are way better looking."

"What should I do? Does he see us?"

Puerto Escondido International was small in comparison to other tourist-focused airports. It had one runway, one gate, one baggage claim, and a terminal with a capacity of only 115 people. It did not take Nick long to spot the two women.

"He's coming over," said Marli. "How do I look?"

"You look fine. Who cares! He looks like shit."

Marli and Tammy waited, both not willing to meet Nick halfway. Something looked familiar to Marli about Nick's new girlfriend, who had now taken a seat among the other passengers waiting to embark on the next plane for Mexico City.

"Hello, Marli. Tammy. What are you doing here?" Nick cautiously asked. His eyes looked like two craters of black lava rock and his chalky skin was paler than when he had arrived in the suntanned city.

"Not looking so good, Nick," Tammy said as she inspected him up and down like he was a John looking for a lay. "Had a bad time in Mexico?"

"Not that it's any of your business, but, yes, I caught a bug or something."

"Montezuma's revenge? What a pity. But how appropriate," Tammy said.

"Marli, I just wanted to tell you that I will have my things moved out of the house as soon as I can. I will try not to disturb you."

"Don't worry about me, Nick," Marli said with satisfaction. "I won't be coming home for another couple weeks, so take your time."

"What?" Nick responded with surprise. "You're staying here longer?"

"That's why Tammy is here. We are going to have some fun for the first time in a long time." The two women exchanged mischievous looks.

"And who is paying for all this fun?" Nick asked. "Not me."

"Go to hell, Nick," Tammy said. "Go get on your fucking plane with your ugly, two-bit whore and fly straight to hell."

"I'll have the divorce papers waiting for you when you get back from your little vacation," Nick coldly stated without regret or remorse as he turned and walked away to rejoin the woman impatiently flipping through the latest issue of *Vogue*.

"Asshole," said Tammy.

"That woman with Nick looks so familiar. I know I've seen her before."

"She's the scum you scraped off your shoe this morning. Stop thinking about her and let's get to those margaritas."

Tammy traveled light. With only one carry-on bag and no checked luggage to wait for, the women quickly caught an airport taxi. On the ride to Hotel Santa Fe, Marli shared with Tammy details of the past week's noteworthy events, including the menacing message about Franklin's death, losing a husband, meeting an attractive veterinarian, and finding a stray street dog, apparently the new love of her life. The two friends counted twelve homeless canines along the way and Tammy finally began to understand the importance of Marli's new mission to help the invisible creatures. When they reached the hotel, the long balmy afternoon had stretched into early evening, and the women had just enough time to step up their wardrobe from shorts to sundresses and relax with a couple of cocktails at the poolside bar before Ben would arrive to pick them up.

"Wait until you see the sunset from here," Marli told Tammy. "It's life changing."

"So is mescal, or so I've heard."

"Yeah, been there, done that already. I'll stick to tequila," Marli replied, looking around for Puerto, whom she last saw right before heading to the airport to meet Tammy but now was nowhere in sight.

Tammy ordered two margaritas on the rocks with two shots of an Añejo tequila on the side from the jovial, English-speaking bartender working behind the bamboo tiki bar. The women found a set of vacant lounge chairs directly behind the white stucco banister that stretched out toward the ocean. A breeze caught Tammy's white paper cocktail napkin and sent it swirling into the air and over the railing.

"What do you think about that message about Frankie's death? Should I contact that detective who talked to us right after Frankie died?" asked Marli, now feeling the effect of her first sip of tequila and allowing the alcohol to intensify her emotions. "Damn, Tammy. Just as I was starting to feel whole again. I can't believe this is happening." Marli outlined the bottom of her eyelashes with her index finger to stop the black mascara from running down her cheeks.

"Someone is trying to tell you something. I would pay attention to it. Did you text back?"

"No. Nick convinced me to let it go. If it is some nutcase, I would only be encouraging him . . . or her."

"Her? You think it might be a 'her'?" Tammy asked hesitantly.

"Who knows? I guess it could be. I just don't know."

"Why would someone go out of their way to tell you that Franklin's death was not an accident if it was a joke? It does not make sense. I think you should text back. See what they say. Then decide if you want to call that detective or not. If that person has evidence to prove it was a murder, then you have to go to the police."

"Murder? That never crossed my mind. Why do you say murder?"

"If it wasn't an accident, what else would it be?" Tammy quickly replied.

"Murder. The thought is just so unbelievable. Why would anyone want to murder Frankie?"

"I don't know. I don't know what I'm saying. I'm sorry. Listen, let's enjoy the evening and talk about what to do tomorrow, OK?"

"OK!"

"Now, tell me more about this Mexican veterinarian," Tammy said, changing the subject. Sipping from her salt-rimmed glass, she sank farther back into her sea-blue lounge cushion. "Is he cute?"

"I don't know. Maybe . . . yes, definitely. Tall, curly brown hair, big soft eyes. Passionate about helping animals, but kind of low-key at the same time. He is hard to read. Anyway, we struck up a friendship of sorts. And he has offered to let me stay at his place."

"What? Have you slept with him already?"

"No!" Marli shook her head emphatically. "But why the hell not? Nick cheated on me and then left me alone in Mexico—piece of shit. So here I am, free to do whatever I want. And Ben is so damn charming and smart and handsome."

"Fuck Nick, that pig," Tammy said a little too loudly. "Bring on *the* Ben," she cheered, raising her margarita glass to Marli's. Several small grains of salt fell between the two lounge chairs as they clinked their glasses together.

"But listen, here's the thing," Marli said. "I want to bring Puerto back to California with me. But we have to wait thirty days after his rabies shot before he can go from Mexico to the United States. I can't afford to stay at the hotel for that long so Ben offered to let me stay at his place—well not *in* his place, but in his rental unit behind his house—if I would help him get the word out about a spay clinic he has planned in a couple weeks." Marli picked up her shot glass and threw back the amber liquid in one gulp. "And I volunteered us both to help."

"Excuse me?" Tammy asked. "What are we doing?"

"Tam, this is really important to me," Marli said. "We will still have plenty of time to lay on the beach and snorkel and shop and all the things we want to do. We just have to help Ben pass out a few flyers and talk to people about the clinic, that's all."

"I'll do anything for you, amiga. I'm here in Mexico with you, right? Plus, I adore that you want to bring home a Mexican street mutt. Nick will hate that. Imagine a dog on those hardwood floors. It will kill Nick!"

"I can't wait." Marli narrowed her eyes like a hired assassin conspiring to bring down a mob boss. "Speaking of Mexican mutts," she said, twisting from right to left in search of the absent pooch. "I wonder where Puerto is."

"Right here." Ben's deep voice floated through the sultry air.

Marli and Tammy swung around in unison to face the fine-looking veterinarian and a tongue-waving street dog panting so hard that the upturned corners of his open mouth made it look like he was in full laughter.

"He came running to greet me in front of the hotel," Ben said.

"There you are!" Marli exclaimed.

Puerto raced up to Marli and leaped into her lap, placing his front paws on the metal frame of the lounge chair. "Tammy, this is Puerto," she said, repositioning the awkward canine who was growing more robust and healthy every day. "And this is Ben."

Ben had switched from his usual beat-up cargo shorts to another pair without tears or stains. For this evening, he wore a salmon-colored polo shirt, untucked, and a pair of faux leather topsiders instead of running shoes. Ben's soft brown locks fell free, unencumbered by his customary hair-band, so his ringlets gently touched his long black eyelashes and tumbled around his ears. He repeatedly ran his fingers through his rebel curls, forcing them to stay back away from his eyes, if only for a second.

"Hell-ooo, doc-tor." Tammy extended her right hand up to Ben with her left still gripping the margarita glass.

"My pleasure," Ben said, returning Tammy's insistent shake.

"Come, sit," Marli said. "Tell us more about Carnaval."

Instead of sitting directly next to Marli on her lounger, Ben pulled up a patio chair from a nearby table.

"It is very similar to Mardi Gras in New Orleans, including the reckless abandon and heavy alcohol consumption." Ben teased them with serious sarcasm, nodding toward Tammy's icy glass.

"Right on!" Tammy laughed. "I picked the perfect time to come."

"It is a last opportunity for *indulgence*," Ben added. "In Puerto Escondido and throughout Mexico, Carnaval is celebrated with pageantry and parades, elaborate costumes with extravagant face masks, live music, and street parties, dancing and drinking typically into the night. It usually begins with the *quema de mal humor* or the ritual 'burning of bad mood' to rid people of unpleasant thoughts so they can enjoy the festivities."

"Burning of bad mood? Just what the doctor ordered," Tammy said as she took the last sip from her cocktail.

"Carnaval is really a way for the Mexican people to take a respite from the seriousness of everyday life, a release from social norms. It has evolved into sanctioned gratification if you will, accepted excess for one weekend, just having fun because you can. Crazy behavior is expected. Today is pleasure, tomorrow is reality."

"Well, let's get this pleasure started." Tammy smiled.

Ben led the way down to the main boulevard, Calle de Morro, leading from Hotel Santa Fe along the Playa Marinero beach, past the endless straight of tourist gift shops, tequila bars, and crowded restaurants. The street was already beginning to come alive with locals and tourists anticipating the annual debauchery.

"My friend is meeting us at Sativa Terraza for dinner," Ben said as he guided the girls in, out, and around tanned surfers, young couples, senior expats, rowdy teenagers, parents with children, and numerous others crowding the sidewalk and spilling out onto the street, which was now closed to vehicles for the evening. Marli slowed to check on Puerto and realized he was not following along behind them.

"Ben. Puerto isn't here," she said, lightly but purposefully touching Ben's arm.

"Don't worry. Street dogs don't like the commotion. They

retreat to their safe places on nights like tonight. Puerto is just hunkering down for the evening. He will be back in the morning."

After another couple of congested blocks, Ben finally came to a stop under a rustic sign made of pine two-by-fours painted with the words "Sativa Terraza . . . Stylish Food & Cocktails" in bright, red letters outlined in black. The eatery and bar resided on the upper level of a rough stucco and wood-planked building decorated with artwork of whimsical palm leaves. Tiny white string lights wrapped around two poles leading up the staircase to the entrance. Angular pendant lights hung above an open patio that extended out from the main floor to an extraordinary view of the Pacific Ocean.

The interior of the restaurant sported a contemporary decor featuring bleached, midcentury-modern fiberglass chairs and polished teak dining tables. The full bar to the right of the entrance was already two bodies deep with beautiful young women in bikini tops, low-rise cutoff jeans, and strapless sundresses. Men, grasping bottles of Mexican beer, wore logo T-shirts and surfer shorts. Ben maneuvered his way through the standing-room-only crowd toward the outside patio where three vacant chairs peered over the railing toward the water.

"Hola amigo," Ben said to his friend as he waved Marli and Tammy in closer. "Cyrano, meet Marli and Tammy."

Cyrano stood and took each of their hands.

"Lovely to meet you," Cyrano said in his limited English. He was beautifully handsome with rich, brown hair trimmed short and a seductive smile.

"This is incredible!" Tammy exclaimed, looking out over the ocean. "I am loving this!"

"Sit," Ben told the ladies as if they were two of his four-legged patients. "What would you like to drink?"

"Double margarita with a shot on the side. You pick the tequila!" Tammy added.

"Sounds good," Marli said.

"We will be right back with menus, too."

Ben and Cyrano retreated through the sea of party-seekers toward the bar. A live reggae-soul-rock band had just kicked in their first set, and the uninhibited crowd moved and mingled to the music.

"Ben! My favorite veterinarian!" the bartender shouted over the crowd. "Everyone, this man saved my dog after he ate rat poison! Let him through! Ben, what can I get you?"

It was only a few minutes before Ben and Cyrano returned to their two female dates with four menus, a pitcher of margaritas, a bottle of Herradura Reposado, and eight accompanying glasses.

"So, Cyrano," Tammy said. "That's an unusual name. Like Cyrano de Bergerac?"

"Remember that old movie from the '50s about Cyrano de Bergerac?" Ben answered for his friend. "It starred José Ferrer. That was Cyrano's mother's favorite movie. That's how Cyrano got his name. His mom said if she had a girl, she would have named her Roxane."

"Fascinating," Tammy said with intent interest. "How did you two meet?"

"High school," Ben said. "We grew up in a small town called Bajos de Chila. It's only four miles from here on the coast. Both our parents still live there."

"Ahhh, nice," Tammy said. "Marli and I met in college. We were roomies. Good to have longtime amigas you can count on."

"What does Cyrano do for a living?" Marli asked.

"He works on the family farm. They grow corn, chilies, cacti, pumpkins, papayas, limes, mangoes, you name it. It's a much slower pace in Bajos de Chila. So Cyrano likes to join me here for a little nightlife. It's a good reason for him to dress up!"

"You two complement each other," Tammy said. "Bohemian meets GQ."

"Ha!" Ben laughed. "I'm wrinkled baggy shorts and T-shirts, and he's pressed khakis and button-up shirts. But we always have each other's back."

Cyrano filled their four shot glasses from the bottle of Herradura Reposado.

"To new friends," Tammy said as they downed the golden liquor.

"So, you were roommates in college," Ben said. "How was that?"

"We were carefree and crazy," Tammy said, the tequila loosening up her inhibitions. "On the first day of each semester, we would play this game. We'd survey our respective classrooms for the best-looking men, then decide which ones we were going to sleep with."

"Excuse me? What?" Ben said.

"Tammy, too much information!" Marli shouted over the music.

"It was great fun," Tammy continued, ignoring her friend. "We had to report back to each other at the end of the week with details on our unwitting male victims-to-be. Hair length and color, height, choice of attire. Then the race was on for who could get a first date and the first, you know, overnight."

"Sounds like you ladies approached dating like a college sport," Ben said after translating Tammy's story for Cyrano. "I'm sure you *scored* a lot."

"We were hot!" Tammy laughed. "Fridays and Saturdays meant drinking at our favorite nightclubs. Last call was two a.m. but they stayed open until four so we could dance and sober up before driving home. It was so much fun!"

"But those days are far behind us, right Tammy?" Marli said, turning to Ben and Cyrano. "Tammy is married now with a sweet four-year-old daughter."

"Oh yeah, right. I forgot," Tammy joked. "Exciting nights are ordering in pizza and watching a Netflix movie. All the more reason to enjoy tonight!"

From their second-story vantage point overlooking the crowd-crazy boulevard, the four friends drank without inhibition, ate dinner with enthusiasm, and marveled at the passing parade. A sea of grandiose displays floated by, each embellished with enormous papier-mâché creatures—unicorns, marlin, dragons, lions, tigers, and giraffes—painted in psychedelic, glow-in-the-dark colors and electrified with thousands of neon lights. Dozens of men and women, most with buff, bronzed bodies, strutted past in extravagant costumes adorned with feathers, sequins, jewels, satin, and lace.

"See what I meant when I said crazy behavior is expected?" Ben shouted, raising his voice above the music and laughter from inside the restaurant, which competed with the street sounds below.

"Let's dance!" Tammy said, jumping up from her chair and grabbing Cyrano's arm as he downed his second shot of tequila.

The restaurant was now revolving with the revelers, the pleasure-seeking crowd on its feet. Tammy and Cyrano fell into their rhythm, swaying back and forth to the band's version of "One Love" by Bob Marley, with their hips pressed up against each other, arms overhead. Ben grabbed the bill from the table and handed it to the waitress with cash for the tab plus a generous tip.

"Thank you." Marli smiled.

"Looks like our friends are hitting it off."

"Yes, well, but she is married. I hope she does not do anything she regrets."

"What happens in Mexico, stays in Mexico," Ben said, taking Marli's hand and joining Tammy and Cyrano on the dance floor. As the reggae song came to an end, the band went directly into a cover of "Shut Up and Dance" and the floor erupted with the four friends sandwiched in the middle at full speed.

"Walk the Moon!" Tammy screamed. "I love this band!"

Still holding Marli's hand, Ben pulled her in closer so their torsos were connected as twisting bodies worked around them. Cyrano and Tammy belted out the lyrics in unison with every other voice in the room, jumping in tandem and shaking their shoulders back and forth into each other's chest.

Still secure within Ben's powerful reach, Marli pulled herself up to his ear. "I can't breathe!" she said, laughing and catching her breath at the same time. Ben grabbed Cyrano's arm. "Let's get some air," he shouted, and the foursome pushed through the ricocheting mob, out the front door, and down the stairs to the street.

"Oh my god! That was too much fun!" Tammy laughed, clearly feeling the effects of the Herradura tequila as she fell into Cyrano's arms.

The parade had ended, but the sidewalk and boulevard were still alive with energetic partygoers, many donning the crazy Carnaval masks—some frightening, some friendly—believed to protect them from evil spirits. To their left,

Mexican music blasted from a large boom box atop a dented newspaper stand. A group of five foreigners, each wearing multiple strands of cheap, plastic Mardi Gras beads, clutched frozen strawberry margaritas as they stumbled past a young man vomiting into a green, metal garbage can.

"Time to go," Ben said.

"Ah! So soon?" Tammy protested, still clinging to Cyrano.

"It's really not safe as the night goes on," Ben replied, apologetically.

"Do you want to come back to the hotel with us?" Marli asked. "We can go for a swim."

"*Excelente*!" said Cyrano, who seemed to understand more English than he claimed.

The poolside patio on the upper level of Hotel Santa Fe was surprisingly quiet. Only two other couples occupied the lounge chairs, and no one was enjoying a moonlit swim. Some of the hotel guests were still out celebrating Carnaval. However, most leaned toward the conservative side and were safe inside their comfortably appointed suites long before midnight. Marli and Tammy excused themselves to go to their room and change into their swimming suits.

"Are you OK?" Marli asked Tammy as soon as she shut the door behind them.

"I'm having an excellent time. Cyrano is soooo cute!"

"Tammy, you're drunk. And you're married. Happily married!"

"Oooohhh, don't worry. I'm just having fun. I'm not going to do anything," Tammy said as she fell backward onto the embroidered Mexican bedspread. "But damn, what if I did?" she said, emphatically sitting straight up. "Men do it all the time. One little meaningless fling. How could that hurt? I want to feel that crazy passion just one more time before

I die. You know, when you kiss someone for the first time and you feel all tingly. When you feel that first penetration—"

"OK! Enough! You've lost your mind in Mexico. No, you're just drunk." Marli chastised her friend. "Do whatever you want. You're a grown woman. But don't blame me in the morning. And make sure he wears a condom."

Chapter Eleven

Ben and Cyrano caught the hotel restaurant manager, Ivan, just in time to order drinks as he was closing up for the evening.

"Big night, Ivan?"

"Sí. Always busy during Carnaval," Ivan responded as he wiped the long elaborate bar top paved with deep sapphire-blue Mexican tiles.

With unimpeded views from the second level, the hotel restaurant was a popular destination to enjoy the pageantry and pomp of Carnaval taking place on the street below. But the enthusiastic crowds had dispersed by now and the three men cheerfully embraced the quiet night air, occasionally interrupted by celebratory firecrackers exploding in the distance.

"The dog is over there," Ivan said, pointing to Puerto curled up on the cool tile in the corner of the bar.

"There you are, amigo," Ben stated, kneeling down to embrace Puerto as he bounded toward him. "Marli was worried about you."

Ivan told Ben that the nervous mutt had laid low all evening to avoid the crazy chaos on the streets. The restaurant manager brought Puerto leftover scraps from diners' dinner plates, but he was too agitated and anxious to be interested in eating.

"He's a good dog," Ivan said.

"Sí," replied Ben. "Very good."

"And Marli is a nice woman," Ivan added with a grin and lift to his voice, as he polished the last of the washed wine glasses with his bar towel.

Ben ordered two snifters of Los Amantes Joven mescal, two shots of Patron tequila, and two cocktails of Kahlúa and Cream so the women could choose whichever they preferred.

"Tammy is also nice," Cyrano said as they waited for Ivan to pour their drinks.

"Sí, she is nice too," Ben agreed, not sure where Cyrano was heading with his observation about Tammy or what exactly his honorable comrade had in mind.

"Sí, mi amigo," Cyrano responded. "But the tipsy American woman is not really my type," he added with a sly smile.

Ben paid Ivan in cash and told Cyrano the next round was on him. By the time they returned to the outside patio, Marli and Tammy were already sitting on the edge of the pool dangling their feet in the clear, pristine water.

"There you are. We thought you ditched us," Marli said.

"Never," replied Ben. "And look who we found." Puerto rushed up to Marli, almost knocking her into the deep end. Marli answered back by tackling the animated mutt to the ground and giving him an enthusiastic belly rub.

Ben set the drink tray on a small teak table between two of the lounge chairs. "You have your choice. Mescal, tequila, or Kahlúa and Cream."

"Nice!" Tammy exclaimed. "Bring on the mescal!"

"Excelente!" Cyrano cheered, picking up the two snifters of tequila's evil cousin and situating himself next to Tammy at the side of the pool.

Marli stood up, slipped on a short, sheer cover-up that revealed her long trim legs, golden from her full week under the Mexican sun, and joined Ben, sitting across from him in one of the lounge chairs, the beverage table between them. The other two couples who were at the pool when they arrived had retreated to their respective hotel rooms, so the foursome had the night to themselves.

An unfettered breeze flirted with the hibiscus bushes that encircled the courtyard. The glow from two opposing lampposts cast a shimmer across the water and lightly illuminated the surrounding patio. Hidden by the darkness, a collection of crickets offered their own melodic chirping to celebrate Carnaval.

Cyrano stood, slid off his brown, suede loafers, and unbuttoned his casual, loose-fitting shirt. After laying it carefully down on a nearby chair, he unzipped his khakis, slipped one leg out and then the other, and strategically placed the pants next to the shirt. His tanned Mexican skin shone like melted dark chocolate next to his stark white briefs. Cyrano sat back down on the pool's edge, swung his long, muscular legs into the water, and slipped in next to Tammy, who was already submerged and waiting. The softly lit night provided a perfect cloak for the twosome as they silently drifted to the other end of the pool.

Ben slowly sipped the Patron instead of throwing back the tawny liquid in one shot. Marli gently swirled the Kahlúa against the ice with her index finger until the coffee liqueur merged with the rich, white cream to become a decadent dessert. Puerto lay quietly next to Marli on the lounge chair, his head resting on her bare thigh. The air was still now, interrupted only by sporadic splashes and muffled giggles emerging from the blackness at the far end of the pool. Like the Carnaval fireworks far off in the distance, they could hear Cyrano and Tammy but could not see them.

"It seems as though our friends are having a good time." Marli smiled.

"Yes, yes they are. But don't worry. We have been friends for many years, and he is always a gentleman," Ben said, hoping the conversation would drift away from their two impetuous friends and what they might be doing.

"You said you grew up in Bajos de Chila," Marli said. "But you opened your vet practice here in Puerto Escondido. Why?"

"There is no business for a vet in Bajos de Chila. Here my clients are rich expats from Canada and the United States, and wealthy Mexicans who are willing and able to spend money on their pampered pets. It's enough to keep the doors open."

"And you never married?" Marli asked.

Ben paused. "I did marry. But she died. Of breast cancer. Two years ago."

Marli's breath retreated back into her lungs. Two years ago. Franklin died two years ago. Should she tell Ben about her own sorrow? *No, not tonight.*

"I am so sorry, Ben," she managed to say.

They sat in silence for a moment, a sorrow now hanging over the night. Tragedy had no veil. It was open and everywhere. It did not discriminate. It had no remorse. It struck whenever, wherever, and whomever it wanted. No wonder the handsome veterinarian was alone, shared his life with no one, and owned a sadness he had no power over and could not escape.

Marli stroked Puerto's soft head and then shook her hand, watching the floating wisps of dog fur, backlit by the glow from the lampposts, dance delicately into the night air.

"The shedding may be hard to get used to when you get Puerto home," Ben said.

"Yes," Marli agreed amiably. "But he's worth it. I've wanted a pet for a long time but Nick refused. He didn't like the hair in the house, the poop in the yard, and everything else that goes along with owning a pet. He is a clean freak. But now I don't have to worry about that any longer. Nick left and Puerto came. Someone or something sent Puerto to me at the exact right time in my life. In a way, I'm not rescuing Puerto. He is rescuing me."

Ben took the last sip of Patron from the second shot glass. "It's late and I really have to go," Ben said. "I have to be at the office early tomorrow morning before the meeting starts. You are coming to the meeting, right?"

Marli looked confused.

"The meeting to discuss the spay clinic," Ben said.

"Yes, of course," Marli replied, jogging her tired, intoxicated memory. "Hopefully, Tammy will be with me if she is not too hung over."

"OK then," Ben said standing up. "I'm sure Cyrano will find his way home."

"Thank you for a wonderful evening."

"*De nada*."

Chapter Twelve

Tammy found her way back to the hotel room long past midnight. Marli woke up when she heard the key turn in the lock. Tammy tiptoed into the bathroom, quickly towel-dried her wet hair, peeled off her swimsuit, threw on an oversized T-shirt, and slipped under the cotton sheets on the left side of the king-size bed. Marli turned toward her friend so they were both laying on their sides facing each other.

"Did you have fun?" Marli whispered.

"Sí, *senorita*," Tammy responded, struggling to keep her eyes open.

"Bueno."

"Marli, do you ever wonder why we can't stay in love?"

"Stay in love?"

"Maybe love is the wrong word. Why we can't stay in lust?"

"I think you need to sleep now," Marli said to her weary friend.

"I mean . . . when I first met Sam, we couldn't keep our hands off each other. I couldn't wait to be with him. I thought about him all day and night. I longed for him." Tammy openly shared about her husband, becoming more alert the more she spoke. "But now, after twelve years of marriage and a child, I don't want to have sex with him anymore. Why is that?"

"I don't know, Tammy. But I'm sure you still love him."

"You know what I think? I've thought about this a lot. I had two real relationships before meeting and marrying Sam. In both of them—just like with Sam—we had wild, mad, passionate sex all the time! And then, after a few years, I just didn't want to do it anymore. I lost the desire. Why?"

"Why?" Marli asked, playing along.

"Because Mother Nature was saying 'enough.' Stop having sex or you will die." Tammy was sitting straight up now, fully awake.

"What?"

"See, in nature, without any birth control, I would have gotten pregnant and had babies. And being pregnant and having babies is dangerous—women can die. They do die! So after having sex with one mate for a period of time, Mother Nature shuts down our bodies so we don't want to have sex anymore, so we won't get pregnant and we won't die. It makes so much sense."

"OK," Marli said, propping herself up on one elbow.

"All those self-help books and women's magazines spouting off on how to add romance back into your waning relationship . . . it's all a bunch of shit. You can't bring back that passion. It goes against nature."

"Why does the passion come back if you change partners?" Marli asked, gaining some interest.

"That's a good question." Tammy candidly continued. "I think, maybe, it has to do with making sure we have diverse offspring to keep the gene pool going. If we mated with only one man, and that man was flawed—as most are—our genes would be in trouble. We are predestined to mate with many different men to make sure we have offspring that live."

"Why don't men lose their passion? They want sex all the time regardless of how long they've been with one woman."

"Because they can't get pregnant. They won't die. So they don't care who they have sex with—their wife or their lover. They just want to keep procreating with whoever is convenient." Tammy flopped back down on the mattress, eyes focused on the ceiling.

"You really have given this a lot of thought, haven't you?"

"Mother Nature is giving me permission to mate with another man. How can I ignore that?"

The next morning, Tammy and Marli took a taxi to Ben's veterinary office to join several volunteer expats and locals for their weekly meeting to discuss the logistics of the upcoming spay and neuter clinic.

"I'm going to respond to that text message now," Marli said to Tammy as she fidgeted for the seat belt in the back of the cab.

"What are you going to say?"

"I am going to say, 'Who is this?' and 'What are you talking about?'"

Marli pulled her mobile phone from her purse and scrolled to the ominous message. Tammy stared out the taxi's window, grateful she left the disposable cell in her luggage back at the hotel.

Ben arrived at his vet clinic at 7:00 a.m. Before the meeting, which began at 8:00, he wanted to feed the two resident felines, clean their litter boxes, and check on an amiable patient recovering in a cage from a broken leg. By the time Marli and Tammy lightly tapped on the front door, the meeting had just gotten started.

"Nice to see you ladies again," Ben smiled, gesturing to the duo to come inside and then relocking the door. He pulled out two more white plastic chairs from the back room and introduced the newcomers to the group.

"Thank you for joining us so early on a Sunday. I know it's probably the last place you want to be," Ben said with a grin.

Tammy stifled a yawn with her forearm.

"As I was saying, our spay and neuter clinic is coming up this Saturday. Thank you to everyone who helped secure the necessary equipment, supplies, and volunteers. Just yesterday, I confirmed two more veterinarians and six vet students from Mexico City."

The group responded with a spattering of applause and head nods.

"This coming week will be our last chance to publicize the event, and we need everyone's help passing out flyers and talking to the community about bringing in their dogs . . . and any stray dogs they are feeding. I've divided the town and outlying areas into different sections to ensure complete canvassing and to avoid duplicated efforts. And I've assigned the sections per your requests and depending on where you live. Please take a look and let me know if you have any questions."

Tammy took the assignment list and scanned for her and Marli's names, secretly hoping that Ben had forgotten to add them.

"For the clinic, all volunteers should arrive by seven a.m. We will begin at eight sharp," Ben said as he passed out a second sheet of paper. "This list has everyone's assignments.

It includes greeting and registering owners and their pets, monitoring the flow of patients throughout the process, assisting the vets and vet students, and overseeing the recovery of the dogs from anesthesia."

Marli fixated on Ben as he confidently led the meeting. His brown curls were pushed back again with his trademark hairband, unlike the night before. He graciously laughed when someone joked about uncooperative canines and/or their owners, and he became softly serious when he spoke about the difference their efforts would make in the lives of so many animals.

The meeting was over by 9:00 a.m., when Ben found the day's first patient—a spoiled, overweight basset hound who had not eaten in two days—with his two worried owners waiting out front for the office to open. Tammy grabbed a stack of spay clinic flyers. Marli checked her cell phone for the tenth time for a reply to her text message. Nothing.

"Thank you for coming," Ben said, as he unlocked the front door to let the meeting attendees out and the basset hound in.

"Hey, I gotta work off my rent, right?" Marli grinned.

"Yeah, right after we ingest major amounts of caffeine," Tammy said. "Hey, great time last night, by the way."

"Glad you had fun. So do you girls have plans for tomorrow evening? There is a place I want to show you. It involves swimming at night again, so wear your bathing suits."

"Nice. Will Cyrano be there?" Tammy smiled hopefully.

The next day, Ben examined his last canine patient at approximately 6:30 p.m. A soft lump on the side of the senior Labrador mix was most definitely a benign fatty tumor, and Ben advised the owners it would be a waste of money to pay for a costly biopsy to confirm his diagnosis. He trimmed the dog's unwieldy toenails at no extra charge and hurried the couple out the door before they could delve into another endless story about the mutt's adorable antics. Ben and Cyrano were picking up Marli and Tammy in front of Hotel Santa Fe at 7:00 p.m. for a quick bite to eat before their evening's adventure.

"Where are you taking us tonight?" Marli asked as she drenched her street taco with the fresh red chili sauce that was promised to be mild.

"You have to wait to find out," Ben said. "But I guarantee you will never forget it."

Following dinner, the foursome headed for Laguna de Manialtepec, approximately eleven miles west of Puerto Escondido. The coastal lagoon was a twisted swamp of giant mangrove trees, providing refuge to brown pelicans, herons, cranes, and iguanas.

Cyrano, with Tammy seated next to him in the front seat, and Ben and Marli in the back, turned his Honda Civic into a dirt driveway, avoiding a deep pothole to the left and a misplaced boulder on the right, and parked in front of an expansive wooden patio scattered with tables and plastic porch chairs. An older Mexican woman wearing a faded blue apron sat with a younger man holding a syrupy-green-colored Mountain Dew can. A narrow muddy path to the side of the building led to a weathered dock where a row of scarred and scraped motorboats, similar to the water taxis at the beach, bobbed restlessly against each other while fighting their tethers. The time was almost an hour past dusk and the water was black.

"Hola, Chris!" Ben shouted to the younger man.

"*Bienvenido*, Ben!" Chris welcomed them, reaching to first shake Ben's hand and then Cyrano's.

"Gracias," Ben replied. "This is Marli and Tammy, our guests tonight."

"Excelente! It's a perfect night to swim because there is no moon!"

The two couples followed Chris down the dirt footpath to the boat ramp. The night air was still muggy from the humidity of the day, but there was promise of a cooling breeze once their open vessel was out on the lagoon.

Chris hopped into the second-to-last motorboat floating in the scattered lineup. *The Maria* was hand-painted on the side in chipped, white lettering. The boat had a navy-blue canopy hovering over three rows of passenger seats. Ben tossed his backpack onto the bow and held out his right hand to help Tammy and then Marli into the boat, while Chris steadied the women with his left. Ben's touch sent an unexpected flutter through Marli's body. Next, Ben and Cyrano unleashed the line and pushed the imprisoned boat to freedom, then took seats behind Marli and Tammy while Chris dropped the rear engine into the water and revved up the motor.

"He is right. There is no moon tonight," said Marli, gazing up into the darkness. "Why is that good?"

"You will see," Ben said.

Slowly and purposefully, Chris glided the motorboat through the pitch-black water for approximately a half mile, far from any lights on shore, and then cut the groaning engine. The vast silence was intoxicating.

"Watch," said Ben, as he leaned over the side of the boat and drew his hand across the still water. Luminous streaks of blue sparkled wherever his fingers touched.

"Oh my god," Tammy gasped. "What is that?"

"The lagoon is filled with microorganisms, plankton, that give off a phosphorescence that is activated by water movement," Ben explained. "The darker the sky, the easier it is to see."

Ben stood and pulled his T-shirt up over his head and kicked off his flip-flops. Marli tried not to stare at his taut torso and the curly dark ringlets against his bronze chest.

"Are you ready?" he asked. "Come on!"

"This is so cool!" shrieked Tammy. "Come on Marli!"

Ben launched off the side of the boat followed by Cyrano, while Tammy and Marli ditched their tank tops and shorts. Tammy dove into the depths without hesitation. Marli swung her legs over the side and slowly slipped into the lagoon, taking a few moments to adjust to the chilly change in temperature.

"Look at this!" Tammy shouted as she waved her arms back and forth through the slate-like water. With each movement, her skin shimmered and glowed, leaving a fanciful path of electric glitter. As the foursome swam, their luminescent bodies sparkled under the moonless sky. When they lifted their hands from the water, the radiant droplets shimmied down their arms, pirouetted off their skin, and flickered back into the dark bay. When they dived below the surface, they could see shiny flashes of light bounce off their eyelashes.

The four friends weaved within the water, splashing and twirling and diving around each other for nearly an hour before exhaustion forced them to surrender. As Marli pushed her way through the dark night toward the waiting boat, a sudden and familiar sensation surrounded her.

"Frankie?" she heard herself say in a hush. "Frankie?" Marli spun around, the still ocean inlet cradling her from below. Something was there, something spiritual, something transcendent. Something or someone.

"Marli!" Ben yelled from back onboard. "Are you all right?" Chris shone a flashlight through the quiet evening air.

"Yes!" Marli shouted back. "I'm coming."

"That was the most incredible thing I have ever done." Tammy radiated as she wrapped an oversized beach towel around her shivering shoulders. Cyrano brought Tammy close into his chest for extra warmth. A brisk breeze kicked up as Chris maneuvered *The Maria* through the night and back toward the dock. Ben pulled a silver flask from his backpack and offered his companions a sip of tequila.

"To warm your soul," he said.

"Gracias," Marli said, taking a long sip.

"Were you OK out there?" Ben asked.

"Yeah, I was fine. I just felt something. Like a presence in the water, in the air. I can't really explain it. I wasn't frightened. I just felt . . . safe? Does that make sense? Like someone was watching over me. I don't know. I sound like I have had too much tequila."

"These waters are magical," Ben said. "Especially at night . . . when there is no moon."

Back at the hotel room, Marli and Tammy took turns in the bathroom and then threw on their extra-large T-shirts. Marli dropped on top of the bed, too high from the night to fall asleep right away.

"Swimming in that lagoon was amazing." Tammy sighed as she slipped under the sheets.

"It was incredible," Marli agreed, falling back onto her pillow, eyes wide open.

"So is Ben," Tammy whispered to her friend with a grin.

"Yeah, Ben is pretty remarkable," Marli sighed. "But what about Cyrano?" she added. "Is Mother Nature still telling you to cheat on your sweet husband?"

"Tomorrow is another day," Tammy said. "But what about Ben?"

"Maybe . . . maybe I was meant to meet Ben. Maybe that is why I insisted that Nick bring me all the way to Mexico, and why Nick chose here to dump me, and why a homeless street dog came into my life, leading me to this incredible animal doctor. Nothing makes sense, yet everything makes sense."

"And it will make even more sense in the morning," Tammy said as she closed her eyes to exhaustion.

The next two days in Puerto Escondido were nonstop for the two women friends. Mornings consisted of block-by-block traversing on foot through business districts and residential neighborhoods to distribute spay clinic flyers, interspersed with shopping for Mexican memorabilia at every opportunity. Ben let Marli and Tammy use his truck to get from one area of town to the next. Afternoons included swimming and sunbathing at Playa Marinero and shopping at the mercados. Evenings meant dinner and drinking with Ben and Cyrano, coupled with dancing at one of the nightclubs along the Adoquin and strolling at the water's edge on Playa Principal.

The black-and-white spay clinic flyers were worded in both Spanish and English and featured a stock photo of a friendly looking collie mix. Even though the poster was self-explanatory, Marli and Tammy still learned to say "*castración perro este sábado*," which meant dog castrations this Saturday.

Expats who took the flyer thanked them for helping the harmless street dogs and promised to spread the word about the spay clinic. Local shopkeepers either smiled and nodded in agreement to post the announcement in their store windows or waved the women away like pesky flies. Canvassing the residential areas proved easier than soliciting business owners. Marli and Tammy mostly got away with leaving the posters on house doorsteps or handing them directly to neighbors chatting on front porches and people strolling along the roadsides. If a discussion arose regarding religious objections, they simply pointed to the talking points on the flyer and said, "*No hablo español.*" If someone said they could not afford the sterilization fee, Tammy would emphasize that it was only one hundred pesos. Then Marli would point to the asterisk on the flyer explaining that the hundred pesos would be waived for those who could not afford it.

"No, no, not my Jabu," said a burly Mexican man in his late fifties. "You will ruin his manhood." A broad-shouldered bulldog mix, with short, caramel-colored fur, sat silently by his owner. A chain collar, attached to a brown leather leash, hung loose around the canine's thick neck.

"Sir," began Tammy in as diplomatic a tone as she could muster, "that is actually a myth. Neutering your dog will not diminish his 'manhood,' as you so eloquently put it. It will, in fact, help him live a longer, healthier life."

"No, no, not my Jabu," the man repeated, shaking his head and waving his hand to reemphasize his conviction.

"What if I pay you five dollars to do it?" Tammy asked.

"Tammy . . ." Marli pulled her friend aside. "You can't do that. What if others find out this guy got paid to bring his dog in, and they didn't?"

"So what? If it gets the guy to let Ben cut off his dog's testicles, why not?"

"A hundred dollars?" the man countered.

"A hundred?" Tammy said. "Ha, everyone has their price. Twenty-five."

"Fifty," the man lobbed back.

"You show up at the spay clinic at eight in the morning on Saturday with Jabu, and I will have fifty bucks waiting for you." She pointed to the address on the flyer.

"Do you think he'll show?" Marli asked, as they moved onto their next stop.

"I don't know. But if he does show up, you'll have to pay him," she smiled. "I'll be on a plane heading home."

"I don't understand why there is no response to my text message," Marli said to Tammy as they stood in line waiting to order lunch at Dan's Café Deluxe, a casual street diner famous for its cheap tacos and exaggerated fruit smoothies. Puerto calmly waited at their feet, expertly balancing on his three good legs and hoping for a snack. An aqua-colored surfboard hung haphazardly above the cash register from a high, wooden crossbeam ceiling. An idle ping-pong table, complete with two paddles and a tiny white ball, was situated among the regular dining tables, as if patrons could pull their chairs up to the net if other options ran short. "Why did that person send it if he or she didn't want to tell me more about Frankie's death?"

"Maybe there isn't more to say," Tammy replied nonchalantly, perusing the Spanish-language menu posted on the wall. "Or maybe the person changed her—or his—mind about telling you."

"Excuse me, ladies." An unexpected male voice came from behind them. "Could I trouble you for a light?"

"Excuse me?" Tammy turned to inspect the person attached to the intrusive voice and retracted slightly upon inspection. "What makes you think we smoke?"

A Caucasian man in his late twenties, tall and gangly, stood uncomfortably close, wearing baggy blue jeans that rested on his distended hips, and a thin, green-plaid, long-sleeve shirt over a yellowing, white T-shirt. An unlit Camel dangled from his lips.

"My apologies," he said.

"Apologies for what?" Tammy replied, irritated.

"For making the assumption that you two lovely ladies smoked. May I buy you a drink to make restitution?"

"Absolutely not," Tammy said, sending a direct message to the unwelcome man who had oddly respectable etiquette. She then turned back toward the restaurant counter just in time for the cashier to take her and Marli's lunch orders.

"Nice dog," the stranger added, now crouching down to Puerto's view of the world. "Too bad about that bum leg. Good thing you got that smart doc helping you."

Undaunted, Tammy and Marli exchanged a quick glance between them, their backs still to the outsider.

"Well," the man said as he stood, "have a fabulous day."

"That was creepy," Marli whispered, turning to confirm that the man had indeed retreated.

"A little too creepy," Tammy agreed. "How did he know about Ben?"

Chapter Thirteen

By midweek, Marli and Tammy had handed out the last spay clinic flyer from the stack they took at the meeting. Stopping for lunch, they devoured fried huaraches with nopales and queso fresco at a popular diner called La Juquileña, a casual destination with bright-orange plastic tablecloths draped over long communal tables surrounded by ubiquitous white plastic chairs. Next, they stopped at Ben's office to pick up more posters for the following day. An older woman with deep creases in her face sat in one of the two chairs in the reception area balancing a wooden produce crate on her lap. The side of the crate displayed a worn sticker with the words "Visit Mexico" and a colorful graphic of a young Mexican girl cradling a basket spilling over with mangoes, pineapples, limes, and bananas in her arms. Inside the crate were five two-week-old puppies of questionable descent. Two were black with patches of white, two were a golden-brown with extra fluffs of fur around their ears, and one was the color of clay dirt. Their eyes were just beginning to split open, and they were relentlessly squealing and crawling over each other in search of their mother's milk.

"Oh my gosh," Tammy said. "Look at the puppies!"

"Does Dr. Rosado know you are here?" Marli asked.

"No hablo *inglés*," the woman responded.

Marli walked past the reception desk and into the back area where she had brought Puerto the first time she visited Ben exactly ten days prior.

"Ben?" she tentatively called out.

The door to another small room on the left was slightly ajar and Marli could see Ben standing to one side of a stainless-steel exam table facing an attractive young lady, startlingly similar to the Mexican girl on the side of the produce crate harboring the newborn puppies out in the waiting room. Curls of long, jet-black hair drifted down to the woman's minuscule waistline, and she clutched a tiny, tan Chihuahua, maybe four pounds at the most, to her breasts. What Marli could hear of their private conversation was in Spanish. Their voices were low and thoughtful. Hoping they were oblivious to her presence, Marli began to quietly back out of the room so as not to interrupt what appeared to be an appointment, when she saw the female reach up, twist a lock of Ben's hair with her forefinger, and softly kiss him on the cheek. Ben took the woman's hand and gently pressed his lips to her palm. Startled by the unexpected exchange of affection between the doctor and his client, Marli quickly turned to exit and knocked a metal canister of little round dog treats off the counter, spilling the contents across the scarred linoleum floor.

"Marli?" Ben called out when he eyed her through the slim opening in the door.

"Oh, yes, sorry. I didn't mean to interrupt," she nervously stuttered, her words stumbling out of her mouth as she attempted to corral the marble-shaped biscuits rebelliously rolling out of her reach. "I just wasn't sure if you knew you had another patient up front. Puppies. Five, I think. Cute. Very cute. So anyway. I'll be going. Sorry about the mess."

"Did you need something? Why are you here?" Ben asked with apprehension.

"Oh yes, more flyers. We ran out. So anyway, where would they be?"

"Let me get them," Ben said. "Excuse me," he told the pretty woman who had kissed him. "I'll be right back."

Ben closed the door behind him, leaving his client alone in the exam room with the smallest canine Marli had ever seen. *Was it even a dog?* she wondered, still recovering from her embarrassment. Ben led the way back to the reception area and pulled a large cardboard box from under the front counter.

"Here you go. Take as many as you think you will need," Ben said. "Thanks for doing this."

"Yup, you're welcome—"

Tammy grasped one of the puppies under its shoulders and brought his tiny head to her face. "Oh, you're so cute! I could just eat you up!" she whined in baby-talk, rubbing her nose on the wiggly pup's exposed pink belly. "Are we getting together tonight?" she asked in her high-pitched voice, turning to Ben.

"Maybe Ben has other plans," Marli quickly said, thinking about the mystery woman in the other room. "We can't expect him to entertain us every night."

"Why not?!" Tammy asked.

"As it turns out, I do have other plans tonight," Ben said hesitantly.

Marli was sure her heart stopped beating. Her smart, good-looking, sensitive doctor must have plans with the flawless, young beauty in the other room. It only made sense, the way he tenderly kissed the inside of her hand, the way she lovingly touched his curling locks of hair. And why shouldn't the handsome veterinarian be in love with this stunning woman? What made Marli think he might be interested in a still-married, middle-aged, pesky, California girl anyway? He was just being hospitable to two tourists in exchange for their help, and nothing more.

"See, Ben is busy," Marli said, trying to sound upbeat and indifferent.

"But how about tomorrow afternoon?" Ben quickly asked. "I can leave work early. Have you been snorkeling yet?"

"No! Not yet," Tammy said. "Great! Tomorrow afternoon it is." She placed the puppy back in the crate among his squirming siblings.

"The puppies are hungry," Ben said, looking down at the pile of cuteness. "I'll be right with you, Mrs. Gonzalez."

"Cyrano will come too, right? I don't want to be a third wheel," Tammy said as her feeble excuse for wanting Cyrano to join them.

"I don't think I will have to twist his arm," Ben said cheerfully.

"Why are you acting so strange about getting together with Ben and Cyrano?" Tammy asked, as they walked back out onto the sidewalk with two new stacks of flyers.

"There was a woman in the exam room. I saw Ben kiss her!"

"What? Are you sure?"

"Yes, I'm sure. They didn't know I could see them."

"Where did he kiss her? On the mouth or on the cheek?"

"On the inside of her hand."

"That means nothing! They could be old friends or even former lovers."

"Maybe. But it sure didn't look that way. And I don't want to be a burden. If he is trying to date someone else, he doesn't want to entertain us all the time."

"If he is trying to date someone else, he *wouldn't* be entertaining us all the time!" Tammy said, lifting her voice in annoyance. "Anyway, I only have two more days here. And I want to get to know Cyrano better!"

"Puerto Escondido is home to several of the most magnificent beaches in Mexico," Ben explained the next day, as they exited Hotel Santa Fe and headed for the oceanfront. "Playa Zicatela is considered one of the world's top ten surfing destinations. The beach is nicknamed the Mexican Pipeline because its powerful waves are similar to the Banzai Pipeline in Oahu."

Marli listened intently, fascinated by Ben's encyclopedia-like mind.

"They hold international surfing competitions here several times a year," Ben said. "Now, east of Zicatela is Playa La Punta, where the waves are more moderate and better for beginning surfers. West of Zicatela is Playa Marinero, a small stretch of sand with water ideal for body surfing and swimming. Adjacent to Marinero is Playa Principal. West of Principal are the twin beaches of Puerto Angelito and Playa Manzanillo—they are in a sheltered cove, both good for swimming, snorkeling, and relaxing on the beach. But even a little more west and a touch more remote is Playa Carrizalillo, which is where we are going."

From Hotel Santa Fe, the foursome walked down to where Playa Zicatela met Playa Marinero. Separating the two beachfronts was a twenty-foot cement sculpture of two human hands jetting out from a pile of boulders, reaching for the sky.

"What does it mean?" Marli asked, handing her cell phone to Cyrano so he could take a snapshot of the two women posing under the outstretched fingers, carefree clouds suspended along the horizon.

"It's a tribute to the people who have risked their lives trying to save others at Playa Zicatela," Ben said. "This beach is famous for surfing but infamous for taking lives."

Ben waved down a water taxi to take them to the secluded Playa Carrizalillo, where the cobalt-blue sea transitioned into emerald-green fifty feet before the water met the golden-sand beach. Rocky outcroppings on each side of the cove provided an ideal habitat for tropical fish and coral. The waves were gentle, the water warm and clear, and the ocean floor smooth, all faultless for friendly swimming and snorkeling. Family-owned palapa restaurants, constructed of dried branches and palm leaves, backed up to the lush hillside. Weathered Adirondack chairs lined up in the sand under the shade of frond-thatched umbrellas. Ben had brought them here, hoping the small bay's difficult access would equal fewer crowds than the neighboring beachfronts, and today he was correct. Only a few sunbathers occupied a scattering of horizontal loungers and beach blankets, and a handful of swimmers bobbed in and out of the water like playful porpoises.

"Margaritas, anyone?" Ben asked as they settled into four Adirondacks connected to one of several beach bars.

"And guacamole," Tammy said.

After ordering, Ben and Cyrano peeled off their shirts, damp with perspiration from the hot afternoon air, and unpacked four masks and snorkels, two they had rented for Marli and Tammy.

"The best area to see fish and coral is by the rocks to the right and left of the beach," Ben said, squeezing the juice from his lime wedge into the salt-rimmed glass. "Today is good. The water is calm, and there are not a lot of people. So shall we snorkel?"

"Sí!" Tammy replied, taking a gulp from her margarita and jumping to her bare feet.

Marli carefully inched into the ocean while the other three frantically splashed their way in without reserve. The waves were soft and warm as they first caressed Marli's calves and then worked their way up her thighs. The ocean floor was silky just as Ben described, and she could see her pink-painted toenails through the crystal water.

"You should spit in the mask first and rub it around so the glass won't fog up," Ben said.

"I've heard that rumor, but I was hoping it wasn't true," Marli said, hesitant to carry out the task.

"You get to rinse the mask in the water before putting it on," Ben said.

After they both spit and rinsed, Ben helped Marli adjust the rubber strap over her blond hair pulled loosely into a ponytail trailing down the back of her neck. The mask was tight but comfortable and angled just enough so the long plastic snorkel would stand straight up when she floated face down.

"Those rocky areas are where we will see the most fish," Ben said to Tammy and Cyrano, who were working on their own masks. "But be careful because the waves can push you against the rocks if you get too close."

Masks and snorkels in place, they all swam single file with Ben in the lead, heading toward the jagged rock outcroppings. Ben and Cyrano did not hesitate to dive deeper for a better view, holding their breaths, rotating their broad bodies so their heads were down and their legs straight up, and then letting gravity take them the rest of the way. When the oxygen in their lungs was almost expended, they would break the surface and expel the saltwater out of their tubes with a quick burst of air like the blowhole on a dolphin.

Marli and Tammy were satisfied with effortlessly drifting on top of the tranquil water as if observing the obscure marine world below from a glass-bottom boat. When Ben would catch a glimpse of something exceptional, he'd get Marli's attention by reaching out to touch her arm or leg and then point toward the specimen. Schools of neon-painted parrotfish danced past, turning in unison through beds of seagrass in search of coralline algae to consume. Luminescent angelfish with their laterally compressed bodies darted in and out of the reefs followed by several slender needlefish sporting long narrow beaks with rows of thorn-like teeth. Two deflated pufferfish, one creamy yellow, the other black with tiny white splatters, hovered near the uneven rock formations. A grayish spiny lobster, sporting long thick antenna, and two chubby, worm-like sea cucumbers nestled themselves on the sand floor camouflaged by the barbed coral. A charcoal-colored sea urchin shielded with long threatening spikes lay half hidden under a ragged outcrop.

"This is incredible!" Tammy shouted, extricating the snorkel from her mouth as a passing motorboat threw off an unwelcome breaker, the surf colliding around her shoulders.

The unexpected upsurge caught Marli by surprise as she brought her head out of the ocean and took a deep, unintentional breath of saltwater. Another wave rose up on the heels of the first and crashed down on her before she had a chance to steady her swim stroke and expel the sea from her lungs. The normally calm beach cove stirred with the unforeseen force for only a few moments and then settled down again into a smooth glass window over the sea.

"Marli, are you OK?" Tammy was a good fifty feet away as she worked her way through the now nearly static water toward her friend.

Coughing uncontrollably, Marli could not respond, fighting to keep her body afloat, her arms frantically slashing the ocean's surface.

"Marli, I got you," Ben said, coming up from behind and wrapping his arms around her chest. "Calm down and just cough. I've got you. You just took in a little seawater. Don't panic. Just cough it out. I'm here."

Ben molded his bare chest into Marli's back as he steadily paddled to keep them both upright. Just his touch, his warm body against hers, triggered a tranquil trust within her. Marli stopped struggling and relaxed into Ben's grasp.

"I'm OK," she whispered through one more exasperated cough. "I'm OK, really."

Exhausted and hungry, the four made their way back to Playa Carrizalillo's beach for shots of tequila before catching another water taxi into town for dinner.

"Sorry, gang," Marli said as she cleared her throat and threw back the smooth, medicinal liquor, letting the top-shelf alcohol coat her embarrassment. "I didn't mean to freak everyone out."

"We just didn't want you to drown," Tammy teased. "Ben to the rescue again."

Chapter Fourteen

Ben had made reservations for 7:00 p.m. at Pascale Restaurant Bar & Grill, an upscale dinner house where they would dine by candlelight under palm trees on an outdoor beachfront deck overlooking the ocean. The two couples had just enough time to retreat to Hotel Santa Fe, shower, and change.

"Let's pick up the dinner tab tonight, OK?" Marli suggested to Tammy as they slipped into the only semi-fancy dresses they each brought and finally had a chance to wear. Marli had purchased her low-cut gown with a fuchsia-colored background and dramatic hibiscus flowers in Hawaii when the airline lost her luggage for the entire seven-day vacation on Maui with Nick. She had to reacquire a full wardrobe for the warm climate at a local tourist shop and soon learned that anyone can make due on the islands with only one pair of shorts, a couple of T-shirts, a bathing suit, flip-flops, and a pretty sundress. Marli never overpacked again.

"Agreed," Tammy said, wiggling into her form-fitting black dress held up by spaghetti-thin straps. "They have spent a lot of money on us, and we can probably afford it more than they can."

They swapped earrings, touched up their makeup, and stepped into their respective rhinestone-studded sandals.

One final check around the room for anything embarrassing, then Ben and Cyrano could shower and change into the extra clothes they left in the truck, while Marli and Tammy waited in the hotel bar.

"All yours." Tammy smiled when they found the two men sitting poolside with Puerto sprawled out by their feet. "Here's the room key."

"It makes me crazy when I don't know where Puerto is all day," Marli said, rubbing the now-exposed abdomen of the mutt, who had submissively rolled over on his bony back.

"We won't be long," said Ben. "Meet you at the bar. I told the bartender to put your drinks on my tab. Then we will head to dinner."

Pascale Restaurant's food reflected the taste of the French-Mexican couple who owned and operated the bar and grill. Daily offerings always included fresh fish from the morning's catch, shrimp and lobster grilled over an outdoor charcoal flame, specialties like paella and handmade pastas, and decadent desserts such as chocolate mousse, soufflé, and fruit flambé. The hostess, wearing a simple black dress and large silver hoop earrings, escorted the friends to a table shaded by a tiered, tan umbrella just at the edge of the deck before the wooden slats fell away to the sand. An ivory taper flickering within a clear, hurricane candleholder sat atop a white linen runner down the center of the table dressed for four with crisp cotton napkins perched on chargers and oversized wine goblets calling out for a robust red. A man with round, wire-rimmed glasses played acoustic guitar on a stool in the far-left corner, accompanied by a woman singing a leisurely Jim Croce song into a microphone. Tiny white lights crawled up several palm tree trunks growing through large circles punched into the wood deck. The view of the harbor revealed a quiet fleet of fishing and tourist boats anchored for the evening. The sunset was still an hour in the distance, but the horizon had already begun its nightly display of gold melting into crimson, then dripping into the sea.

"This is beautiful," Marli said as she took a seat across from Ben.

"Spectacular," Tammy added.

Puerto curled up in the salt-fine sand next to their dining table, technically not within the boundaries of the restaurant.

"That is why I requested this table." Ben smiled as he nodded toward the reposing pup.

They ordered two California reds, a 2005 Hahn Estates Central Coast cabernet sauvignon, followed by a 2009 Bogel Vineyards Old Vine zinfandel. Cyrano and Tammy dined on grilled shrimp and red snapper accompanied by a layered potato gratin and stuffed baked tomatoes with oregano and feta. The restaurant's chef created a special paella for Ben and Marli with roasted baby artichokes, portabella mushrooms, and crookneck squash seasoned with saffron threads and fresh rosemary.

"So, Ben," Tammy asked after her third generous glass of cab. "You don't eat anything with a face or a mother? What about oysters?"

Ben lifted his head with a grin. "Fascinating thing about oysters," he said. "They actually do have a mother. Just not in the typical sense. You see the female oyster releases her eggs into the water—millions at a time. And the male oyster releases his sperm, and they fuse in the water. It's called external fertilization."

Tammy and Marli exchanged eye rolls.

"You asked," Marli said.

"That doesn't sound like much fun," Tammy said.

"You see, the oyster larva floats around in the water for weeks," Ben said, his enthusiasm growing. "When ready, it drops to the ocean floor and looks for a hard surface to attach to—like an empty oyster shell or a clam shell—any hard surface. Then it secretes this cement-like substance and slowly metamorphoses into an adult oyster. It's really quite fascinating."

"OK, then," Tammy said with a sigh. "Let's get dessert!"

The four shared bites of lavender crème brûlée with toasted hazelnuts and house-made vanilla bean gelato garnished with caramelized almonds. The waiter, in a short-sleeved, white shirt with the Pascale logo emblazoned across his back, brought warmed snifters of cognac as a finale to the evening. Several other diners had risen from the chairs and were now moving to the musical duo's cover version of "Dancing in the Moonlight."

"King Harvest! Oh, we gotta dance to this," Tammy shouted, feeling the effects of the night's libations, as she took Cyrano's hand and they joined the others on the impromptu dance floor. Marli and Ben followed suit, and everyone mouthed the words karaoke-style.

The sky and water were black now. Lights shining from shore reflected off the boats hovering in the harbor so they looked like glowing blue oysters suspended in darkness. The air had cooled and a breeze rolled off the tide, across the beach, over the wood deck, and squeezed between Marli and Ben, who were pressed together on the dance floor. Tammy wrapped around Cyrano so he could hold her up like they were contestants in the last minutes of a twenty-four-hour dance marathon.

"I think it's time for bed," Marli whispered to Ben, nodding toward Tammy.

"I'll get the check."

"All taken care of. This time it's on me and Tammy," Marli said, still dangling her arms around Ben's neck. "I gave the waiter my card when I went to the restroom."

"Well, thank you. You did not have to do that."

"We wanted to. You and Cyrano have been so wonderful. It's going to be hard to leave."

"Let's go swimming!" Tammy shouted, revived by the cool ocean air as the group meandered along the now-vacant beach back toward the hotel, crossing over the rocky crag that separated Playa Principal from Playa Marinero, its sultry silt ideal for dancing among the waves.

"Excelente!" agreed Cyrano.

"Are you crazy?" Marli sighed. "We don't even have our suits."

"Oh, come on! We don't need suits! It will be fun. Please! It's my last night here!"

Marli and Ben obediently followed their two friends as they raced each other to the water's edge, simultaneously flipping their sandals into the air. Tammy pulled her tight, spaghetti-strap dress off over her head, revealing her black bikini underwear and ample breasts. Cyrano yanked his button-up Hawaiian-print shirt apart with one hard pull, stepped out of his now unzipped khakis, and tackled Tammy as they fell together into the first ascending wave.

"Oh my god. Be careful!" shouted Marli, dropping down into the sand next to Ben. "If you drown, I will be so pissed off!"

"Cyrano will save her," Ben said.

"She is crazy. And I am so tired I can barely keep my eyes open," Marli said in a barely audible whisper.

"It's been a long week for you."

"Thanks for saving my life today," Marli said with a tease.

"Think nothing of it. I really did it for Puerto's sake. He can't get to America without you."

"Can I ask you something personal?"

"Please do."

"Who was that woman in your exam room the other day? The one I embarrassed myself in front of."

"That was an old girlfriend, Jenna. We had to put her dog to sleep that afternoon."

"I'm so sorry. I didn't know. I didn't mean to snoop."

"It's OK. I was just consoling her. It's never easy to say goodbye."

Marli considered, for a half second, that Ben meant it was never easy to say goodbye to an ex-girlfriend. Then she quickly realized he meant saying goodbye to a dying dog. It really was time for bed.

She hesitated. "How long did you date?"

"Only a few months. She was the first woman I dated after my wife died. Jenna did not want the relationship to end, but we really were not meant for each other. We are just friends now."

After a few quiet moments, Marli realized she could not see nor hear their two impetuous friends. "Where did Tammy and Cyrano go?"

"They are laying in the sand over to the right. You can barely see them," Ben said. "Don't worry, they did not drown."

Marli pictured Tammy and Cyrano dramatically embracing each other in the sand as the frothy waves curled up over their bodies, like Burt Lancaster and Deborah Kerr in the 1953 movie *From Here to Eternity*.

"Maybe we should go?" she said more as a question than a statement.

Ben stood up and offered Marli his hand. Just like every time before, there was a rush from the touch of his skin to hers. They brushed off the sand clinging to their clothes and headed back up to the beach, Puerto keeping up with their awkward, sinking steps. They passed the statue of the "two hands," crossed the street, and walked up to the hotel, leaving Tammy and Cyrano to do whatever it was they were doing. The time was approaching midnight, still early for a Friday evening in Puerto Escondido, and they could hear the beat of dance music drifting up from the nearby beach bars.

"I hate for the evening to end," Marli said as they walked down the paved garden path toward her room.

"Would you like something?" Ben asked, gesturing toward the hotel bar.

"Yes. One of those Kahlúa drinks you got before."

"Wait here. I'll be right back."

With a shot of Don Fulano 100-proof tequila in one hand and a Kahlúa and Cream in the other, Ben returned to find Marli fast asleep on the pool lounge chair where he left her, lying on her side, knees pulled up toward her chest. Puerto was snuggled at the end of the cushion, his back pressed up against the bottom of Marli's feet. Ben threw back the tequila and sat down next to her. The single lamppost nestled among the hibiscus bushes shone down like a full moon settling on Marli's face, giving her an angelic glow. She really was beautiful, Ben considered. She was smart and kind and funny. He wanted to wake her up and kiss her and make love to her right there without thought or hesitation.

"Time for you to go to bed," he whispered.

"Yes," she replied, not opening her eyes.

Ben helped Marli to her feet and wrapped one arm around her small waist as she leaned into his strong torso, and they walked up the tiled steps to the landing of her hotel room door. Ben still had her key from earlier that evening. He unlocked the door, pushed it open with his right foot, and struggled in the dark until he found the light switch along the wall to the right. Escorting Marli to the king-size bed, he pulled down the embroidered Mexican bedspread and then the cool white sheets. Still fighting to keep her eyes from sealing shut, Marli collapsed onto the mattress and fell back into the soft, faux-down pillow. Ben carefully pulled off her sandals and brought the sheets back up over her still-dressed body.

"Thank you," Marli whispered.

"I don't want to leave the door unlocked, so I'm going to lock you in and give the key to Ivan at the bar." Ben spoke softly, unsure if Marli was aware enough to hear him. "You can fetch the key from him in the morning." Ben then stepped out onto the landing and closed the door behind him.

"Come on, Puerto. Let's go home."

Marli was deep in an unshakeable sleep, still wearing her binding bra and favorite sundress, which was now scrunched up and entangled around her hips. She was incapable of moving while a relentless tapping kept beating on her brain. Seconds seemed like hours before she fully realized the persistent drumming was reverberating from her hotel room door.

"Marli, let me in." Tammy impatiently exhaled, trying to keep her voice low enough to not disturb guests in the adjacent rooms but high enough to summon Marli from inside.

"Tammy? Is that you?" Marli asked, stumbling to the door, still lost in her grogginess.

"Yes!"

"What time is it?" Marli pulled open the door just enough for Tammy to squeeze in.

"I don't know. Sorry to wake you. I left my key in the room."

"Where have you been?" Marli fell back down on the bed. "Oh my god, I fell asleep in my dress." She looked down at the pile of wrinkles in the hibiscus flower print.

"What a great night!" Tammy said, pulling her little black dress off over her head for the second time that night. Her hair was slicked back in a sea-salty mess and her eyeliner and mascara were now under her eyes instead of over them. She tossed her wet bra on the floor and squirmed into the same oversized, 1990 James Taylor US concert tour T-shirt she had slept in all week. "I don't have the energy to brush my teeth," Tammy said, finding her way under the covers on the other side of Marli.

"That's OK. Neither did I."

They turned to face each other lying on their sides, each with an arm cradled under their respective heads.

"Did you sleep with Cyrano?" Marli kindly demanded to know, now fully awake and aware of how late it was.

"No! Well, I would have," Tammy said. "But he's gay."

"What?"

"Yeah. Who would have known!"

After staring into each other's eyes for several seconds, they both burst out laughing so hard Tammy had to run into the bathroom to relieve her bladder before it burst.

"Can you believe it?" she said, still chuckling as she slipped back under the sheets. "I finally meet a guy worth having an affair with and he turns out to be a homosexual."

"That is priceless. I wonder why Ben didn't tell me," Marli said.

"Maybe he's gay, too."

"No way," Marli quickly said. "He told me that he was married before. His wife died of cancer."

"Thank god! . . . I didn't mean it that way. I am just relieved. I was beginning to think there was something wrong with him. Like he couldn't get it up. There is no way a good-looking, truly nice, smart doctor doesn't have a girlfriend unless something is wrong with him. Now we know."

"Yeah, that crossed my mind, too," Marli said. "I also asked him about that woman I saw him kiss in his exam room, and he said she was an old girlfriend."

"Well, there you go," Tammy said. "Isn't life weird?"

"You know, you would have regretted sleeping with Cyrano anyway. You have a wonderful husband and beautiful kid. No need to screw that up."

"Yeah, funny how things work out," Tammy said, her eyelids gradually giving way to slumber.

"Tammy?" Marli nudged her friend. "I finally remembered why that woman at the airport looked so familiar—the one that Nick was with when I picked you up last Saturday."

"OK, why?" Tammy asked drowsily.

"She's the same woman who was at the restaurant Nick and I ate at on our first night here. When Nick got up to use the restroom, that woman followed him. And they were both gone a really long time. You don't suppose they were having sex in the bathroom while I sat there, do you?"

Tammy reached across the bed and gently rubbed Marli's tan bare arm. "I'm sorry. I am really, really sorry."

Marli had no way of knowing that Tammy's genuine remorse encompassed far more than she was willing to reveal, at least not yet.

"Yeah, me too," Marli sighed.

Tammy took a deep breath. "So how many more days until you can bring Puerto home?" she asked, changing the subject.

"Today is day twelve. Eighteen to go. Eighteen," Marli said. "Sounds like such a long time."

"Eighteen more days to spend with Ben." Tammy flashed her friend a smile.

"Yeah. And there's Ben." Marli exhaled. "Sleep now. You have an early plane to catch."

Tammy wedged her way around the rotund businessman wearing a navy-blue suit in the center seat and settled in next to the window of the Boeing 737. From one international airport to another—Puerto Escondido to Mexico City to Houston to San Jose—Tammy had a good eight hours of flight time to contemplate what, if anything, she was finally going to expose to her best friend, Marli, after two long years of keeping her agonizing secret. But if she couldn't tell Marli the truth after a full week together in Puerto Escondido, when could she tell her?

When Tammy had decided to join Marli in Mexico just the week prior, she had every intention of confessing the entire reality to her longtime, dear friend. Tammy planned to disclose that she was the one who sent the mysterious text message about Franklin's death because she could not keep it locked up inside her any longer. Spending time in Mexico, just the two of them, would be the ideal opportunity to be honest with Marli. Nick had just left her for another woman. Now Marli needed—deserved—to know the truth. But when Tammy arrived in Puerto Escondido, she found Marli not broken but instead resolved, even happy for the first time in a long time. Everything changed.

Now Tammy just wanted to stow away the past, to rewind. She longed for them to be the same two unencumbered college roommates who trolled the trendy bars and popular nightclubs on their long weekends, looking for fun and unfettered love. Ben and Cyrano were godlike gifts that helped Tammy forget she had a life back home, a past she regretted, a secret that was destroying her. The time was not right to confess to Marli. Would the time ever be right?

Tammy was far from innocent. She never meant to have sex with Nick. At least not in Marli's own bed. It just happened. She was drinking way too much that evening. Eggnog spiked with rum followed by Jägermeister shots. The holiday party at Marli and Nick's house was one for the record books. They invited everyone they knew—neighbors, coworkers, family, friends, and friends of friends—the more, the merrier. The overly decorated house was filled with festive party people. Marli, always the diligent hostess, was busy making sure appetizer platters were replenished and every guest had a full libation in hand. Tammy and Sam, her attentive husband of twelve-plus years, had just finished a spin on the makeshift dance floor. Tammy wanted to check her makeup and fix her hair, but the guest bathroom was occupied. So she found her way up the staircase to the master bedroom to use the en suite, not knowing Nick was taking a break from the crowd with a spoon up his nose. It had been a long time since Tammy had done cocaine. That was in her past. She was a wife and mother now.

"Want to join me?" Nick asked.

"What the hell," Tammy said. "It's Christmas after all."

Tammy sat down next to Nick on the satin duvet. The silky fabric was cool against her smooth, bare legs dangling out from her short black skirt over the side of the bed. As Tammy tipped back her head and wiped the white residue from her nostril, Nick placed his hand on her exposed thigh. Tammy didn't pull away. Nick, now more determined, guided his hand under her skirt and into her red lace panties. Two of his fingers made their way into her warm vagina and then his tongue into her mouth. She did not resist. It was too good. She was too high. Tammy unbuckled Nick's belt, unbuttoned and unzipped his pants, pulled down his underwear, and led his penis into her. It was over in less than a minute, but Nick had neglected to lock the door. When they looked up, Franklin was standing just inside the doorway, expressionless as he stared at his father and his mother's best friend, then turned and left the room without a word.

Tammy arrived home in San Jose at 9:00 p.m. At the bottom of the airport escalator, she could see Sam balancing their four-year-old daughter on his slightly slanted shoulders, her chubby little legs dangling around his neck. Dressed in hot-pink tights and a ketchup-stained T-shirt with a fluffy white kitten on the chest, the young girl caught sight of her mother and started screeching and waving with such excitement that Sam almost lost his balance and tumbled over.

Just as Tammy had left him a week prior, Sam was still losing his hair, his remaining strands graying and his paunch undeniable. His faded, baby-blue polo shirt was tucked into his tan jeans, even though it would have been more stylish to leave it hanging out. Staring down as she descended the escalator toward her haphazard family, Tammy beat back the tight fist swelling up within her throat—the same emotional choke from watching television commercials about homeless dogs rescued by the Humane Society, or listening to stories on public radio about children who had beaten leukemia, or reading about women who had overcome cancer to run a marathon. Tears were inevitable.

"Holy shit," she said to herself. "What am I going to do?"

Chapter Fifteen

It was an early call for the long-anticipated spay clinic. Marli and Ben met several other local volunteers at his vet office at 7:00 a.m. to begin setting up the surgery tables and prepping the equipment and supplies. The two other veterinarians and six vet students from Mexico City, plus the one vet from California, joined them at 8:00 a.m. Owners were told to arrive with their dogs between 8:00 and 9:00 a.m. Reservations were encouraged but not required. The goal was to alter as many canines as possible regardless of whether the owners were last-minute walk-ins or how much they could pay. Normally for a routine spay or neuter, owners would drop off their dogs and return when the canines were ready for pick up. However, a shortage of space, cages, and volunteers at Ben's small shop required owners to stay with their dogs until they were taken in for surgery, wait until the procedures were completed, and then monitor their pets while they came out of anesthesia.

By 8:15 a.m., a line began to form at the front door of the clinic and soon stretched past the wooden bins of fresh vegetables and tropical fruit for sale outside the neighboring market. By 8:45, owners and their dogs twisted down the block. Marli and a young American woman named Manda greeted each person with a clipboard, pen, and sheet of paper that explained in Spanish and English the spay/neuter procedure and its risks.

"Fill out your name, address, and phone number, por favor," Marli said. "Also your dog's name, male or female, breed, and an estimated age if you know it. And sign at the bottom, right here." Marli pointed at the place on the form.

Manda, who was fluent in Spanish, communicated with those who did not speak English. Marli helped owners juggle the paperwork as large dogs pulled on leashes and smaller pups wiggled anxiously in their owners' arms. With only ten clipboards available, owners passed along the boards to the next person in line as soon as they completed their form. By 9:00 a.m. Marli counted eighty-five wagging tails waiting in line for surgery.

Spirits were high. No one complained about the wait. Owners and dogs alike came in all shapes and sizes and ranged in age from teenagers to seniors. While some people claimed to actually own the mutts they came with, others said they were just caretakers who put out food and water for a stray in need.

Ben popped his head out the front door. "OK. We're ready," he said to Marli and Manda. "Bring the dogs in six at a time."

The morning air was still cool but showed promise of a long, warm afternoon.

The first half dozen owners and their dogs entered the building with paperwork in hand and were escorted by volunteers into a side room. After each dog was weighed, a female vet student injected a sedative into a rear flank muscle to relax the animal before general anesthesia. The first dog was assigned the number one. A volunteer wrote "01" with a large, black felt pen on a wide piece of masking tape and stuck it to the top of the dog's head. The pet parents then turned their dogs over to a volunteer and were asked to wait outside the clinic—their name would be called when the sterilization surgery was completed in approximately thirty minutes, and then the owners would need to sit with their dogs until they were awake and alert enough to return home.

"You will take good care of my *bebe*?" an older woman asked and demanded at the same time as she handed her five-pound, toothless Chihuahua to an eager volunteer.

The next stop for the motley group of sedated patients, legs wobbly and eyes half shut, was a lineup of folding tables where each dog received a general anesthetic to block the pain and prevent the canines from moving during surgery. Once the dogs were unconscious, the vet students checked their ears for mites and cleaned and treated them if needed. Severe mats in the fur were cut away. The canines' bladders were expressed into a bucket. The surgery areas—abdomens on females and scrotums on males—were shaved and disinfected with an iodine solution. If the dogs were small, the vet students could prep two dogs on one table at a time.

When ready, the immobile mutts were carried one by one by volunteers to the larger adjoining room at the back of the clinic that served as a surgery suite where the veterinarians were waiting to perform the ovariohysterectomies and castrations. Two people—one to cradle the front half and one to heft the rear end—were required to move the heavier hounds.

Everyone was aware of the primitive, low-budget accommodations. The vets did not have the ability to intubate their patients or use inhalant gas anesthesia monitored with high-tech EKGs. They did not enjoy luxuries such as oximeters to gauge blood pressure and heartbeats, single-use autoclaved instrument packs, overhead surgical lighting, or highly trained veterinary technicians. Blades, scissors, and forceps were sterilized by hand washing in hot water and detergent and reused. Without proper surgery-table equipment to stabilize the patients, volunteers were needed to hold the dogs steady on their backs so they did not roll over during the operations.

"It is what it is," one vet said, as she delicately sliced through the abdomen of a female German shepherd mix. "Sterile scalpels are overrated," she said, and everyone chuckled under their surgical masks.

Marli stood by to assist in whatever manner she could. She helped turn a golden retriever from one side to the other so the vet student could shave away several tangled mats that were tearing at the dog's tender skin. She was asked to clean away the black encrusted dirt, so thick it resembled tar, from the ear canals of a tan Labrador with a horrific case of mites. She restocked tubes of flea treatment and piles of cotton balls. She refilled syringes from vials of rabies vaccine that were kept in a small, dented refrigerator in the corner of the clinic. When a shaggy white terrier was ready to be moved to the surgery room, Marli slid her arms under the sleeping dog's torso, carried him to the waiting surgeon, and gently placed the mutt on the operating table scattered with steel surgical trays, rolls of suture material, and piles of gauze pads.

"Have you ever seen a castration?" Ben asked.

"Not that I can recall," Marli responded.

"Feel free to stay and watch if you want."

"Oh, I don't know," Marli said with hesitation. The fresh blood and organs she had already caught glimpses of as she moved in and out of the surgery room were unsettling.

"I would not have pegged you for squeamish," Ben said.

Marli let loose a deep sigh and stepped up to the surgery table. Ben made a small incision at the front of the lifeless terrier's scrotum. With his gloved right hand, he pushed the left testicle out through the incision, clamped off the spermatic cord, tied the cord with an absorbable suture, cut the testicle free, and repeated the procedure on the right side. He completed the castration in less than five minutes by closing the incision with more absorbable sutures.

"Neuters are easy," Ben said, stripping off his blood-stained latex gloves and replacing them with a fresh pair. "You should stay to see a spay, too."

Marli watched with both fascination and revulsion as Ben executed surgery on a female patient, a much more complicated and lengthier procedure that involved removing the ovaries, fallopian tubes, and uterus. However, when two volunteers carried in a pregnant black lab at almost full term, the puppies soon to be aborted, Marli elected to exit the operating room and make herself useful at other tasks.

"Pizza is here!" an enthusiastic volunteer called out. "Come and get it!"

A stack of cardboard pizza boxes waited on a makeshift dining table just outside the reception area. Four hours into the day with at least four more to go, everyone was more than ready to get off their feet and grab some nourishment. The aroma of melted cheese and spicy tomato sauce mingled in the warm air with wet fur, rubbing alcohol, and blood.

"How can you eat?" Marli asked the first set of hungry lunch-takers stretched out around the table. "The smell is making me sick."

"You would not have made a good doctor," one of the volunteer veterinarians said, wiping red sauce from his mouth with a piece of paper towel.

Following surgery, the altered canines were moved to the recovery area. Large, mismatched blankets, throws, and towels were strewn across the linoleum. While still unconscious, each dog was given a rabies vaccination and a dose of topical flea treatment. Anxious owners were then summoned back in to sit with their pets as they slept, to watch their breathing, and call for help if an animal began to vomit or show signs of distress. A mosaic of mixed breeds from bull terriers and pinchers to collies and spaniels littered the floor, each wrapped in a thick blanket or towel to keep their core bodies warm as they came out of anesthesia. The strips of masking tape with each dog's assigned number still clung to the fur on top of their heads. Some owners cradled their animal companions in their laps, softly speaking to the sleeping hounds in both English and Spanish.

"Perhaps he can hear my voice and it will help him feel better," one elderly gentleman said, stroking his snoozing boxer's short, reddish-brown fur. Other pet parents and volunteers sat or laid next to the slumbering dogs, intently watching for signs of consciousness.

Puerto was the last pooch to be neutered, and Ben made sure he performed the surgery himself. Marli busied herself with the other resting canines and waited anxiously for Ben to carry the sleeping mutt to her in the recovery area.

"All is well," Ben said to Marli. "He will begin to wake up soon."

It was a successful day. Six by six, the mongrels came in and moved along in the clinic, a steady, well-organized assembly line with minimal disruptions and no surgical complications or deaths. Forty-seven female dogs were spayed and thirty-eight male dogs were neutered—a total of eighty-five in eight-plus hours. The three guest veterinarians and six vet students had packed up and departed. The other volunteers had left one by one throughout the afternoon as their assigned duties winded down and they were no longer needed, and the remaining few finally said goodbye. Marli finished sanitizing the folding tables used for surgery with a mixture of lemon-scented bleach and water, while Ben swept up stray Q-tips and chased wispy balls of fur that floated across the worn linoleum floor.

"You must be exhausted," Ben said to Marli as he placed the weary broom into a standalone closet with particleboard doors that did not quite meet in the middle to close properly.

"You must be tired, too," she replied. "But it was worth it."

"Yes, no doubt." Ben ran his left hand through his long, thick, dark curls, catching his woven hairband in his right hand and placing it back into position behind his ears.

"I know it's late, but would you like to recap the day with a glass of wine?" he asked while reaching inside a metal cage to stroke one of his overnight patients recovering from a broken front paw. "Unless you need to get back to the hotel," he added, providing her with a ready reason to decline his invitation. Marli had one more night in Hotel Santa Fe before she would move her belongings to Ben's rental unit for the remaining seventeen days in Puerto Escondido.

"I think we should go over the details of the day while they are still fresh in our minds," Marli said with a smile. "You keep wine here?"

"Only for emergencies." Ben grinned. He washed his hands in a small, makeshift kitchen at the back of the clinic and grabbed two mismatched wine glasses from the cabinet above the sink. "I'll meet you out back. It's cooler there."

"I'm just going to use the restroom first," Marli said. Looking at herself in the bathroom mirror, she repositioned her hair clip so her bangs fell in a more flattering manner around her fatigued face. She checked to make sure her black eyeliner rested along the curve of her eyelids and her mascara clung to her lashes rather than creating even darker circles under her eyes. She touched up her lips with the pink-tinted moisturizer she kept in the front pocket of her jeans. A small crack weaved across her reflection in the glass, as if splitting her already tenuous personality.

The day was reaching dusk now and the air was sweet from a flowering jasmine clinging to a drooping chain-link fence at the back of the property. Just off the backdoor of Ben's veterinary office was a small slatted porch with uneven steps that led to a patch of dirt and nothing else. The deck was home to two old rocking chairs Ben had found by the roadside—he assumed they must have fallen off of someone's truck because they were in fairly decent condition. The chairs were constructed of unfinished knotty pine and held hand-sewn seat cushions with competing floral prints. Between the rockers sat a square side table with a dusty glass top. Ben attempted to wipe the grime away with a damp cloth but instead left a thin muddy film that revealed a swirl pattern when the muted porch light, coated in cobwebs, hit the table's surface at just the right angle.

Ben was already rocking in his chair with a groggy Puerto at his feet when Marli joined them. "I hope you like zinfandel," he said, pouring the rich red wine into the two glasses.

"That's perfect," Marli said as she picked up her vino and sat back against the vertical wooden slats. She did not realize how the long eventful day had taken its toll on her until she allowed the old rocking chair to accept the weight of her achy body.

"It feels so good to sit down," Marli said, twirling the wine until the deep crimson liquid reached the rim and then flowed back into the goblet, coating the interior like a red velvet curtain. "So what is it about animals? Why do you do what you do for them?"

Ben sat silent for a moment, his brown eyes focused on his own wine glass. The chapulines began their nightly mating calls as the sun slowly surrendered to nightfall.

"I believe animals are more intelligent than we give them credit for," he softly responded. "They know more than we think they know. Their spirits are more resilient. Their hearts are truer."

Ben took a long sip and swallowed. "Have you ever looked into the eyes of a street dog? I mean really looked into them, through them? Wondered what that dog was thinking, what did he know? What had he seen? Cruelty? Love? Hunger? Compassion? What does he remember? Does he remember the person who took pity on him and gave him something to eat? Does he remember the shopkeeper who chased him away when he merely stopped by for a scrap of food or soft place to sleep?

"When he does find sleep, what does he dream about? Running? Playing? Or is he on guard all the time? When he awakens, is it with a growl and a snap just in case danger found him while he was finally at rest? And when does he rest? How does he rest when he is hungry or hurt or afraid?" Ben sat forward in the chair and gazed across the weed-laden dirt yard.

"I do what I do for animals because so few will," he whispered under his breath, as if to keep anyone from hearing him. "When my wife died, I thought it was the end of the world. I honestly didn't think I had any reason to go on. Then I found Escondido. He was so afraid. So helpless. He needed someone to believe in him. To give him another chance. At living. At trusting. At getting by in this really harsh world. A world that can be so unkind, so unforgiving.

"I believe animals are mankind's last chance to be human." He then paused again and smiled, realizing that he had just shared with Marli what he had never revealed to anyone before, maybe not even to himself.

"That must sound so corny." Ben grinned in an attempt to bury the awkwardness.

Marli put her wine glass down on the grime-smeared table and took Ben's free hand in hers. A nervous excitement flowed over and through her body, a kaleidoscope of emotions spinning within her.

"You're a pretty amazing man, Ben Rosado," Marli whispered back.

"You think so? Then would you like to go home with me tonight instead of tomorrow?"

Ben and Marli were silent for most of the short drive to Ben's house only minutes from his veterinary office. Marli rubbed Puerto's silky chest as he lay sprawled out on the vinyl upholstery between his two people, head on Marli's lap. The soft wind from the open passenger window drifted across her face. She watched the passing shops, restaurants, and homes littered with people and pets preparing for the evening ahead. Marli let the aftereffect of the wine temper her nerves as she imagined where the night would lead when they reached their destination.

Ben parked his Chevy in his usual place on the street adjacent to the cement walkway leading to his front door. Puerto, still unsteady from his neuter surgery, crawled across the truck's front seat to Ben, who helped his patient down from the driver's side because the passenger door continued to be wedged shut. Marli and Puerto followed Ben into his small, single-story home, and waited while he opened the back door to welcome in his own patiently waiting pup. As usual, Escondido bounded inside with the enthusiasm of a child on his first visit to Disneyland.

"OK, settle down Big Guy," Ben said, scratching the dog's favorite spot at the base of his long, whipping tail. Escondido greeted the groggy Puerto with a sniff to the butt and then went back to his human for further affection.

Marli set the multicolored Mexican handbag she purchased from a street vendor on the coffee table.

"Would you like something to drink?" Ben asked.

"No, not really."

"You must be starving. It was a long day."

"Yes, I am starving," Marli said, slowly moving closer toward Ben. It had been such a long time since Marli was comfortable letting the world and all its complications disappear. She wanted to embrace what was good and right and gratifying that night. She wanted to forget the tragedies of her past life and hold onto something that was safe from pain and sadness. She was strong and smart and sexy when she was with Ben. She savored the sensations. She ignored her doubts and hesitations and was ready, willing, hoping to let Ben Rosado into her life. She crossed the room and stopped inches from Ben's body.

Ben was also ready. He saw something in Marli that had eluded other women he had spent brief moments in time with since his wife's death. He longed to hold Marli, to touch her, to kiss her skin, her mouth, her breasts. He wanted to be selfish and enjoy her for the sheer pleasure of feeling her body against his and making love to her throughout the night, then letting tomorrow take them wherever they wanted to go.

Ben stepped closer to Marli until their faces were almost touching and then pressed his lips to her mouth, letting his tongue touch hers. She was perfection. She was warm and sweet and silken. He held her shoulders and kissed her again, harder. Her hair was soft and her arms firm. She was what heaven would be like. He took Marli's hand and led her through the door to his bedroom. Escondido and Puerto would have to wait for their dinner.

Chapter Sixteen

Early the next morning, Ben drove Marli and Puerto back to Hotel Santa Fe to pick up her luggage and bring her bags back to his place, where the girl and her dog would be staying for the next sixteen days as they waited for Puerto's thirty-day rabies hold to end. It was still several hours before the hotel's noon checkout so they decided to take their time. First, they showered, taking turns pressing the lavender-scented soap between their chests and thighs while the pulse of the water jets caressed their backs and buttocks. Then they made love again on the freshly made bed.

"I have a surprise for you," Ben said, as they lay under the cool, white sheets. He pulled Marli into his naked torso so he could kiss the back of her tanned shoulders.

"A surprise? What is it?"

"You will see tonight."

Leaving the room at noon, Marli and Ben stopped by the Hotel Santa Fe restaurant to bid goodbye to Ivan and the reception desk to check out and thank Rosa.

"You are leaving us, sí ?" Rosa said to Marli.

"Sí. I just wanted to thank you for everything, Rosa," Marli said, attempting to suppress tears while handing Rosa one hundred dollars in American bills.

"No, no. It was my pleasure," Rosa said, waving the money away. "Puerto, have a great life in America," she added, running her hand from the top of his furry head, down his charcoal-black back to his long, extended tail. Puerto reciprocated by licking her painted pink toenails and turning three times in a circle.

On their way back to Ben's house, they stopped for soft tacos and grilled corn on the cob at a street vendor along the Adoquin. A flimsy, blue tarp provided adequate shade for a square, white-washed table wrapped in a hand-painted vinyl banner that served as a sign for the simple menu. Three large, round, aluminum pots, sunk into holes cut out of the wooden tabletop, each held a different spicy taco filling—seasoned pork, chicken, and crooked-neck squash. Ben and Marli helped themselves to the red and green salsas, pickled cacti, and sliced jalapeño peppers lined up in plastic containers. A young woman with her black hair pulled back tight in a rubber band squeezed fresh chunks of guava and pineapple from a handcrank juicer.

After returning home, Ben brought in Marli's chartreuse suitcase with the black scuff marks and her carry-on shoulder bag and set them on the worn living room floor, the hardwood in need of a good refinishing.

"Where would you like me to put these?" Ben asked. "I don't want to be presumptuous, but if you would like to stay here with me in the house instead of out in the rental unit, I would not object."

"What do you think?" Marli smiled back, picking up her carry-on and heading toward Ben's bedroom. After sleeping and making love for most of the remainder of the day, Ben revealed his surprise.

"Tonight, we are going to release sea turtle hatchlings

into the Pacific," Ben said, pushing away Marli's hair and pressing his lips to the back of her naked neck.

Mazunte was a small coastal town located approximately forty-five minutes south of Puerto Escondido where monumental efforts took place year-round to help preserve the endangered sea turtle population, Ben explained to Marli.

"By the 1970s, Mazunte was the center of sea turtle hunting in Mexico," Ben said as they drove along Highway 200 toward the quaint, quiet beach town. The time was two hours before dusk.

"Mazunte had its own turtle slaughterhouse. The meat was popular and the eggs were considered delicacies," Ben continued. "The severe decline in sea turtles eventually led to a complete ban in 1990. It is now illegal to kill turtles for their meat and/or their eggs in Mexico. The Mexican National Turtle Center is located on the same site as the turtle slaughterhouse. Poetic justice in a way."

"What is the Mexican National Turtle Center?" Marli asked.

"An aquarium. A research facility. Where they study turtles—marine, freshwater, and land turtles."

Ben reached across the worn truck seat and took Marli's hand. The warm wind mingled with dust from the dry landscape and pushed through the open windows.

"We are going to visit the Palmarito Sea Turtle Preserve," Ben said. "Volunteers and employees from the National Turtle Center patrol Palmarito Beach three times every night—nine p.m., midnight, and four a.m. They are searching for sea turtles that come ashore to nest.

"Once the females lay their eggs, they leave and never return. Then the workers will collect the eggs and take them to the turtle preserve, where the eggs are buried again," Ben continued. "Approximately forty-five days later, the eggs hatch and the newborn turtles work their way to the surface of the sand. The hatchlings, only hours old, are collected and placed in a large bucket until sunset when they are released. The researchers wait until sunset because the seabirds are less likely to prey on the turtles as they make their way to the ocean.

"If the eggs were not relocated to the preserve, many would be dug up by poachers to sell on the black market. The eggs also fall prey to dogs, birds, even crabs. So taking the eggs to the preserve increases their chances of survival."

Ben turned his truck off of Highway 200 onto a quiet street leading toward Mazunte, then veered onto a dirt road scattered with deep divots and bumps, forcing Marli to hang on to the grab bar mounted above the passenger-side window.

A short fifteen minutes later, Ben pulled off the road and parked next to a small weather-beaten sign that read "*Campamento Tortuquero Palmarito*." The time was approximately 7:30 p.m., only forty-five minutes until sunset.

"It's just a short walk," Ben said, taking Marli's hand as he led her along a narrow, pebble-strewn path crowded on both sides with waist-high grasses, dry and withered from the infinite heat. The end of the trail opened up to Palmarito Beach, a pristine piece of secluded, sea-front property free of hotels, high-rises, shops, restaurants, and bars. Patches of olive-green vegetation mingled with driftwood and ocean rocks that lay neatly where Mother Nature deposited them. A flag of Mexico fluttered on a small pole outside of a roughly constructed, palm-thatched hut that served as a base camp for the preserve. A roof-to-ground yellow vinyl banner hung from the shack, reading "*Cuidemos Nuestro Medio Ambiente*."

"It says, 'Let's take care of our environment,'" Ben translated.

Next to the hut were the two large beach corrals, each enclosed by a six-foot-high chain-link fence braced with irregular wooden posts to keep out animal and human predators. Inside the corrals were dozens of rows of wire mesh circular cages, each atop its own sea turtle nest. In the middle of each mesh cage, inserted in the sand, was a thin stick bearing a white plastic tag, hand labeled with the type of sea turtle eggs that were buried below and the date the eggs were laid.

"Alfonso!" Ben called out. "*Buenas noches*!"

"Buenas noches, amigo! Bienvenido!" Alfonso was a jovial man in his late sixties. He had worked for the Mexican National Turtle Center since it opened in 1991. He wore light-tan cargo shorts and a bright-red polo shirt with a small round logo on the left side of his chest. The logo's words, "Centro Mexicano de la Tortuga, Mazunte, Mexico," encircled an image of a green sea turtle. Alfonso stood about five feet, six inches tall in his bare feet and his large wide smile revealed unnaturally white teeth against his dark Mexican skin.

"Gracias," Ben replied. "Alfonso, this is Marli."

"Ah Marli! Nice to meet you. You picked a good night to join us. We are releasing 212 Olive Ridley sea turtle hatchlings tonight!"

Dusk was beginning its descent. Several other people—university students, center volunteers, travelers—had arrived and were gathered around Alfonso as he explained the history and mission of the turtle preserve, as well as the guidelines for the release.

"Now, you must thoroughly wash your hands to remove dirt, lotion, or anything else that might harm the hatchlings," Alfonso said as he gestured to a nearby bucket filled with seawater.

"Next, we will form a single line right here. This is approximately forty feet from the ocean's edge. This is where we will release the turtles," Alfonso continued. "The hatchlings must be strong to make it to the water. So we do not help the strong ones. They have a better chance at survival. We are here to help the weaker ones—the turtles that are struggling. We are just giving Mother Nature a little assistance."

Two younger men carried over two round plastic containers, one red and one blue, each filled halfway up with three-inch hatchlings, squirming and crawling over each other, not unlike the crate of newborn puppies that awaited Ben in his reception area the week before.

"These hatchlings were born earlier today deep in their protected beach chambers," Alfonso said. "Then they fought their way to the surface in a united effort to get through the sand to the top."

"Look at how small they are," Marli said in amazement. "They look like little toy turtles."

"See how the flippers in the front are larger than those in the back," Ben said. "They need those bigger front flippers to push up through the sand, out of their deep nests, and then to reach the ocean."

The two young men carefully tipped the buckets into the sand a few feet in front of the line of human spectators and spread the anxious, energetic infants out in one long row. Cameras feverishly clicked.

"Remember, no photo flashes," Alfonso said. "The bright light will disorient the hatchlings."

The once-tranquil, benign beach came to life as the determined newborns, their tiny greenish-gray bodies powerful against the dense sand, spread out in an unrelenting race to the ocean's edge, the impatient tide still shimmering from the sun's last rays.

"We will wait and watch for a few minutes and let the baby turtles make their way to the water," Alfonso told his audience. "Then we will assist those that are struggling. It is critical that you do not walk in front of the line or you may step on a hatchling."

"This is amazing!" Marli exclaimed to Ben. "How do they know which way to go? How do they know to head toward the ocean?"

"Sea turtles are phototactic," Ben replied.

"Photo-what?"

"Phototactic. They are attracted to light. They are guided by the brightest light they can see, which is usually moonlight reflecting off the sea or the natural light of the ocean horizon."

"Oh my god. They are doing it! They are heading toward the water!" Marli shouted as they watched the fledgling chelonians battle their way across the granular ground.

"Now," Alfonzo called out after several minutes. "You may carefully pick up the hatchlings that are struggling to go in the right direction. Take them to the ocean's edge and carefully set them down. The current will pick them up and take them away."

"Look! I'm holding a baby sea turtle!" Marli said, stretching out the palms of her upturned hands, cupped together just enough to keep the hatchling from falling through.

The sky was nearly dark now and it was getting difficult to see the tiny turtle bodies against the sand. Marli took the long way around the line of marching infants to ensure no one met the bottom of her bare feet. She set the newborn down inches from the surf and stood mesmerized as she watched a wave roll in, scoop up her tiny ward, and carry the helpless creature into the powerful arms of the sea.

"Will he make it?" Marli asked Ben, who had followed behind her with his own hatchling.

"Unfortunately, only about one in a thousand sea turtles survive to adulthood."

"What?"

"I guess I shouldn't have told you that," Ben said. "But I'm sure *your* hatchling is the one who will make it." He pointed out toward the restless waves that now embraced Marli's first rescue.

One by one, Marli, Ben, and the others picked up the wiggling sea babies and safely escorted them to their new world in the ocean, watching as the turtles began their swimming frenzy into the depths of the saltwater and away from the dangerous shoreline, where predators were abundant.

"Now their 'lost years' begin," Ben said calmly, looking out to the bronze-painted horizon that had engulfed the sun. "No one knows where they go from here. And they will be gone for as long as a decade. Then these turtles will return and continue their lives. The lucky ones will live to be fifty years old or more. Pretty cool, huh?"

Ben turned toward Marli to find her kneeling in the sand, her hands covering her wet face, elbows tucked into her bent-over body.

"Marli? What is it? Are you OK?"

"My son died," Marli calmly said, looking up at Ben. Her tears dripped relentlessly down her cheeks as she wiped her nose with the back of her hand.

"What? When?" Ben asked helplessly.

"Two years ago. It was an accident. He was eighteen."

Ben sat down next to Marli and wrapped his arm around her sunken shoulders. "Oh my god, Marli. I am so sorry."

"Urrrgggh!" Marli screamed, grabbing a fist of sand and squeezing the fine grains in anguish against her palms. "I am just so angry! Why my baby? Why?"

"I don't know, Marli. Why didn't you tell me?"

"I just don't talk about it. I keep it bottled up. There's never a good time to tell someone that your child died. I didn't mean to keep anything from you. It's just . . . just these damn sea turtles," she said, raising her voice again and waving her arm toward the water. "These helpless baby turtles. Only one percent will survive? They are the 'lucky ones'! I guess my Frankie was just not one of the lucky ones."

"Was that his name? Frankie?" Ben asked.

"Franklin. I called him Frankie."

"I didn't mean to upset you, Marli. I didn't know."

"No, please, Ben. I'm the one who is sorry. I am just so tired. Nick leaving me, finding Puerto, thinking about Frankie . . . meeting you. I am just feeling overwhelmed." She let her tears fall freely into the fragile sand.

Ben brushed a rebellious strand of Marli's blond hair away from her sorrow-stricken face and tucked it around her ear.

"But I loved tonight," she quietly added. "Releasing the turtle hatchlings was one of the best things I have ever done. I wish Frankie were here. He would have loved it. He loved all animals."

Marli and Ben thanked Alfonso, and Ben placed two one-hundred peso notes in the preserve's donation box.

"I want to show you something when we get back to Puerto Escondido," Ben said as he turned his Chevy onto Highway 200.

"Another surprise?" Marli asked, inspecting her tear-smudged face in the mirror of the truck's visor.

"Yes, but this one is quite different."

Dusk was behind them now, but a gradual glow lingered in the air. As Marli studied the vast fields of grass and cacti rolling past her open window, she visualized the turtle hatchlings alone in the infinite darkness of the ocean, each struggling to stay alive and facing an uncertain future. Not unlike Puerto, she considered. Not unlike Frankie. Not unlike herself.

"Do you want to talk about Franklin?" Ben asked.

"Sure. What do you want to know?"

"What was he like? Did he go to school? Did he work?"

"He was a great kid. Never gave us any trouble growing up. Handsome. Curly blond hair. Girls loved him. And he was smart. He could talk to anyone about anything. Like a walking encyclopedia. We used to tease him. He had a good sense of humor," she said with a grin.

"He sounds like a good guy."

"He was. He is," she hesitated. "I like to think he is still here with me."

"He is. He always will be," Ben said.

Ben's Chevy truck continued down the moon-dim highway; the headlights of oncoming traffic flashed past like a series of flickering lightbulbs about to burn out.

"Frankie had just enrolled at the community college," Marli said. "He loved photography. He wanted to be a photojournalist. He took his camera everywhere. We bought him one of those fancy digital cameras, a Canon I think. No, a Nikon. I can't remember. And a couple of zoom lenses."

"What did he photograph?"

"Everything. You name it. Flowers, buildings, bugs, people. He would post them on his Facebook page and ask friends to tell him what they thought."

"I would love to see them sometime."

"Oh, I have lots of his photos on my cell phone. You will be sorry you asked," Marli said. "We used to talk about going into business together—the writer and the photographer. We were going to freelance for National Geographic. Can you imagine? Well, at least that was our dream. But I told him he had to finish college first. Because there was plenty of time . . ." Marli bit her lip.

"Marli, how did he die?" Ben asked with trepidation. "I know you said it was an accident, but how? If you don't mind talking about it."

"He fell off a ladder in his apartment."

They were both silent.

"He was alone," Marli said. "Hanging Christmas ornaments on his first Christmas tree. So stupid. Why wasn't he more careful?! He wanted the apartment to look nice for us. He was having the family over for Christmas Eve. To his first apartment. He wanted everything to be nice. So stupid! Such a stupid way to die! I was so angry with him. I'm still so angry."

Marli squeezed her eyes shut with her thumb and forefinger, suppressing the tears as best she could.

"And here's another thing," she said after taking in a few deep breaths. "The first night here, in Puerto Escondido, I got this text message from a number I didn't recognize. The message said, 'Franklin's death was not an accident.' Out of the blue, two years after his death, I get this message!"

"What?"

"Yeah, isn't that weird? But Nick tells me to forget it. He says it is just some sick nutcase and I should just ignore it."

"Did the police determine it was an accident? I mean, what else could it be?"

"I don't know. There was no struggle. No forced entry like a robbery gone bad or anything."

"But anyone could have covered that up," Ben said. "There was no investigation?"

"I was pretty distraught. But I remember questioning how quick the investigator ruled it an accident. Nick insisted that we let it go. He said I was grasping at straws. That I was making things worse and I needed to just accept that Frankie was gone and move on."

"Well, he was probably right," Ben quietly replied. "But what if he wasn't?"

Ben turned the truck off of Highway 200 and continued inland another few miles after reaching Puerto Escondido. Streetlamps lit up the gravel-gray street paved with concrete hexagons and fronted by red-brick buildings with wide, metal, rollup doors. After another mile or so, he pulled up to an empty dirt lot with an eight-foot-high, chain-link barrier encircling the property. Dried thistles and dandelions worked to escape along the fence line. A fan palm stood guard in the corner where the land met the sidewalk.

"This is where I hope to build an animal shelter, vet hospital, and spay/neuter clinic one day," Ben said, walking up to the galvanized-steel fence and peering through the diamond-shaped openings. Marli took his hand.

"I have been working with city officials to secure this piece of land for the building. Now I'm just waiting to hear if they will do it or not. If the city appropriates the land, then it will be just a matter of raising the funds to construct the shelter and clinic."

"Wow. You are full of surprises. This is incredible."

"We just have to get this land," Ben said. "I even provided the city with a financially self-sustainable model based on income from the veterinary hospital to keep the shelter and clinic operating. The hospital will treat all strays, but owned pets, too, on a sliding scale based on the owner's income. The focus will be on sterilization and adoptions." The passion and excitement in Ben's voice began to build. "There also will be an educational component and a volunteer program for kids. It will be great. It could be great."

"When will you hear if you get the land?"

"Supposedly, any day. If the city decides not to dedicate the land for a shelter and clinic, then the government is going to start rounding up the street dogs and killing them."

"Jesus," Marli said under her breath, wondering where Puerto was at that moment.

Chapter Seventeen

On their way back to Puerto Escondido, Ben stopped at a local market to pick up the ingredients for dinner. He carefully selected the fresh, handmade corn tortillas, dried chili de arbol peppers, pungent garlic, vine-ripe tomatoes, green scallions, Romaine lettuce, and queso fresco cheese that he needed to create his famous enchiladas, an authentic regional recipe handed down from his mother. He added a bouquet of fresh sunflowers and a bottle of chardonnay, while Marli marveled at the exquisite Mexican pastries behind the glass dessert case.

"Pick out something you would like," Ben said.

Marli opted for the Mexican wedding cookies, heavenly spheres made of butter, flour, sugar, vanilla, and walnuts, baked until slightly golden and then dusted in powdered sugar so they resembled tiny, sweet snowballs. She could feel the flurry of buttery snowflakes already melting on her tongue.

"I rarely cook for myself," Ben said as he arranged the groceries on his laminate kitchen counter, stained and scarred with age. "But when I do, it usually turns out pretty decent. I credit my mother for any talent I have in the kitchen."

As Ben began to prepare the enchilada sauce, Marli arranged the sunflowers in a shiny, black, clay vase.

"This is beautiful," she said.

"It's called *Barro negro* pottery," Ben said, snapping the stems off the thin, dried chilies and placing them to briefly soak in water in the only saucepan he owned. "This style of pottery was born in Oaxaca. The metallic sheen is achieved by polishing the pottery with a quartz stone before it's fired. Each piece can take up to three weeks to complete. This vase was given to me as a gift from a friend whose family makes the pottery. I helped their cat."

"Of course you did." Marli smiled.

"The chilies need about fifteen minutes to simmer," Ben said, cutting the foil away from the rim of the chardonnay bottle and artfully removing the cork like the skilled surgeon that he was. He filled two wine glasses halfway up with the chilled vino, the bouquet beginning to emerge as the grape warmed up to the night's heat.

"I want to show you something I bought," Marli said, disappearing into Ben's bedroom and returning with a shopping bag bulging with an item she had acquired during one of her adventures with Tammy in Puerto Escondido. Marli lifted out her acquisition, carefully peeled away the clear packing tape, vehemently affixed to an immense amount of bubble wrap, and proudly unveiled her prize—a carved, neon-painted, winged wooden animal she had purchased at the Mercado Benito Juarez.

"Wow, look at that!" Ben exclaimed. "It's an alebrije."

"Yes, I know! Isn't it great?"

"It's a great example of traditional Mexican folk art," Ben said as he turned the brightly colored sculpture over in his hands. "It looks like a giraffe on heroin. I like it!"

"My mom and I bought one in Mazatlán years ago, and my goal on this trip was to find another one. I think it's going to bring me good luck."

"Then let's leave it out until you have to leave. My place could use a little color," Ben said, gently setting the crazed creature on the coffee table.

"Hey, did you hear that?" Marli asked as she moved toward the front door that stood between her and a barely audible whimpering followed by a light scratch.

Marli and Ben looked at each other. "Come on in, Puerto," Marli said, opening Ben's door to the hungry hound. "Look who found his way home? My psychotic animal sculpture is already bringing us good luck."

When the chilies were ready, Ben poured the scalding mixture from the saucepan into a blender and added a clove of fresh garlic and a pinch of salt. The crimson puree pulsed up the sides of the glass pitcher normally reserved for margarita making. Next, Ben pressed the bright red sauce through a metal strainer into a sunny-yellow mixing bowl.

"Is it going to be hot?" Marli asked with a touch of skepticism.

"Medium," Ben answered. "Chili de arbol peppers have a smoky flavor that enhances Mexican cooking. They are not too hot, depending on how sensitive you are," he said with a teasing inflection. "Did you see how the pepper was bright red even though it was dried? That is why artists use these types of peppers in decorative ristras and wreaths. They stay bright red."

Next, Ben poured a full cup of vegetable oil into a heavy, cast-iron skillet and turned the gas burner up to medium-high.

"Here's a trick my mother taught me," he said to Marli. "Stick the handle of a wooden spoon into the oil. When it's hot enough for frying, tiny bubbles will form around the wood."

"Well look at that," Marli said. "I never knew that." Marli had never deep fried anything in her life.

One after the other, Ben submerged the corn tortillas in the molten red sauce, thoroughly coating each one along with the tips of his fingers, and placed the Mexican crepes in the hot oil, a mere five seconds on each side so they would still be pliable. Then he stacked each on top of the other on a plate lined with paper towels. When all the tortillas were coated and fried, he cradled the golden discs one at a time in his left hand, added a heaping spoonful of the queso fresco and chopped green onions down the center, rolled them up, and placed them seam side down on a large ceramic platter.

"My mom taught me a few tricks of the trade in the kitchen, too," Marli said. "She is a great cook. Was a great cook. She doesn't cook much anymore."

"Tell me about your mom," Ben said as he assembled the four remaining enchiladas.

"She is an interesting woman. Not your typical mom," Marli said, setting the small round dining table with two handwoven placemats and neatly folded napkins. "She likes things that are out of the ordinary, like the alebrije. When I was little and we would go on vacations, she would make Dad pull over to the side of the road so she could jump out to pick up dried tumbleweeds and thistles. She would say, 'Isn't Mother Nature beautiful?'"

"I think that's fantastic," Ben said.

"We had this huge piece of driftwood hanging on the living room wall. Mom picked it up in Mendocino when it was still OK to take Mother Nature home with you. Mom would hang little gold birds on it at Christmas. She was so different than other moms. Other women wore pearls. Mine would wear strand on top of strand of American Indian trading beads—like ten or twelve strands at one time—around her neck." Marli laughed.

"Where did she get them?" Ben asked.

"Garage sales. Estate sales. Flea markets. But never paid full price, of course. She was the queen of bargain shopping."

"Sounds like my kind of woman," Ben said, smiling.

"And she loved anything tribal or primitive. One day Mom came home from visiting her brother in San Diego with this huge African mask," Marli said. "It must have been five feet long and three feet across. It was so scary. You really had to see it to believe it. It had animal hair and seashells and bone fragments all over it. But the worst part is that it was just encrusted with mud. It had dried black clay embedded in every nook and cranny. The store owner told Mom it was an ancestral tradition to bury dead tribesmen with face masks to protect them from evil spirits. Mom thought the mask was just beautiful. She loved it. But Nick, of course, hated it. I remember Mom said, 'How can you not love it?! It's so interesting. It tells a story.' And Nick replied, 'All it says to me is I'm filthy and ugly. Maybe we can bury it again in the backyard.'"

"I love your mom," Ben said.

"Yeah, there is little that Nick and Mom saw eye to eye on." Marli paused and then added, "Including pets. We always had a dog or two when I was growing up, usually a stray that Mom took in. But Nick didn't want anything to do with animals."

Ben finished the enchiladas by dressing them with a little more sauce, a layer of sour cream, a handful of shredded Romaine lettuce, several tomato slices, and a scattering of the crumbled cheese. Then he found a tapered candle and its holder in the kitchen cupboard where he kept them on hand for electrical outages or, as in this case, special occasions.

"This is really nice, Ben," Marli said, pulling her chair closer to the table as she sat down. "Thank you."

"My pleasure. It is one of the only things I know how to cook so I hope you enjoy it."

Ben could tell Marli was nervous. He was also. He wanted to reach across the table, kiss her perfect lips, and tell her it was all going to be OK. Before he had a chance to speak again, he could tell something was wrong. Marli's eyes widened as tears careened down her cheeks.

"Hold on! Don't drink any water! It will make it worse!" Ben jumped up from the table and flung open first one kitchen cabinet, then another and then another until he found what he was looking for—a small, clear, plastic bear filled with honey. "Squeeze this into your mouth," he said.

The sweet, thick syrup varnished Marli's burning tongue and the tender skin on the inside of her cheeks, instantly taking away the pain like an intravenous injection of morphine. Marli wiped away the tears that had pooled in her eyes and took a long sip of chardonnay.

"Whoa! Ben, that was so hot!"

"Marli, I'm so sorry," Ben said. "I didn't think it was that hot. I guess I'm just used to it."

"And who knew honey would help?" she said, sucking in more of the heavy amber liquid just to be safe.

"Yes, isn't it interesting? The sugar in the honey dissolves the capsaicin, which is the chemical compound in the chili peppers that causes the burning sensation." Ben rambled partly out of embarrassment, but mostly caught up in his own fascination with the science of it all.

"Fat in whole milk, olive oil, and peanut butter will all do the same thing," he continued. "But water just spreads the burn around your mouth. Water won't dissolve the capsaicin. You see, the chili burn stems from a chemical reaction that occurs when capsaicin bonds with the pain receptors on the inside of your mouth—"

"Ben?" Marli said, trying to bring her dinner mate back into her world.

"Actually, honey has been used for hundreds of years to treat ailments . . . ulcers, open wounds, first-degree burns."

"Burns?"

"Yes. Honey's antibacterial and anti-inflammatory properties actually promote healing. One study in 2006 found that non-serious burns healed faster when treated with gauze and a spot of honey than those treated with antibiotic ointment."

"Ben," Marli said.

"You see, honey has high osmolality. The sugar draws the water from inside the bacteria cells and kills them through dehydration. Honey also is somewhat acidic—"

"Ben! I got it. Enough with the chemistry lesson."

"I'm sorry. I get excited about these things. Bad habit. We can go out and get something else to eat."

"No, it's OK. I'm really not hungry anymore. Just tired."

"How about a Mexican wedding? I mean a Mexican wedding cookie."

"Yes, that would be perfect."

"Are you really OK?" Ben asked, lowering his voice.

"Yes. I've never been better."

Fifteen days remained before Marli could return home with Puerto. But did she really want to go back to California? Nothing was waiting for her there except a pending divorce and an overly formal and fussy house, one she never really liked and was now hopefully void of anything related to her husband, which probably meant void of everything. If she returned home to San Jose, she would have to suffer selling the house and either finding an apartment or moving in with her mother while enduring the dissolution of her marriage, which was sure to prove unpleasant. So why face it? Here, in Puerto Escondido, she had found purpose with Ben. She could volunteer at his vet office. Continue to assist him in his mission to rescue street dogs. Help at more spay clinics. Support his quest to open an animal shelter. She could do all of this while freelance writing to bring in a little money to pay her share of the bills. But what would Ben think? Did he want Marli to continue living with him? Maybe he liked being a bachelor. Maybe he only agreed to let her stay with him because he knew she would be leaving at the end of thirty days. Maybe she was beginning to fall in love with someone who did not return her feelings. In the end, none of it mattered. It was too soon for Marli to put her heart on the proverbial line again anyway.

By midweek, Marli had adjusted to staying in Ben's home. He was neat but not obsessive like Nick. He did not have many possessions and certainly no clutter. His lifestyle was simple. Ben preferred to read the latest veterinary journal over watching something mind-numbing on his antiquated television set. His refrigerator was what you would expect from a single man, amply stocked with beer, peanut butter, and frozen bean burritos. Dishes and drinking glasses were mismatched, but they were clean and in the cupboard, not dirty and in the sink. His computer and printer were set up in the second bedroom, which acted as Ben's home office. The small single bathroom had zero counter space but was sufficient for the short amount of time Marli would be living there. Best of all, the toothpaste tube was always squeezed in the middle.

Ben had a full day ahead at his vet office, including three dog dentals to perform in the morning plus a benign tumor to remove from an agreeable feline. In the afternoon, he had eight scheduled appointments and several follow-up phone calls to return to anxious pet owners.

Puerto had been restless earlier in the week. He paced in front of Ben's front door until Marli finally succumbed to his whimpering and released her furry friend from his comfortable captivity. Puerto then disappeared into the night without looking back. By morning when he had not returned, Ben assured Marli that their vagabond friend would come home when he was hungry.

On his way to the office, Ben dropped Marli off at the Mercado Benito Juarez, where she hoped to purchase an airline-approved dog crate in which she could transport Puerto home. The mutt was clearly too large to travel in the cabin with Marli and would have to ride in the cargo hold.

"The kennel has to be constructed of hard plastic with a solid roof and floor and have a metal door and ventilation on four sides," Ben said to Marli. "Airline regulations require that the crate be large enough for Puerto to sit down and stand up in without his head touching the top. He also must be able to turn around and lie down comfortably. It should have two dishes, one for food and one for water, that can be attached to the inside of the crate but also accessible from the outside so they can be filled without opening the door. Remember to get labels that say 'Live Animal' and 'This End Up.'"

Ben recommended purchasing the kennel as soon as possible so Puerto could become familiar with the enclosed space, especially since the canine, to the best of their knowledge, had never been in such a small confinement. "Puerto could panic and try to escape if he feels trapped," Ben said. "We'll put dog treats in the crate at home and prop the door open so Puerto can get used to going in and out of it."

"What about a sedative?" Marli asked. "Won't that help ease his anxiety?"

"So little is known about the effects of sedation in animals that are under stress or traveling in pressurized cargo holds," Ben said. "Increased altitude can create respiratory and cardiovascular problems in dogs that are sedated. The temperature in the belly of the plane can significantly fluctuate. The noise can be tremendous and the air pressure can dramatically drop."

"What?" Marli said in horror.

"Don't worry. I read somewhere that only an average of seventeen animals die each year on US commercial airlines."

"Only seventeen?"

"Yes, but remember, two million animals travel by flight annually. So seventeen really is an insignificant number."

"Sorry, that does not make me feel any better."

Ben suggested that Marli revisit the Mercado Benito Juarez, where she acquired her mythical-animal wood carving, because a fairly reputable vendor operated a pet-supply store along the perimeter of the market.

"Ask for Lucas," Ben said.

It was Wednesday, one of two days a week considered a "market day," when merchants from all over the state of Oaxaca bring their numerous products to sell. The mercado would be busier than other days and the roads more congested. But, because there were additional vendors, Marli had a better chance of finding an airline-approved dog crate from another merchant if Lucas did not have the one she needed.

As anticipated, the buyers and sellers making their way to the mercado, both by vehicle and on foot, were so numerous that Ben had to drop Marli off several blocks away. Ben double-parked his Chevy on the side of the street and stepped out of his truck.

"It should not be difficult to catch a taxi when you are ready to leave," he said, helping Marli down from the driver's side, shielding her as best he could from oncoming traffic.

"You know, it's been three days since we've seen Puerto," Marli said, turning to Ben. "I'm worried about him."

"He must be pretty hungry by now unless he's finding somewhere else to eat," Ben said, trying to hide his mutual concern. "But I'm sure he's fine. He'll be home tonight."

"I hope so," Marli said reluctantly. "See you tonight," she added with a smile as she turned toward the sidewalk and headed north, squeezing past anxious street dealers, animated food vendors, and hordes of pedestrians paving the way to the Mexican marketplace. An errant cloud drifted across the Oaxacan sky, threatening to release an unforeseen shower over the idyllic coastal town.

Marli could have spent all day at the mercado, not only for the sheer pleasure of shopping for anything and everything she could possibly want but to take in the sounds, sights, and smells of such an extraordinary gathering of humankind. Just as on her first visit three weeks earlier, only more intense because of the greater number of vendors and crowds vying for merchandise, the mercado was the quintessential bargain shoppers' paradise. It was easier to list what she could not find there than what she could. The task-oriented locals were interested in the just-harvested vegetables, the early-morning seafood catch, hot tortillas steaming up their twist-tied plastic bags, fresh-baked Mexican pastries, and on-the-spot squeezed juices, sprays of exotic flowers for church altars and birthday parties, and various household necessities. The leisurely tourists wanted logo T-shirts, beaded handbags, leather belts and sandals, silver jewelry, hand-painted pottery, and souvenir tchotchkes to take home as gifts and remembrances.

Thin, elderly women with deep, whiskey-brown crevices carved in their sunken cheeks sat quietly behind tables laden with bowls of dried beans, spices, and chilies. Younger women filled canvas tote bags with limes, tomatoes, and ears of corn as they bartered for better prices. Dark-skinned children with well-rounded stomachs ran about unattended, sucking on jewel-toned popsicles. Groups of Mexican men wearing sweat-stained cowboy hats and pointed animal-skin boots nodded to each other on their way to the livestock corrals.

Despite the multiple distractions and excessive shopping sidetracks, Marli finally came upon the vendor that specialized in small and large animal supplies. Hefty bags of dry dog and cat food rested outside the shop entrance. Black iron bird cages hung from the rafters, hamster and guinea pig pens were stacked in the corner, a barrel of colorful stuffed dog toys sat by the cash register, and carpeted cat trees lined the far wall. Steel shelves housed food dishes, carriers, litter pans, puppy training pads, poop scoops, pet shampoos, and flea- and tick-control products. Back walls were lined with provisions for rabbits, horses, pigs, chickens, ducks, goats, cows, and sheep. There were salt licks, bales of grass and straw, bags of alfalfa pellets, and pine, cedar, and aspen shavings. Bulk bins contained chicken scratch, goat chow, and whole, cracked, and rolled corn. Just past a peg board holding collars, harnesses, and leashes, Marli found several hard plastic pet crates of various sizes haphazardly stacked on top of one another. She brushed away the layer of dust coating the top of one kennel that looked large enough to meet airline requirements for Puerto's weight and dimensions and schlepped it to the cash register.

"You would like to buy this dog crate?" asked the stout gentleman behind the counter with a gap between his tobacco-stained teeth.

"Sí. Ben Rosado told me to ask for Lucas."

"Ah, Ben! Sí! I am Lucas!"

"Hola. So I need an airline-approved crate. Is this crate airline-approved?" Marli asked, extending her arms apart like the wings of a bird just in case Lucas did not understand.

"Sí, sí, for airplanes."

"Sí. Great. So how much?"

"For Ben, only 500 pesos."

"Done."

Marli was relieved to find a taxi waiting for a potential customer directly in front of the main entrance to the mercado. She did not have to maneuver the awkward dog kennel down the crowded sidewalk still paved with zealous shoppers searching for bargains from the transient vendors lined up outside. She pushed the crate across the backseat of the cab and settled in beside it. She then handed a piece of paper with Ben's home address to the smiling driver wearing a beat-up baseball cap with a Corona logo and was startled when her cell phone rang unexpectantly through her handbag strapped across her shoulders.

Marli fumbled to find the phone before it stopped calling out to her. "Aunt Abbey?" she asked. "Are you there?"

"Marli? Is that you?" Abbey replied in an elevated voice as if she forgot who she called.

"Yes. Hi. How are you?"

"I'm fine. Listen, honey. I did not want to disturb you on your vacation but I thought I should call. I thought you would want to know. Since we don't know when you are coming home."

"What is it?" Marli asked, her voice shifting from surprise to concern.

"Your mom isn't doing well. I don't mean to worry you, but she went to the hospital again yesterday. They are running more tests. You know those doctors. Test after test after test, but never a definitive answer—"

"Aunt Abbey!" Marli interrupted. "What happened? Why did she go to the hospital?"

"I had to call 911. She was having trouble breathing. It came on so suddenly. Those nice paramedics were here so fast. They did all this stuff, took her blood pressure, gave her oxygen, and then they whisked her off to the hospital. I had to follow in Alice's car—"

"Are you at the hospital now? Can I speak to her?"

"The nurse just came and took her for another test, a CAT scan, I think. But listen, Marli. You should come home. Your mom is not well. You should come home, honey. I think you should come home."

Abbey could have repeated it a million more times, but it would not have mattered. All Marli could hear were her own thoughts racing around like synapses from one nerve cell to another inside her brain, trying to reconcile how her mother could be laying in a hospital bed while Marli was more than two thousand miles away in a foreign country.

"I will, I will. I will catch the next possible plane. I will let you know when."

Marli searched the bottom of her cluttered purse until she found the pack of matches she had taken from Hotel Santa Fe and dialed the number on the tiny box as calmly as she could.

"Rosa, por favor."

"Sí. *Esta es* Rosa."

"Rosa? This is Marli May."

"Marli? How are you?"

"Rosa, I need your help. My mother is sick. I have to get home right away. I don't know what to do. Can you find out if there is a flight to San Jose today?"

"Sí, sí! I am so sorry. Hold on while I check."

The taxi driver was impatient with other motorists. He pulled up fast behind other cars and slowed down so abruptly that Marli had to hold the dog kennel with her left arm to keep it from falling forward. Mariachi music melted from the cab's radio. Marli fixated on a gash in the upholstery on the back of the front passenger seat while she waited for Rosa to come back on the phone.

"Marli. There is a flight in two hours to Mexico City where you can transfer to Houston and then to San Jose. Do you want me to book it for you? You can give me your credit card number over the phone. And I can email you the boarding pass."

"Sí, yes!"

"OK, but you must hurry."

"Rosa, I have not seen Puerto for three days. Can you keep your eye out for him and call Ben if you see him?"

"Sí, of course. Don't worry."

By the time the taxi pulled up in front of Ben's house, Marli had left six voicemails and two text messages on his cell phone. He must still be in surgery or with patients.

"Wait here, por favor," Marli said to the driver, holding up the palms of her hands to his face to signal "Stop, don't go." "I will be right back."

There was no time to leave Ben a note. There was no time to look for Puerto. All she could think to do was collect her belongings and leave the new dog crate in the middle of the living room floor, a symbol that she would be back.

"Airport, por favor," she told the smiling, impatient cab driver.

Chapter Eighteen

Ben Rosado was behind a closed exam room door with a former street dog named Max, who had hit the canine equivalent of the lottery. A retired couple from Canada took in the homeless lab-size hound as their precious pet two years prior, just as construction was wrapping up on their new, Mediterranean-style condo overlooking Playa Manzanillo. Max went from begging for leftover scraps of food from sympathetic tourists to dining on homemade meals of free-range roasted chicken lovingly mixed with steamed carrots and brown rice. Instead of sleeping on cement sidewalks and gravel driveways, he lounged on a custom-created doggy couch covered in royal, burgundy-red velvet to match the Canadian couple's living room furniture. Fleas, ticks, ear mites, worms, and other assorted parasites were a thing of the past. Max was one of the lucky ones, and he showed his appreciation for his new status in life with unconditional exuberance for his people and by inhaling a pound of premium dark chocolate off the kitchen counter when no one was looking.

While Ben was busy monitoring the mischievous mutt's vital signs, he heard Jenna Gonzales, his former girlfriend, call his name from the front of the vet office.

"Dr. Rosado? Ben? Are you here?"

"I'm here," Ben said, pushing open the door from the back room to the reception area. Jenna sauntered past the front desk toward Ben in her four-inch stilettos and fitted, purple miniskirt. Half of her mocha-colored tresses were casually clipped high on her head, while the other half purposely trickled down in ringlets over her accentuated breasts.

"What are you doing here?"

"Oh, Ben," the ex-girlfriend cooed, moving in closer. "I was just looking for you. I was wondering if you wanted to share a bite to eat. I am lonely without my precious Chica. Maybe you can come over tonight. We can share a bottle of wine."

"I can't, Jenna. I'm seeing someone else now. You really need to go. Listen, I have to get back to a patient. So please go." Ben turned and exited the reception area, shutting the door behind him with a definitive slam, hoping Jenna would take that as a signal to leave.

As Ben headed back to his four-legged patient, he overheard Jenna still in his reception area.

"No hablo ingles," Jenna said. "Esta es Jenna."

"Are you still here?" Ben asked, returning to the reception area and picking up his cell phone. "I heard you talking to someone." He looked down at the screen, void of any calls or text messages.

"Nobody of concern," Jenna said.

"Jenna, please—"

"I miss you, Ben. This thing with the American is just a fling. You miss me, too. I know you do."

"That's not really any of your concern, Jenna. Come on. Please, let's go," Ben said, escorting his ex to the front door. "What you need is another dog. I know where you can get one."

Marli sat alone at the Puerto Escondido International Airport waiting to board her flight to Mexico City. Several Mexican families began to fill the seats around her. Marli faced a woman, maybe in her sixties, wearing a stylish maroon blouse that crisscrossed her chest and left just enough cleavage to be tasteful. A dramatic drop necklace lay eloquently around her neck with matching earrings hovering above her shoulders. Her tailored black pants stopped two inches before her gold-toned sandals accented with crystal rhinestones. The woman held a clear plastic container filled with cut-up pineapple, strawberries, and mango purchased from one of the airport's few walkup food vendors. She hand-fed the fresh pieces to two small children, most likely her grandchildren, Marli supposed. The little girls were dressed in matching purple tights and sparkly T-shirts and twirled and danced about between bites of fruit, sometimes crashing into the woman's legs with uncontrollable giggling. Marli could hear but not understand the Spanish they shared, so it did not seem quite like eavesdropping when she could not stop watching and listening to their contagious happiness.

Marli's mind wandered back to the telephone call she had made to Ben. *Jenna? Jenna? Why does that name sound so familiar? Of course*, Marli remembered. *Jenna is Ben's ex-girlfriend. Why did Ben's ex-girlfriend answer his cell phone? Was she at his office again? Or were they somewhere else together?*

By 7:00 p.m., Ben Rosado was exhausted from his long day of slobber, scratches, vomit, fur, and excrement, and eager to see Marli and relax with a glass of zinfandel over dinner. Escondido responded to Ben's truck pulling up to the house with his usual irrepressible barking. Ben took note of the large dog crate in the middle of the floor on his way to the back door to save Escondido from any self-inflicted injury stemming from his uncontrollable, seizure-like excitement. As usual, it took several seconds of head scratches and belly rubs, coupled with a peanut butter-flavored dog biscuit, to calm the enthusiastic mutt down.

The unassuming home seemed strangely empty. "Marli?" Ben called out as he pushed open the bedroom door. He could immediately see that the few belongings Marli had brought with her were gone. The chartreuse luggage, carry-on case, and shopping bags had disappeared. The straw hat and extra pair of sandals were missing. The wire hangers she used for her sundress and shirts hung empty in the closet. Her toothbrush, hairspray, and makeup bag were absent from the bathroom counter. The only trace of the girl from California was the wild wooden animal—the cherished Mexican folk art that Marli said would bring her good luck—still standing alone on Ben's meager coffee table.

The halls of Good Samaritan Hospital in San Jose were quiet at a quarter past midnight when Marli finally arrived. She did not go home first from the airport. She took a taxi directly to the hospital with her travel bags in tow. Marli knew it was way past official visiting hours, but when she called Aunt Abbey back to tell her that she got a flight home, Abbey informed her that the hospital was lenient about the rules in favor of letting families and friends visit patients as much as possible.

Marli hung her carry-on and shopping bags over the outstretched suitcase handle and wheeled her possessions through the automatic sliding glass doors into the hospital lobby. She went past the unoccupied patient registration desk, across the linoleum floor lined with armchairs upholstered in a purposefully busy orange and maroon pattern to camouflage stains, and toward two sets of elevator doors. Uplifting plexiglass posters hung on the stark walls. One poster featured a woman holding a laughing baby. The words "Compassionate Care for You and Your Family" hovered over their heads. Another showed a young boy running through an open grass field. "We Believe in Your Total Health" ran across the bottom.

"Well, that's reassuring," a good-natured stranger said, nodding his head toward one of the posters as he and Marli waited patiently for the elevator doors to open.

Marli followed the man into the elevator, taking note of the empty candy bar wrapper in the corner, and pushed the button for the fourth floor, where Aunt Abbey told Marli she would find Alice's room. The doors opened up to a fluorescent light show that made the bags under Marli's eyes even more pronounced. The hallway smelled like disinfectant. Leftover cafeteria food lay unpleasantly on dinner trays that had yet to be picked up. A slightly overweight middle-aged woman, wearing medical scrubs decorated with cartoon kittens playing with stethoscopes, sat behind a computer screen at the nurses' station.

"May I help you?" the woman asked Marli.

"I am looking for Alice Stewart's room."

"Are you a relative?"

"I'm her daughter."

"She is having a bad night. Another nurse is in with her now. Room 412."

Marli dodged a large hamper of soiled bedsheets and maneuvered around a portable imaging machine. An elderly woman in a light-blue patient gown tied across her back shoulders and buttocks shuffled along in hospital-issued socks while holding on to her IV bag pole. Marli made her way down the antiseptic hallway, averting her eyes from open room doors so as not to intrude on private matters taking place inside. With each step closer to Alice's room, Marli could hear her mother's voice growing louder and clearer. Pushing the heavy wooden door open, Marli stepped inside and rolled her bags into an empty corner. An obnoxious plastic curtain hanging from a metal track in the ceiling separated Alice from her sleeping roommate. A tall, Black woman in a light-yellow nurse's top and matching drawstring pants hovered over Alice, making a dent in the curtain with her curvaceous rear as she tried to adjust the bedsheets and blanket that were wrapped around her patient's legs.

"Stop it!" Alice shouted at the unfazed nurse. "Leave me alone!"

"Mom, Mom. It's OK," Marli said softly.

"Marli! Is that you? You're here!" Alice said as she reached for her daughter's hand, straining the intravenous tubing connected to a venous catheter in the vein above Alice's wrist. A small drip of dried blood peered out from under the medical tape holding the catheter to her tissue-paper skin.

"Yes, I'm here, Mom. It's OK. It's going to be OK," Marli whispered, feeling Alice's cool, soft fingers wrap around her hand, the grip tight without apology. With her free hand, Marli reached back to pull the visitor's chair closer so she could sit next to the bed, face-to-face with her mother, and rest her arm over the bed rail, still clutching Alice's hand. A dingy, brown, over-the-bed hospital table with a water pitcher and box of tissues was shoved to the side of the room out of Alice's reach. A small bouquet of tulips and daffodils from Aunt Abbey rested on the nightstand. A tiresome light blasted out of the top of a long, fluorescent wall lamp hovering over the hospital bed, smothering the acoustical ceiling tiles before falling to the floor like a dense, gray fog.

"You must be Marli," said the nurse, whose hospital badge clarified that her name was Gisselle and she was a registered nurse.

"Yes," Marli replied, almost ashamed to admit she was the absent daughter.

"She has been calling for you all night. Seniors do not do well here at night. It's not their home. They get confused. It's called 'sundowning.'"

"Sundowning?"

"Yes, or Sundown Syndrome," Gisselle said. "It's when patients become more confused and restless, sometimes violent, after the sun goes down. It's usually associated with dementia or Alzheimer's." Gisselle wore her dark hair very short, almost shaved to her head. She had a stethoscope dangling around her neck so each end rested at the top of her breasts. Pinned onto her name tag was a small round metal button that said "50 Years of Caring for Our Community."

"Mom does not have dementia," Marli said.

"Then it's probably just what we call a senior moment. Anyway, it's good you are here. She will be much calmer now, won't you Alice?" Gisselle said, lifting her voice as if talking to a child. "I'll be back to check on her. Push the nurses' station button if you need anything."

"When can I talk to the doctor?" asked Marli.

"He usually makes his rounds around ten in the morning. Or you can also leave a message with the desk nurse to have him call you."

Marli fell asleep hanging over the bed railing, still gripping Alice's fingers in her right hand and holding her cell phone with her left.

The morning-shift nurse came into the room around 6:00 a.m. to replace Gisselle's name with her own on the dry-erase board hanging over a large, army-green garbage can. Startled awake, Marli sat up and stretched her back out of its twisted position and checked for messages. Still nothing from Ben. Why hadn't he called? Why was that Jenna person answering his phone? The battery light flashed its 5 percent warning. Alice lay sleeping, curled up in a half-moon with her bottom arm cradling her head despite the IV tube being stretched to its limit. Her breathing was deep and steady with a hint of a soft snore that Marli could hear when she bent over the bed to kiss her mom's warm cheek.

"Good morning. I'm Gypsy," the perky morning-shift nurse said, shaking Alice's IV bag so the fluid inside sloshed about, and then flicked the connection from the bag to the tube with her forefinger. "I will be Mrs. Stewart's nurse today. Are you her daughter?"

"Yes," Marli replied in a gravelly voice, thinking Gisselle and Gypsy sounded like a vaudeville act. "What is she getting through the IV?"

"Right now, it's just a sterile saline solution. It is set up in case the doctor wants to give her a pain med or something else later on."

"Right," Marli said. "Hey, I don't seem to get any cell phone reception here."

"Nope. You won't. It's the walls. You have to go out into the lobby or outside," Gypsy said. "Weird, I know."

"Great. OK, I'll be right back. I won't be long." Marli wanted perky Gypsy and all the other nurses to know that Alice was not one of those patients whose family never came to see them, who had no one to watch their backs, who were all alone in the world. Alice was not alone.

"Hi, Aunt Abbey. It's Marli."

"Oh, hi dear. Did you make it home?"

"Yes, I'm at the hospital now. I stayed with Mom last night."

"Oh, good. I'm so glad. How is she doing?"

"She's sleeping now. What did the doctors tell you? Why is she here?"

"Well, you know. It's the cancer. But you should talk to the doctor, sweetie."

"Yes, right. I will when he gets here. Are you going home?"

"Now that you are back, I think I will head home, honey. I will see if I can get a plane out this afternoon and take a taxi to the airport. You call me if you need anything."

The morning crawled by as Marli waited for the doctor to make his rounds and stop by to check on Alice. Breakfast was scrambled eggs, dry wheat toast with a pat of butter on the side, a container of strawberry yogurt, an overripe banana, a carton of orange juice, and black coffee with packets of white sugar and powdered creamer. The smell made Marli nauseous. Alice removed the plate cover, allowing the liquid steam to drip down and puddle onto the plate. She fumbled to free the plastic utensils, paper napkin, and salt and pepper packets from their clear sterile packaging. She peeled back the lid on the yogurt, took one bite, and placed the container back on the food tray.

"I'm not hungry," she said.

"Hospice?" Marli repeated back to the young Asian doctor as they stood in the hospital hallway just outside of Alice's room.

"Yes, hospice," said Dr. Chu, who looked like he'd just graduated from high school. "There is really nothing more we can do for your mother." He took off his thick, black-rimmed eyeglasses and placed them in the breast pocket of his white, pressed physician's coat. "Her tumor is inoperable, as we discussed before. I am discharging her today and I will have someone contact you about setting up home hospice. Does she live with you?"

"But she is sick. How can you send her home? She will wonder why you are not doing more for her here in the hospital. How can I tell her you are recommending hospice? That's like giving her a death sentence."

"I understand how difficult this must be. We will also arrange for a home-care nurse to visit at least once a day to check her vitals and a home-care aide to help with bathing and physical activities."

Hospice. Hospice. Hospice. The word kept repeating in Marli's head. The slick, color brochure Dr. Chu located behind the nurses' station defined hospice as "a facility or program designed to provide a caring environment for meeting the physical and emotional needs of the terminally ill." *Terminally ill. Terminally ill. Terminally ill.* Marli stared down at the cover photo of the glossy pamphlet. Was the smiling senior, being comforted by a seemingly concerned loved one, dead now? Or perhaps the elderly hospice patient was really a paid model who was not near death at all.

"Mom, they are discharging you this afternoon," Marli said as she handed Alice a plastic cup of ice water, helping place the clear straw to her mother's dry, colorless lips.

"But I don't feel good. Why are they sending me home?"

"I know. They think you will feel better at home. You don't want to stay here. You will feel much better in your own bed. So instead you will have a home-care nurse to help you. OK?"

"Will you stay with me?"

"Yes, of course."

Chapter Nineteen

Ben checked his cell phone over and over again for a text or voicemail from Marli as if he could have missed a message from her the first time he looked. He searched for a note in the living room, maybe it slipped under the sofa; in the bedroom, it could have fallen behind the nightstand; in the kitchen, perhaps she thought that was the first place he would go when he got home. Nothing. *Why did she leave so abruptly? Why didn't she tell him she was going? Why would she leave Puerto behind?* Ben decided to let it go, to stop trying to understand why Marli left without explanation. He would not call her. If she wanted to talk to explain, she would have called him by now. Marli was free to do whatever she wanted to do. If she changed her mind about taking a street dog home to the States, that was her decision. If she decided that a relationship with a Mexican vet was not in her best interest, no harm done. She was in a mixed-up emotional frame of mind, so she probably came to her senses. And she believed that leaving with no notice and no goodbyes was easier. Besides, a long-distance relationship—Puerto Escondido, Oaxaca, to San Jose, California—was not practical. Ben knew the time they shared together would have to come to an end. Marli could not stay in Mexico permanently. Ben could not move to California. So maybe she was right. This way was easier.

Dr. Chu's official discharge order took several hours to trickle down to the nurses' station, giving Marli enough time to arrange for Tammy to pick her and her mom up from the hospital around 4:00 p.m. and drive them to Alice's house.

"Hospice?" Tammy repeated back to Marli as they stood next to Tammy's 2008 silver Toyota Solara parked in the passenger loading zone at the front of the hospital. They were waiting for the nurse to bring Alice down in the mandatory discharge wheelchair. "I am so sorry. I had no idea she was so sick."

"Neither did I," Marli said. "I mean, we knew she had cancer and the options at her age were limited, but I never thought it would come to this. But honestly, I'm not going to panic. The doctor said hospice usually means six months to live, but some patients live for years. I know Mom has lots of time left."

Heavy commuter traffic at the end of the workday on Highway 85 North turned what should have been a ten-minute drive into almost an hour by the time Tammy turned off onto the South De Anza Boulevard exit. Alice rode in the front passenger seat because it was too difficult for her to get in and out of the backseat of the two-door sports coupe. Marli rested her head against the back window, cradling between her knees the vase of flowers that Aunt Abbey had brought to Alice in the hospital, and watched the other cars pass like they had somewhere important to go. Marli let Tammy, who was driving uncharacteristically cautiously in the slow lane of the freeway, manage an innocuous conversation with Alice.

"How was the hospital food?"

"Did you like your nurses?"

"The flowers Abbey gave you are lovely."

San Jose's enviable Mediterranean climate was predictable for March at a pleasant 77 degrees, almost 20 degrees lower than the flush temperature at that very moment in Puerto Escondido.

As soon as Alice had settled into her own bed—one of those adjustable king-size monstrosities with a remote control so she could lower and raise her head and feet at will—Marli asked Tammy to take her home, the home she used to share with Nick, so she could take a long-overdue shower and gather some things for staying with her mother.

"I have not had a chance to talk to you about Ben," Tammy said, pulling her seat belt across her chest and snapping the buckle in place.

"He has not returned any of my calls or text messages," Marli said matter-of-factly.

"That does not sound like Ben. Maybe he didn't get them."

"Or maybe he just wants to let it all go. It's not like we were ever going to be a couple anyway. I live here and he lives there. He's probably not the kind of guy for long goodbyes, so it's just better this way."

"What about Puerto?"

"Yeah, I know. I don't know what to do. I just have to hope he will be OK and Ben will watch out for him. I have to focus on Mom now."

"I'm sure he will be fine," Tammy comforted her friend as she turned the silver sports coupe back onto Highway 85. "You did so much for that mop of a dog."

"Mom, hospice. Nick, divorce. Puerto, still in Mexico. Ben, not returning my calls. And that message about Frankie. Doesn't get much better than that, does it?"

"Speaking of . . . what about that message about Franklin?" Tammy asked, her eyes fixated on the road ahead.

"I found out that the number came from one of those disposable cell phones."

"How did you find that out? When did you have time?"

"While sitting with Mom at the hospital," Marli said, pulling down the car visor and examining her weary face in the passenger-side mirror. "I searched on the Internet for how to trace a text message. There's a couple of websites. One is a cell phone registry. The other is some kind of tracing website—it traces cell phone numbers. When I put the number in, both websites said it came from a prepaid phone. No way to trace it." Marli paused. "It's just as well. I'm sure it was a prank. But someone went to an awful lot of trouble for a sick joke."

"Marli, there is something I have to tell you," Tammy said, just as Marli's phone sent out its irritating chime. Marli scrambled to find the cell hidden within her purse, still holding out hope that it would be Ben calling at last.

"It's Nick," Marli said, disappointed, looking down at the flashing screen.

"Don't answer it!" Tammy said. "You've got nothing to say to him."

"What if it's about the divorce? Or the house?"

"He can text or email you. No need to waste your breath on that piece of shit."

Tammy pulled her car into Marli's painted, concrete driveway, stamped with grout lines to mimic oversized decorative tile. Nick had insisted on a traditional, two-story, colonial-style home with a half-circle porch, Georgian columns, and gridded windows on each side of the front door and across the second floor. The perfectly symmetrical house was painted "wedding veil" white and the raised panel shutters were "midnight dream" black. The brick, herringbone walkway leading to the classic red door was lined with boxwoods pruned into squares and mature agapanthus ready to explode into globes of blue-and-white, trumpet-shaped flowers. The expansive lawn was embarrassingly lush due to the automatic sprinklers Nick refused to limit despite the irrepressible drought.

"Do you want me to come in?" Tammy asked.

"You were going to tell me something," Marli said.

"It can wait. You need to rest now."

"Thank you for everything. You're a good friend. I don't know what I would do without you."

"You're my partner in crime, remember? I'm here for you."

Tammy popped open the car trunk and pulled out Marli's exhausted suitcase and bags.

"I'll call you," Tammy said, pulling Marli in for a long everything-will-be-OK hug. "Have a glass of wine. Or better yet, some mescal."

Tammy waited while Marli fumbled for her house keys, pushed open the stately front door, and slipped safely inside. Then Tammy crumbled over the steering wheel like a scattered pile of brittle fall leaves, weeping uncontrollably. What kind of a person was she? How could she be so deceitful to her friend, her best friend? Marli deserved better.

Marli dropped her luggage onto the Carrara marble entryway, its twisting, river-like, black veins leading into the sweeping living room. The house was stuffy from being closed up for so many weeks. But nothing seemed out of place like Marli imagined it would be. She had pictured walking into a vast, open space void of furniture, artwork, and decor. She just assumed Nick would take everything. After all, he paid for most of their joint belongings. And he *was* an asshole. Maybe he was being kind for now but would demand splitting up the contents when the house was sold. Yes, that made sense.

Too tired to free open the windows and summon in fresh air, she dragged her travel bags up the red-oak staircase to the master bedroom. Now she could see that Nick had actually come and gone. The hand-carved, mahogany jewelry box where he kept his Movado watch and sterling silver money clip was not in its usual place on top of the tall, six-drawer, maple-wood chest. His dresser was empty except for the musk-scented paper with which Marli had lined the drawers. The fancy trophies he won three years in a row at the San Jose Sharks Foundation Golf Classic were missing from the bookshelf, along with the autographed 49ers football on which he was the high bidder at a recent charity auction. The right side of the spacious walk-in closet where Nick kept his suits, slacks, pressed shirts, ties, and shoes was bare. Everything related to her soon-to-be-former husband had also vanished from the en suite bathroom.

Marli let the pair of faded blue jeans she had been wearing since the prior morning fall to the honey-colored, wall-to-wall carpeting. She sat on the edge of the bed and laid back on the cool satin comforter, gazing up at the recessed light fixtures. There was nothing about the stodgy, pretentious house that Marli would miss. She hated the dirt-brown granite countertops and the custom, cherrywood cabinets in the designer kitchen. She loathed the stiff leather sofa and matching chair with their rolled arms, carved wood frames, and nail-head trim that the saleswoman called an "Old World look that will never go out of style."

Marli wanted to take a sledgehammer to the gilded metal coffee table with its ornately scrolled legs and beveled glass inserts that never failed to slam into her knee when she tried to walk around it. She dreamed of setting fire to the giant, antique, reproduction china cabinet that conspired against her with the three-leaf French provincial dining table and its eight pompously curved chairs. What if she fetched the long-handled shovel from the outdoor garden shed and bashed in the French Empire chandelier that leered down from the entryway ceiling? Does anyone except Nick really decant their designer liquors into crystal carafes anymore or need a sub-zero, dual-zone, stainless-steel cooler just to store their overpriced wines? What if Marli took those out, too? One swing and it would be over.

As she let the warm shower water wash away any unproductive thoughts of destruction, she considered how fast life changes without care or concern for anyone who gets hurt.

One day you are taking an overdue vacation to a foreign country to reconnect with your seemingly faithful spouse; the next day you are embracing a fantasy life with a foreign lover and a four-legged reason to live; the next day you are alone with a dying mother.

Marli wiped a circle in the steam that had coated her bathroom mirror and stared into her tired reflection. "I miss you, Ben," Marli whispered to no one there. "I miss you, Puerto. Why haven't you called?"

Chapter Twenty

The older gentleman introduced himself as Dennis, but Marli forgot his name immediately after he said it. The woman with him was Kay. They were with the hospice care program that the discharge nurse at Good Samaritan Hospital had arranged for Alice. Dennis was a volunteer. Kay was a hospice nurse. They were right on time the day after Alice returned home from the hospital when they knocked on the large, double, redwood doors that opened up to Marli's childhood home.

"Greetings," Dennis cheerfully said to Marli as she pulled open the front door. "We are from hospice care. Are you Marli May?"

Dennis was in his late seventies with silver-gray hair cut so short it stuck straight up like a military crew cut. Kay was in her mid-fifties and overweight by any medical definition. When she teetered down the two steps from the black, slate entryway into the sunken living room, Kay had to hold onto the wall to maintain her balance. She favored her right leg, which made her rear rock from side to side like a child's red hopper ball.

Dennis wore an old tan cardigan scattered with sweater fuzz balls that begged to be shaved off. They both wore faded blue jeans, Kay's on the tight side, while Dennis's could be removed with one swift tug.

"Please have a seat. Would you like anything to drink?" Marli obligingly asked.

"No, but thank you," the two hospice care workers replied in unison.

"We realize this is a difficult time for you right now," Kay said in her most sincere sympathetic voice. "Do you have any other family who can help you?"

"No, not really."

"Well, that's where we come in," Kay said, opening up the white plastic binder that she had been clutching to her ample chest. "The doctor has ordered a home-care nurse to visit your mother twice a week. She will take your mom's vital signs and monitor any medications she is taking. Does your mom take any meds?"

"Oh, yeah, for high blood pressure, her thyroid, arthritis," Marli said. "She's also on the blood-thinner Coumadin and a diuretic. I'm sure I'm forgetting something. But don't you know all that already?"

"Alice has also been assigned a physical therapist twice a week and a home health aide three times a week," Kay continued. "The aide will help your mom bathe, wash her hair, and any other personal tasks that Alice needs assistance with. Does your mom have a bedside commode or a raised toilet seat?"

"No," Marli said, a little unnerved.

"We will have those delivered right away. How about a walker or a wheelchair?"

"No, we never needed them. She just uses a cane."

"Well, as your mom grows weaker, she may need one or the other. So we will have those delivered, too. The physical therapist will discuss the appropriate way to use these assistive devices. The doctor has also ordered oxygen. So we will have an oxygen tank delivered this week as well."

Marli sat quietly and listened as Kay explained how the hospice program worked and what she could expect in services.

"Alice will receive a care plan created by her hospice doctor that focuses on pain and symptom management." *Makes sense.*

"The home health nurse will bring over any prescription and non-prescription medications and monitor her blood levels." *Excellent, no more waiting in line at the drive-up pharmacy or trips to the Coumadin clinic.*

"A hospice physician will visit at least once a month or more if necessary." *Say goodbye to endless doctor's appointments*, another perk that went through Marli's mind.

"An on-call registered nurse will be available twenty-four hours a day, seven days a week." *Nice to know.*

"If you need someone to talk to, you can call on our chaplain or a hospice volunteer, such as Dennis here, most of whom have had similar experiences with loved ones." *No thank you.*

"Now, does your mom have DNR?"

"A 'Do Not Resuscitate'?" Marli replied.

"Yes, exactly."

"Yes, she does."

"Oh, good. Now, Ms. May, there is one more thing you will have to decide. As you know, hospice provides palliative or comfort care, which means we treat pain and other symptoms without trying to cure the patient. The focus is on palliative care with no extraordinary or curative measures."

"OK."

"You will have to decide, when the time comes, if you will call the paramedics to intervene or not. Remember, you will be able to call the hospice nurse at any time, day or night. But to call 911 would be out of the program."

"Out of the program?"

"Yes, it would not be covered by insurance. So you have to be comfortable with no extraordinary measures. Since your mother has a DNR, we can assume that is what she would want."

Assume away. All this does not matter because Alice is not going to die any time soon.

"I understand," Marli managed to say.

"Great. May we meet your mother now?"

Marli led Kay and Dennis down a long hallway. While the halls of most other homes were plastered with a hodgepodge of family photos, Alice's hallway wall was adorned with hand-embroidered Hmong tapestries, each telling a tale of war or village life in Laos. Alice had collected the colorful story cloths from art shows and estate sales over the years, and Marli's father, Allan, had mounted the textiles on wooden rods.

"Aren't these interesting," Kay said, reaching out to touch the fabrics. "Did you make these?"

Marli stopped at the end of the hallway, just outside of Alice's bedroom, and turned to the annoying duo. "Listen. Please do not use the word 'hospice.' I have not told Mom anything about it. Just say you are part of the home care program, OK?"

Kay and Dennis left shortly after meeting Alice, assuring Marli that she could call either of them at any time.

"Nick left me, Mom."

"What? Oh, honey. That's terrible."

"Yeah. Pretty shitty."

"When did this happen?"

"When we were in Mexico."

Marli sat down next to Alice on the giant adjustable bed that nearly swallowed up her five-foot-tall mother.

Marli's father had died of complications related to his Alzheimer's disease. Basically, among other things, he did not know how or when to wipe his ass any longer. The assisted living home let him sit in his diapers too long, which gave him a urinary-tract infection, making him sick enough to move to a skilled-nursing facility, where he languished until he died. Alice, however, did not have Alzheimer's or any other form of dementia. She was as sharp as a razor-blade. Her body was giving out, but not her mind.

"Did you have a fight?" Alice asked.

"No, he met another woman."

Mother and daughter sat silent.

"What are you going to do?" Alice finally said.

"I don't know. Stay here with you for a while?"

"That's wonderful, honey. I would love that. You can sleep in your old room." Alice paused before adding, "Isn't this nice. You don't usually share personal things like this with me."

"I love you, Mom."

"I love you, too, Marli."

The hours of 5:00 a.m. to 7:00 a.m. were when Marli found her "perfect sleep." She rarely slept throughout the night, often waking up three, four, even five times before morning to stare at the backlit clock, frustrated to find only an hour had passed since the last time she checked. So, exhausted by daybreak, she would descend into such a deep slumber that she would actually experience an intense euphoria while in her state of suspended consciousness. Her perfect sleep was pure nirvana.

But this morning, scalding cries for help ripped through Marli's perfect sleep. Frantically fighting to free her mind from the intense slumber, the unnerving disruption finally brought her into focus, and she realized it was Alice screaming from another part of the house.

"Marli! Marli! Help!"

"Mom! I'm coming. Where are you?"

"I'm in the kitchen!"

Marli found Alice sitting, bare legs stretched out in front of her, on the ceramic tile floor by the gas stove. The right sleeve of her pink terrycloth robe was blackened and shredded around the edges. A faint smoke with the smell of burning fabric hovered in the air. A fine silver ash floated about and fell onto Alice's chest and lap.

"Mom, what happened? Are you all right?!"

"I burned myself! It hurts!"

"OK, OK. Let me see," Marli said, pushing the kitchen chair out of the way and kneeling down to Alice's level to get a better view of her blistering forearm. "It's not too bad. Just some swelling. Where do you keep the honey?"

"Honey?"

"Yes, honey."

"In the cupboard above the toaster. Why?"

"Take your arm out of your robe so it's not in the way."

Marli grabbed the glass jar of organic honey from the shelf, then ran to Alice's master bathroom for gauze and medical tape.

"You're going to put honey on my burn?" Alice exclaimed out of panic and pain.

"Yes, trust me. It will make it feel better immediately and help it heal," Marli said to her distraught mother as she dripped a dab of the liquid amber onto the gauze pad, pressed the sterile square against Alice's injury, and secured the bandage with the cloth adhesive tape. "Mom, what happened?"

"I was going to make myself a fried egg and I got the sleeve of my robe too close to the gas flame," Alice said. "Oh, Marli, I'm so sorry!"

"It's OK. Don't be sorry. Hold my hand and let's get you up."

Alice braced herself against her daughter with her left arm and used the stove to pull herself up with the right.

"I'm so stupid," Alice said, dropping into the black vinyl kitchen chair.

"You're not stupid. It's OK. You'll be OK. Why didn't the smoke alarm go off?" Marli asked.

"I took it down because the darn thing kept going off whenever I toasted a piece of bread."

"Oh, Mom. That's not good."

"You know, my arm feels so much better. Where did you learn that smart trick with the honey?"

Peter and Paul without Mary. Whenever Marli mentioned that she had purchased tickets to the Peter and Paul concert, people would scrunch up their faces in confusion. To clarify, Marli began adding "without Mary" so everyone would understand she was talking about the American folk-singing trio from the 1960s. Peter Yarrow and Noel Paul Stookey were performing in San Jose and Marli lucked into two seats to the sold-out performance when she was one of the first to respond to an email from the local public radio station that had just released extra tickets.

"I have a surprise for you, Mom," Marli said as she brought a cup of hot Earl Grey tea to Alice, who had gone back to bed after her traumatic encounter with fire. Marli pushed aside the half-empty box of tissues on the nightstand and set down Alice's favorite hand-thrown ceramic mug. "We are going to see Peter and Paul."

Alice looked perplexed at her daughter.

"Without Mary. Peter and Paul without Mary."

"Where is Mary?" Alice asked.

"She died."

"She died? When?"

"I'm not sure, Mom. A few years ago. Maybe longer. Of cancer. But that's not the point. I got us tickets to see Peter and Paul tomorrow night."

"Oh, I don't know, Marli. I will be too tired. I don't think I want to go out."

"Please, Mom. It will be great," Marli said. "You would love to see Peter and Paul. Remember how Dad would play their records over and over again when I was growing up? I remember one of the album covers had a photo of the three of them standing in front of a brick wall. 'If I Had a Hammer' and 'Lemon Tree' and 'Where Have All the Flowers Gone.'"

Alice began to sing "Blowin' in the Wind" in a painfully low, cracking voice, one that Marli did not recognize coming from the vibrant woman who used to serenade her in such a clear, sweet tone.

"See, you remember," Marli said, taking Alice's hand in hers. "Please go with me."

"Let's see how I feel tomorrow."

❋ ❋ ❋

The next day the home-care nurse arrived at 10:30 a.m., calling first to say she was running twenty minutes late and waking Alice from her morning nap. Cici was in her early thirties and almost seven months pregnant. She wore a flowery, polyester blouse with elastic at the bottom and a pair of blue maternity jeans with a black stretch panel that poked out from under her shirt when she reached across Alice's bed. Her straight, chestnut-brown hair was pulled back in a loose ponytail and she carried a black case with all her necessary equipment.

"How are you feeling today, Mrs. Stewart?" Cici asked, looking down at the second hand of her Casio watch while pressing two fingers on the bulging vein of Alice's thin wrist.

"Tired. I'm always tired," Alice sighed, searching for her eyeglasses among the defiant bedsheets. Alice's fickle mood quickly changed from weary to upbeat when she focused in on Cici's protruding stomach.

"Oh, you're going to have a baby! How nice. When is she due?"

"Two more months to go," Cici cheerfully responded, now listening to her patient's beating heart, gliding her stethoscope from one spot to another over Alice's light, cotton nightgown. "Take a deep breath and let it out slowly. How did you know it was a girl?"

"I just had a feeling. Girls are wonderful. Boys are nice, too. I had a grandson, but he passed away," Alice added with resilience.

Marli sat in silence, watching from across the room. A familiar wave of grief reached up from her heart and gripped at her throat.

"I am so sorry," Cici managed to say.

"Do you have other children?"

"This will be our second child. We have a two-year-old boy, too."

"Well, you're very lucky," Alice added. "Children are a blessing."

"Well, they are not for everyone. A lot of work," Cici replied, standing upright and placing her right hand at the base of her aching back.

"But worth it. My Marli is taking me to see Peter and Paul tonight."

"Peter and Paul?" Cici repeated, scrunching up her face.

"Without Mary," Marli said, happy to know Alice had finally agreed to accompany her to the concert.

"What happened to Mary?" Cici asked.

"She died," Marli and Alice said simultaneously.

"Oh. That's too bad. Well, it's nice to hear that you feel up to leaving the house," Cici said as she opened her black medical case and took out a small white monitor used for checking INR levels in patients taking blood-thinning medications. She swabbed the tip of Alice's middle finger with an antiseptic wipe, removed a lancet from its sterile packaging, and skillfully pricked her patient's senior skin almost before Alice even knew it was happening. Cici eased a tiny drop of the hanging blood onto a test strip and inserted the strip into the INR devise. A digital number emerged onto the monitor's screen.

"I will call this in and be right back," Cici said to them both.

"So we are on for tonight?" Marli asked as soon as Cici stepped out of the bedroom.

"I guess so. I'll do my best. But we may have to leave early if I don't feel good."

"Fair enough."

Cici returned to pronounce that Alice's INR level was in the safe range.

"Now remember, any new medications or diet change could affect these numbers," Cici said. "Stay away from food that is high in iron, like spinach."

But Alice already knew all there was to know about taking a blood thinner. A heart-valve transplant in 1985 left Alice on medication for the remainder of her life. How brave Alice was. A cardiac surgeon, more than thirty years ago, held her ailing heart in his hands. He sliced away her failing aortic valve and replaced it with a manmade mechanical substitute.

"You know, the most vivid memory I have of the entire ordeal was being asked by the nurse if I wanted to see my mom in the intensive-care unit after the surgery," Marli had confided to Ben one evening back in Mexico.

"Mom's lips were so dry and chapped. An oxygen tube was coming out of her mouth and I remember the white medical tape stretched across her face, pulling at her skin. Her cheeks were a pale gray. But the worst part was her face and body were so puffed up and swollen. I barely recognized her. She looked like a beached whale bloated from gas swelling up in its decomposing body. I know that sounds horrible, but that's what I remember. Why did the doctors and nurses think I would want to see my mom like that?"

The Peter and Paul concert began at 7:00 p.m. at the California Theatre on South First Street in San Jose. Marli made a tofu scramble with sautéed shitake mushrooms and green onions for dinner. They ate at 5:00 p.m. so Alice could take a nap before they left for the theater at 6:15. The tickets would be at the will call.

"Mom, you look so nice," Marli said to her mother as she emerged from her bedroom wearing a long-sleeve blouse with loose matching pants in an exotic burgundy and tawny pattern that resembled a Turkish kilim rug. Alice finished off her evening attire with a tribal necklace of turquoise, amber, and round brass beads from Africa and large dangling earrings tarnished with a jade patina.

"I never get to dress up anymore." Alice smiled.

The California Theatre was similar in opulence and history to the Crest Theatre in Sacramento where Marli and Nick had met. Considered one of the most lavish motion picture houses in the state, the California Theatre, built in 1927, also went through a series of owners and a full closure before the palace was renovated in the early 2000s. At one time, Allan and Alice had season tickets to all the shows.

"I never grow tired of seeing these gorgeous gold columns and archways," Alice said, gazing up at the ornate ceiling and elaborate glass chandeliers.

Their royal red velvet seats were five rows from the stage and thankfully on the aisle, since there was a high probability that Alice would have to use the restroom during the performance. Marli looked around and took note that she could very well have been the youngest person in the audience.

"The program says Mary Travers died in 2009 from the 'consequences of leukemia treatment,'" Alice read to her daughter. "What a tragic loss to have such a strong woman leave this earth so prematurely. And to take all those beautiful harmonies with her," Alice whispered. "Remember when they sang 'Blowin' in the Wind' at the March on Washington? Oh, you were too young to remember. When was that? 1963? '64? Oh, your father loved Peter, Paul and Mary, but especially Mary." Peter and Paul without Mary were like fine bone china hurled to the unforgiving ground, shattered into a million heartbroken pieces that eventually could be glued back together but would never be the same.

Peter and Paul (or Noel, which was Paul's actual first name and what Peter called him) took the stage a few minutes past 7:00 p.m.

"They look so old," Alice said in a loud whisper, unconcerned that everyone around them could hear. Marli bit her lip.

The concert was billed as "Celebrating 50 Years of Peter, Paul and Mary," and the folk duo did not disappoint in their song selection or political and social commentaries on everything from human rights, the environment, and education to fracking and universal health care. Peter Yarrow appeared especially frail at seventy-seven and rambled on several times, leaving the audience to speculate on whether he was having senior moments on stage. The singer/songwriter would then follow up with something witty in a purposeful effort to bring his incongruent sentences together in a meaningful way, and the crowd would erupt in applause.

Peter and Paul encouraged audience members to sing along with them, and Alice was more than happy to oblige, raising her voice especially high to "Where Have All the Flowers Gone" and "Lemon Tree." The encore was "Blowin' in the Wind."

Marli pulled up to the passenger loading zone where she'd left Alice before hurrying to get the car. The time was approaching 10:00 p.m. and the theater's backlit marquee of California poppies encircled with white chase lights cast a golden glow to the ground. Alice wrapped her hand-knitted shawl from Ecuador tightly around her frail shoulders.

"Did you enjoy the concert, Mom?" Marli asked as she helped Alice snap the seat belt in place across her lap.

"Yes, honey. Couldn't you tell? Thank you for taking me."

"I'm just glad you had a good time. So, what was your favorite song?"

"My favorite song? I would have to say 'Have You Been to Jail for Justice?'"

"What? I didn't even recognize that song. Really, that was your favorite?"

"Well, it had special meaning to me and your father," Alice said. "You know we almost went to jail for justice."

"What? When? How?"

"When we were living in Washington, DC. It was the early fifties. Segregation was still legal. There was a theater house, I can't remember the name. But it would not allow Negros."

"Blacks." Marli corrected her mother.

"OK, Blacks," Alice repeated. "Anyway, your dad got all his college buddies together. You know he went to law school at Georgetown University. And he was very active in civil rights on campus," she continued. "He got all of us together, and the white boys invited the Black girls to the theater, and the white girls invited the Black boys, and we all showed up at the theater doors at the same time and demanded to be let in."

"Oh my god. That is so cool." Marli praised her mom as she turned onto the freeway on-ramp heading home. "What happened?"

"Well, the theater manager called the police. By the time they arrived, we were walking in a circle on the sidewalk in front of the theater with our picket signs chanting, 'We will overcome.' Things got a little heated and many of the protesters were arrested."

"Wow, Mom. I never knew that. You and Dad picketed for civil rights in Washington, DC. That is so cool. How does that song go again?"

"Have you been to jail for justice?" Alice began to softly sing, her voice cracking again with age. "I want to shake your hand. Cause sitting in and laying down are ways to take a stand. Have you sung a song for freedom or marched that picket line? Have you been to jail for justice? Then you're a friend of mine."

"That was pretty awesome, Mom."

"What's the matter, Marli? I didn't mean to make you cry."

"I'm OK, Mom. I'm just feeling a little overwhelmed. I love you, Mom."

"I love you, Marli."

Chapter Twenty-One

Ben was getting a late start on Monday morning. The weekend was a blur of mescal and mania. If not for Cyrano, Ben might have done something in his alcohol-induced state, such as sleep with his ex-girlfriend Jenna Gonzales just to forget Marli May, which he would have regretted for a very long time, maybe his entire life. But Cyrano helped his good friend put the past month's diversion into perspective.

"Marli lives in California," Cyrano reminded Ben, adding that she was not even divorced yet. In fact, she was still committed to her marriage when she first met Ben. Cyrano convinced his friend that Marli's seemingly genuine interest in him, and even the stray street dog, was just a distraction from what she would have to face when she returned to California. Marli merely needed a fantasy until her reality kicked in. And that fantasy was Ben. Why she left Puerto behind was something Ben would have to sort out for himself and eventually come to terms with.

Three days of mail sat unopened on the reception desk of Ben's veterinary office. Bills, medical supply advertisements, animal-welfare solicitations, and the latest veterinary journal were the norm. Ben's first appointment of the day, a Siamese flame point that had developed an unwelcome habit of urinating on her owner's freshly washed laundry, was not until 11:00 a.m. Ben pulled his chair up to the rusty metal desk, began at the top of the pile, and stopped when he came to an envelope with a return address of the Agencia Municipal de Puerto Escondido. Inside was a response to what he had worked so long and hard for. The Municipal Agency of Puerto Escondido had granted Ben's request for real estate to establish a privately run animal shelter and low-cost veterinary hospital. The letter said to contact the city office to finalize the terms of the agreement and operational contract.

Marli could see her mother was growing increasingly weaker in the six days since Marli returned to San Jose from Mexico. Following the Peter and Paul concert, Alice had no interest in journeying outside her home. After establishing hospice, the endless series of doctors' appointments had come to a halt. The home-care nurse brought over a walker and a wheelchair, but Alice would not get out of bed except to use the bedside commode that hospice provided. The home health aide had to plead with her patient to take a shower, which consisted of Alice sitting on a white plastic stool in the shower stall while the aide washed Alice's thinning hair and body, and then rinsed away the lavender-scented suds with the handheld chrome faucet that Nick had installed. Marli was grateful she did not have to face the task herself and endure the awkwardness of having to wash under her mother's breasts and between her legs and buttocks just like Alice had done for Marli when she was a baby. At least Alice was still capable of wiping away the remaining excrement from her bottom after a bowel movement, although Marli had to dump the contents of the commode into the toilet and rinse out Alice's soiled underwear and nightgowns before putting them in the washing machine. When did her mother become the child and Marli the adult? Why didn't anyone warn her of the sting of growing old?

After his last four-legged appointment of the day, Ben read the succinct correspondence from the Agencia Municipal de Puerto Escondido two more times just to make sure the words were real and not an illusion. After more than a year of meetings and negotiations with city officials, the dedication of land to build an animal shelter and spay clinic was finally going to become a reality. Ben realized it was just the first step of many. The land was obviously critical, but now he faced the daunting battle of raising the funds necessary to construct and equip the building. It was too late in the day to call the number provided in the letter to set up an appointment to "finalize the terms of the agreement." The agency's office would surely be closed by now, so he would phone first thing tomorrow morning. When he got home, Ben would send out a group email to the many volunteers who had been instrumental in helping collect data and formulating a proposal to submit to the city in an effort to secure the land for the shelter and clinic. Everyone had dedicated many hours, days, years—some their lives—to helping the street dogs of Mexico, and it was finally time to deliver some good news.

Ben made sure his one ward, a five-pound miniature Yorkie recovering from dental surgery that resulted in thirteen teeth extractions, was fully awake from the anesthesia, breathing normally, and comfortable in his cage for the evening. He locked and dead-bolted the front door, turned off the lights one room at a time, and headed out the back to his truck, looking forward to getting home, where Escondido would be waiting. Someone to greet him with unconditional enthusiasm. As Ben reached to open the driver's side door, he was startled by an unfamiliar voice from behind and the distasteful smell of cigarette smoke.

"Ben Rosado?"

"Sí," Ben said, turning to face an unfamiliar man wearing a green plaid shirt and baggy blue jeans. An unfiltered Camel was situated between his lips.

"My English is better than my Spanish," the man said as the cigarette bobbed up and down, dropping ashes with every syllable.

"OK, how can I help you?" Ben asked warily, aware that dusk was lowering the lights of the day and the crickets were beginning their nightly calls from the dark corners of the parking lot.

"I know where the dog is. The one you have been looking for. The one with the bad leg."

"Puerto?"

"Is that what you call him? Puerto? He's the one who has been escorting those two lovely American women around town."

"How do you know that?"

"I just do."

"Where is he?"

"It would be easier if I showed you," the man responded, looking down at the dust-covered gravel. "You can follow me in your truck. But I will need gas money, if you know what I mean."

"Who are you?" Ben began to feel like he was caught up in a bad, B-grade mobster movie. He didn't know whether to laugh it off or be frightened for his life.

"I'm just a friend who wants to help you get your dog back. I'm just short on cash right now and I was hoping you could help me out. Think of it as a reward for finding your dog."

"How do I know it's my dog?" Ben impatiently asked, deciding to go along with whatever game the strange, unwelcome man was playing.

"Is this him?" he responded, holding up a shadowy picture on his cell phone to Ben's face.

The light from the corner streetlamp was dim and the quality of the low-resolution photo was grainy, but Ben could see through the smudged screen that it was a dog, his head hanging below his shoulder blades with a chain around his neck secured to a metal post embedded in the ground. Ben fumbled for the wire reading glasses in his front pocket, dropping the specs into the dirt in his haste to pull them free. Quickly picking up the eyeglasses, he wiped the lenses clean with the bottom of his button-up shirt and slipped them over his ears. The image came into focus. The photo was most definitely of Puerto, his eyes glaring into the camera with such terror that Ben almost dropped to his knees in disbelief.

"What the hell? Where is this? Where is Puerto?" Ben's anger and anxiety grew.

"Like I said, it would be easier if I showed you," the stranger repeated calmly, taking a last drag off his cigarette and tossing it to the side without bothering to stomp out the burning ember.

"OK, OK, " Ben said, trying to stay calm. "How much?"

"Two thousand pesos should do it." The man grinned, revealing a gap between his two stained front teeth.

"Two thousand!"

"You want your dog back, don't you?"

"How do you know he's my dog? How do you know any of this?"

"Let's just say I see a lot. I watch. Waiting for opportunities. But this time, I got myself involved in something that don't sit right with me. So I want to make it right, OK?"

"I don't carry that kind of money. I have about a thousand on me. Half now, half when I have Puerto," Ben said.

Still shaken from the brutal photo, Ben anxiously pulled his worn fabric wallet out of the back pocket of his pants and extracted two five-hundred-peso notes. "It really is all I have on me," he said, closing up the wallet and pushing it back into his trousers before the would-be thief could catch a glimpse of the other bills tucked inside.

Ben passed the peso notes to the stranger. "There, you have your money. Where are we going?"

"It's about fifteen minutes away," the intruder said, turning toward a weathered Pontiac pointing west on the street in front of Ben's veterinary office. "Try to keep up."

"Wait," Ben called out after the undesirable visitor. "Did you take my dog?"

"No way, man. I wouldn't do something like that. I like animals. That's why I'm trying to help you. The guys who took your dog are going to use him as bait for dog fighting. You know, because he is weaker with that bum leg. That's just fucked up."

Chapter Twenty-Two

Ben kept his sweating palms tight on the Chevy truck's steering wheel and his eyes cemented to the dented bumper of the Pontiac in front of him, driven by a madman he did not know. Ben's outrage and nerves were battling it out in the pit of his stomach. "Puerto used as bait for dog fighting!" he hissed to himself. "Yes, that's fucked up!"

Ben needed time to think. What if he was driving directly into danger? The degenerates running the dog-fighting ring would not want an outsider to know about their cruel criminal activity. What if Puerto was not where this maniac was taking Ben and the thugs tried to blackmail him for more money? What if they won't give up Puerto? What if they have guns? Ben could not do this alone.

The crazy man in the car ahead made no effort to drive at a speed that would allow Ben to easily trail behind him. The road grew darker and more obscure the farther the two men got from town and Ben had to strain to keep the taillights of the Pontiac in view, making it even more difficult to extract the cell phone from his back pocket and dial Cyrano.

"Cyrano, este es Ben," he shouted into the speaker phone, his voice bordering hysteria.

"Hola, amigo," Cyrano sluggishly replied, attempting to muffle an exaggerated yawn.

Ben tried to suppress the panic in his voice as he quickly recapped the past thirty minutes of the bizarre encounter and the potentially disastrous scenario that lay ahead. He and Cyrano decided that Ben would stay on his speaker phone for as long as possible, providing Cyrano with step-by-step driving directions until Ben reached the dreaded destination.

Then, knowing Ben's location, Cyrano would call the police and explain that his friend was a veterinarian on his way to a dog-fighting ring and that he may be in danger and would need assistance from law enforcement. Dog fighting was rampant in Mexico. Many authorities looked the other way. However, where there was dog fighting, there was also the high probability of drug trafficking and organized crime. Ben hoped that the opportunity to expose a Mexican cartel would be enough to bring out the state, if not the federal, authorities on an uneventful Monday night.

The paved asphalt under Ben's tires gave way to a narrow dirt road after several curves and turns at least ten miles out of town. Ben was able to make out all the street signs, even with a diminishing number of lampposts shedding a trivial amount of helpful light, and recited them to Cyrano over the phone, up until the last turn down a gritty driveway that offered no obvious street address.

"I think it was the third driveway on the right," Ben said to Cyrano in Spanish. "There were three black garbage cans right where I turned in. OK, he's parking in front of what looks like a barn. I have to go. Call the police!"

Ben followed the Pontiac off the path and parked on a patch of dried grass at the left-hand side of what appeared to be a working barn, not an abandoned structure used for criminal activity as he expected. The walls of the barn, topped with a rusty pitched roof, bowed in some places from years of weathering the elements and settling into the foundation. Light from inside escaped through the slivered gaps in the vertical wooden planks. But the building looked sturdy, strong, and active. The scent of fresh hay mingled with manure. A metal awning provided cover for a trio of horses tied up in side-by-side stalls just to the right. Several hens and roosters scurried about, pecking at the earth. Ben immediately wondered if cock fighting was another trade these bastards delved in. The night air carried the muffled voices of several men speaking in Spanish coming from within the barn and, with further to travel, the sporadic sound of barking dogs.

Ben stepped out of his truck. But before he could slam the door shut, the stranger, carrying industrial-size bolt cutters, held up his index finger to his flaky thin lips and motioned Ben to stay quiet.

"The dog is around back," the nameless man whispered, his breath and clothes heavy with tobacco. "But listen, let's just keep this between you and me. No need to bring anyone else into it."

"You mean whoever is in the barn?" Ben whispered back.

"Exactly. They might not take too kindly to us being here."

If Ben was not panicked before, he was now. He could feel his heart punching at his chest from inside as if it was trying to escape through his ribs. They were going to die, he was sure of it. Why hadn't he taken Cyrano's advice years ago and stowed a gun in the glove compartment of his truck for situations just like this? *Because things like this only happen in the movies*, he thought to himself.

"What are the bolt cutters for?" Ben cautiously asked as he followed the man around the side of the timbered structure, gingerly placing each step as if he were walking on shards of glass.

"You'll see."

A cool breeze settled in and helped to evaporate the nervous sweat drenching Ben's cotton shirt. As they approached the back of the building, the smattering of random dog barks became stronger. Then, as they rounded the corner, Ben saw what he feared most—row after row of imprisoned canines. Each wore a thick iron shackle bolted around its neck and attached to a heavy link chain, no more than three feet long, that was hooked to a metal stake pounded into hardpan. One filthy plastic bowl, void of food or water, belonged to each dog. The smell of feces, urine, and rotting flesh coated the air. The ingredients of the day's lunch lurched from Ben's stomach and up into his throat as he tried, but failed, to stifle his unforeseen vomiting.

"Jesus!" Ben shouted in a whisper, as he wiped his mouth on his shirt sleeve.

"Yeah, pretty horrible," the stranger mumbled in sympathy.

"I've only heard about places like this. I've never seen it." Ben's head was spinning.

The helpless mongrels, at least a couple dozen, mostly medium to large of varying breeds—many of pit bull descent—had barely enough room to stand and lay down at the end of their heavy chains. Ribs protruded through mange-infected skin on those who were clearly starving, while others were at fighting weight sporting nothing more than solid muscle. Untreated open wounds, gashes, and scars were painfully visible.

"Some are used to fight. Some are used as bait to teach other dogs to fight," the man said under his breath. "Your dog is going to be used for bait. He's over there."

Ben's eyes followed the stranger's pointed finger until Puerto, chained like the others, came into focus. "Oh god," Ben whispered.

"Listen. We gotta do this right," the man insisted. "As soon as the dogs see us, they will start barking. A little barking won't be suspect to the assholes inside the barn, but a lot of barking will bring at least one of them out here to see what's up. So, we have to work fast. I'll cut the chain and then we run like hell to the cars. The dog will follow you, right?"

"Yes, yes. I think so," Ben said hesitantly.

"You better hope so."

"Why can't we do this when no one is around?"

"There is always someone around. This is the best time to do it—under the cover of darkness. Hopefully, they will already have imbibed in too much mescal and won't be good shots."

"Shots? Shit! I don't want to get shot! Why can't we call the police?"

"You want to see your dog again? The police will confiscate him as evidence. He will be locked up worse than this, believe me. Are you ready or not? I'm risking my life, too, for a lousy two thousand pesos."

"OK, but I want to see what we're dealing with. Give me a minute," Ben said as he quietly walked toward the barn. Peering through the rotting wooden slats, he could see five men gathered around a rickety table. One of the men folded his hand of cards from an ongoing card game, threw back a shot of tequila, and pushed himself out of the cheap folding chair. His rotund belly, which had pushed past several buttons on his army-green shirt, extended out over his leather belt, and he had to yank on his pants to keep them from falling around his boots. Half circles of sweat seeped from his armpits, and a wide strip soaked his back.

"OK, let's do it!" Ben said, returning to his accomplice and growling like a psyched-up soldier ready to ramrod the door of an enemy stronghold.

The static night exploded with the rabid snarls of nearly twenty raging dogs. They heaved against their iron shackles until the metal embedded in their throats. Saliva dripped from their incisors and whipped through the stagnant air. Even the mongrels that were weak from starvation and beatings managed to throw forth a defensive growl, while a handful of the timid "bait" dogs stayed low, shaking from fear, two of which were Puerto and a whimpering pit bull mix, his flea-bitten tail planted between his legs. The stranger led the way, maneuvering past several of the crazed canines, staying only inches away from having one of his skinny arms ripped from his body.

Puerto recognized Ben immediately, coming to a stand on his three good legs with his tail, offering a weak wag in his tentative excitement.

"Puerto, we're going to get you out of here. You'll be all right, boy."

The stranger wielded his military-grade, SWAT-certified, heavy-gauge bolt cutters into place over one link of the metal chain that imprisoned Puerto and clamped down on the thirty-six-inch, steel-enforced handles with all the force he could command.

"Shit! I can't do it! I ain't strong enough!"

"Haven't you done this before?!" Ben screamed over the incessant barking. Whispering was no longer necessary.

"No! These are my brother's bolt cutters. He's ex-Marines!"

"Give them to me!" Ben shouted as he wrenched the bolt cutters from the stranger's hands. "I'll do it!"

With one adrenaline-induced rush, Ben squeezed the handles together and snapped the steel link in half as easily as the dead branch of a dying tree.

Ben looked up to see the grizzled man from inside the barn standing at the back door with firearm in hand, scanning the howling canines. He came eye to eye with Ben, who was now upright, bolt cutters still in hand.

"Run!" Ben's partner shouted, freeing Puerto, as the echo from a shotgun sliced through the thick humidity. But the blast did not come from the enemy. Ben looked up and saw Cyrano, knees locked, feet firm, shoulders squared to a 20-gauge shotgun pointed directly at the intoxicated man on his way to a fast sobriety still standing at the back barn door.

Ben, Puerto, and the stranger lined up behind Cyrano, who still had his shotgun focused on the startled criminal. The four quickly rounded the side of the building and sprinted to their respective vehicles before the Mexican and his drunken compadres inside the barn could negotiate the situation. Ben motioned Puerto to jump in through the driver's side door of his truck and then slid in next to him. Cyrano tossed the shotgun on the passenger seat of his car and revved his engine. The stranger put his Pontiac in reverse, backed up without regard for anything that might be in his path, and left deep trenches under the car's wheels as he launched down the dirt driveway with Ben, Puerto, and Cyrano close behind.

"Gracias, amigo!" Ben shouted into his cell phone to Cyrano, who was now trailing in his Honda Civic as the three vehicles sped down the highway to safety.

As soon as the two friends were back in Puerto Escondido, still high on adrenaline, they pulled into the parking lot of the first open cafe in sight and ordered a bottle of the best anejo tequila on the menu, two shot glasses, and a medium-rare ribeye steak for Puerto, who remained curled up and exhausted on the front seat of Ben's truck.

"Where the hell were the police?" Ben asked Cyrano as he filled each shot glass to the rim.

"The police did not seem to think it was urgent," Cyrano replied. "So, I decided to take matters into my own hands."

"Excelente!" Ben responded as they bumped glasses in triumph.

The next morning, on the drive to the police station to report the dog-fighting ring and multiple counts of animal cruelty, Ben considered the nameless stranger with bad teeth and the stench of cigarette smoke on his breath. He hoped he would see him again so he could thank him for his efforts to rescue Puerto from an unfathomable situation. Ben still owed the man one thousand pesos and was more than happy to pay the remainder of the ransom. Despite the stranger's less-than-noble ultimate gain, he had risked his own life to save Puerto. If the stranger was interested, Ben might offer him a job at his future animal shelter.

Chapter Twenty-Three

Marli watched her mother die, in her own home, at 11:20 p.m. on Wednesday, just three days after the Peter and Paul concert. Alice Stewart had remained in bed all day, declined dinner that night, and later became unresponsive when Marli brought her mother her multiple medications. Alice's breathing became labored. She lay still, unable to move or be moved. Marli sat in the wingback chair in the corner of the bedroom and watched as saliva began to bubble out of Alice's mouth and down her neck, soaking her mother's nightgown and pillow.

"The foaming is a sign that Alice is dying," the hospice nurse told Marli over the phone. "The end will be soon."

Marli wiped the thick froth away from her mother's lips and chest with a warm wet washcloth, trying to prop Alice up as much as she could so her mother would not choke on her own fluids. Alice lay unconscious. And then she was dead.

"Mom, please don't leave me. What am I going to do without you?"

The on-call hospice nurse arrived at Alice Stewart's home approximately twenty minutes after Marli telephoned her again. The nurse was in her late forties and appeared weary from being called out at midnight. Marli was not looking for kindness or compassion from this outsider, and the nurse was not offering any. She was sobering and exacting as she confirmed that Alice Stewart had indeed passed away.

"I will need all of your mother's prescription medications," the nurse requested straightforwardly. One by one she unscrewed the childproof caps and dumped the contents of each bottle into a clear, plastic Ziplock bag. The nurse then phoned the funeral home to come retrieve the body.

Two gentlemen, one in his late fifties and the other in his mid-twenties, arrived at Alice's home in about forty-five minutes. The hospice nurse had left. The men both wore skinny neckties and ill-fitting wrinkled black suits that bagged up too much around their ankles. They had their hands clasped in front of their bodies when Marli answered the knock on the front door.

"I am so sorry for your loss," the older man said as they followed Marli down the hallway to Alice's bedroom. "I think it's best if you wait in the living room," he added.

The two men methodically went about transferring Alice Stewart's body from the bed to a stretcher and then out to their hearse parked in the driveway. Marli wondered how often the two undertakers were awakened in the middle of the night, put on black suits, and took away dead bodies. The older man offered Marli his business card and asked her to call in the morning to make final arrangements. Then they left and Marli was alone.

Marli lay on the mattress where Alice Stewart had died only two hours earlier. She had been told that when people die, they often lose control of their bowels, but that had not happened to her mother.

The pillowcase and sheets were still wet from Alice's saliva, but Marli did not care. She wanted to be as close as possible to her mother for one last time. She held the pillow to her face and took a deep breath. She could smell Alice's hair, her skin, her sweat. Clutching the pillow close to her chest, Marli drew her knees up and curled onto one side. The room was lit only by an unassuming wall sconce and the back porch light outside the sliding glass door to her mother's garden. The house was silent. The air was still. Alice's small taupe handbag sat on top of the dresser next to an inlaid Japanese jewelry box she had found at a flea market. Mom would want to know where her purse was. She left without it. She never leaves without her purse.

When Marli opened her eyes again, the porch light was quiet and the morning sun was trickling through the sliding glass door, lighting up a flawless spiderweb that had formed overnight between two branches of a pink camellia bush.

"Mom?" Marli whispered, but no one was there.

Chapter Twenty-Four

"Hola, Rosa."

"Hola, Dr. Rosado. Cómo estás?" the hotel concierge inquired from behind the reception desk. "What brings you to Hotel Santa Fe?"

"I'm meeting a friend for lunch. You know how much I love this restaurant."

"Ah, sí . Está bien."

"Well, I just wanted to say hi."

"Dr. Rosado . . ."

"Por favor, call me Ben."

"Ben," Rosa repeated. "Have you found the dog? Puerto?"

"Sí, he is staying with me now."

"That's wonderful news. Have you told Marli?"

"Marli? No. I thought she left."

"Sí, she left to go back home. But I'm sure she would want to know. She asked me to call you if Puerto ever came back to the hotel."

"Marli asked you to call me?" Ben responded with nonchalant interest. "When?"

"Right before she left. Didn't she tell you?"

"No, she left without telling me anything. I haven't heard from her."

"Her mother became ill. She had to leave right away. When she could not find Puerto, she asked me to call you if he came back. I'm surprised she did not tell you."

Ben did not know what to say. Marli's mother was sick. That was why she left Mexico so suddenly. But that did not change the fact that Marli did not contact him or leave a note. She just vanished without a word or a goodbye.

Two days and two nights had crawled by since Marli's mom died. As difficult as it was to watch her mother leave the weary world, Marli was thankful that Alice had passed away in her own home, not in a sterile hospital or skilled-care facility where Marli's father, Allan, had succumbed to death.

It had been a Monday night when her father had passed. Marli had spent most of the afternoon and early evening at the nursing home, sitting with her dad, who was lost in his own world, seemingly unaware of Marli's presence. Could he feel her cool soft hand against his? Could he hear his daughter's familiar voice or understand her words? How could she know? The dementia had shattered his mind and the infection ate away at his body, leaving him in a comatose state, thin and fetal.

Marli left the nursing facility around 6:00 p.m. to grab a bite to eat with Alice, who had already worried most of the day away at her husband's side and was back home resting. Marli planned to return to the nursing facility after dinner to sit with her absent father a while longer before heading home to Nick. Allan stopped breathing only minutes after Marli left his room, almost as though he had willed the timing of his demise, not wanting his only child to witness his hollow passing.

Rosa searched the guest contact folder on her computer until she found Marli May's email address. She wanted to inform her American friend that the homeless mutt had returned.

"Hola, Marli," Rosa's message began. "I wanted you to know that Dr. Rosado found the stray dog—the one you called Puerto. Dr. Rosado did not know your mother was ill. He said you left without saying goodbye and that he has not heard from you. Anyway, I thought you should know. I hope all is well. Take care, Rosa."

Marli stared at her smudged computer screen, the sun's reflection from the window behind her obscuring some of the words. She read Rosa's email message again, and then a third time, to make sure she understood it correctly.

I just got an email from Rosa, Marli texted Tammy. *Ben told her I left without saying goodbye. But I left him several voicemails and text messages. Why didn't he get them? That's why I have not heard from him. He thinks I just left him and Puerto behind.*

Call him! Tammy immediately texted back.

"Your mother had several bank accounts, annuities, and a generous life insurance policy," the trust attorney told Marli as she sat across from him engulfed in a large, brown, leather chair. "As the sole beneficiary, you stand to inherit close to one million dollars, plus Alice Stewart's home and all its contents."

"You look tired," Tammy commented, sitting next to Marli on her stately, overstuffed sofa. Now on the fifth day after Alice's death, Tammy had stepped into the role Nick should have been playing, calling friends and distant relatives with the inevitable news, stocking the vacant pantry, cooking the meals never to be eaten, holding Marli tight as she wept.

"I would give everything I own to have my mom back again." Marli had paraphrased a Bread song as she clutched one of the fussy, fringed pillows piled on the couch.

"You know, David Gates wrote the song about his father after he died," Tammy shared with her distraught friend. "It's OK to grieve, Marli."

"I just don't know what I'm supposed to do now."

"With the money Alice left you, you could do just about anything. But for now, let's go work out. There's a class starting in thirty minutes. You will feel better," Tammy said, wrapping her arm around Marli's gaunt shoulders. "We can leave if it's too much, too soon."

Marli reluctantly changed from her raggedy, gray sweatpants and torn Beatles T-shirt into workout attire—stretchy black shorts, a purple sports bra, and the only clean tank top she could find.

At class, Marli reached down to pull hand weights from a blue plastic container, struggling to pry each intertwined weight from under the next one, leaving her already drained mind and body even more exhausted before class had started.

The infantile warm-up routine was ridiculous to Marli as she weighed the heaviness of her grief against the frivolity of the moment.

Her mind strayed through the white aluminum mini blinds and out onto the plush grass of the sprawling neighborhood park adjacent to the community center. Even though the expansive lawn was not officially designated as a dog park, families and friends gathered early on the weekends with their best canine buddies. As the pet parents, hot coffee mugs in hand, exchanged information on the latest trip to the vet, a new grain-free kibble they just discovered or which flea-prevention product they preferred, their furry wards would play the field like a soccer team without a ball. A golden retriever at full speed, followed by a black lab mix and several mini mutts trying to keep up, faked a step in one direction then a quick reverse, leaving a trail of barking confusion. Next came the "step-over" executed by two wire-hair terriers hurling over a red powder-puff Pomeranian in a counter-clockwise spinning motion. Not to be outdone, the border collie/Australian shepherd performed a skilled "fake cross," cutting in and out of a Dalmatian who looked to be right out of an animated movie, all white with splotches of black paint across his muscular body, two paws on the ground and his rear in the air.

But today was Monday. Most of the good residents of the safe, quiet neighborhood were at their nine-to-five jobs or schlepping kids to school. The unofficial dog meet-up was reserved for weekends when social opportunities were high. The pristine park was empty now except for a few young mothers and their babies gathered on the cement benches near the multi-colored slides and swing sets.

Just as the class began the fourth high-impact drill, something caught Marli's eye out the side window. A man and a dog, maybe fifty yards away in the middle of the park's freshly mowed lawn. At that distance, it was difficult to determine the man's age, maybe mid- to late-forties. He was dressed in baggy blue jeans and a burnt-orange T-shirt and had a canvas knapsack strapped across his back. The dog looked like a medium-size Staffordshire bull terrier, aka pit bull. His honeycomb brown fur stretched tight across a solid mass of muscle, ribs protruding. A strip of white extended from his chin to his chest like an extra wide necktie. His bow-legged stance was laughable, his broad shoulders miles apart. When he panted, his wide jawline looked like an irrepressible smile.

Marli looked back at the instructor just in time to execute her next command to move right, barely avoiding a collision with the athletic woman beside her looking like she was directly out of an exercise marketing video.

Marli looked across the field again, this time unable to turn away. The bull terrier's leash was attached to a silver choke chain, like a medieval torture device used to strangle a misbehaving dog into submission. The kind of collar that no one used anymore, yet pet stores still sold. Then the man yanked hard on the leash, once, twice, three times, constricting the metal links around the dog's neck tighter and tighter with each jerk. The ensnared pit bull was not cooperating. The man choked the dog again, once, twice, three times. Marli could feel her face begin to burn; her already elevated pulse started to pump harder. What should she do? What could she do? Walk out to the middle of the grass and confront the man?

"What the fuck?!" Marli heard the words jet out of her mouth like an ear-piercing siren headed toward a car crash. "Did you see that?!" she shouted, whipping around to Tammy, who was in mid leg-kick behind her.

"Yup! Let's go!"

Marli and Tammy bolted toward the side emergency exit, leaning on the steel push bars in unison and shoving open the heavy double doors leading out to the park.

"Hey!!" Marli screamed, the violence in her voice assaulting the man before he could get off another punch at the now cowering canine. "What the hell are you doing?"

The man looked up, startled to find two crazed women, energized by exercise-induced endorphins, bolting straight at him.

"Mind your own business!" the man shot back.

"This is our business!" Tammy screeched.

The man turned toward Marli and Tammy, readying for a fight with the oncoming duo, when the two women warriors turned into three, and then four, until the entire class of demonized divas was descending on him.

"Jesus! You are all crazy!" the man panicked. "Come on, boy! Let's get out of here!" he cried, straining against the leash as the strapping canine now lay limp, deadweight at the end of the rope, the choke collar cutting into his fur, the steel rings riding up under his wide jawbone. The pit bull was going nowhere. "Screw you, dog! You're on your own!" The man turned to run, tether falling to the ground, the chain releasing its galvanized grip from around the terrified dog's neck.

"Run, you asshole! And don't come back!" Marli shouted after the oppressor just as she and Tammy reached the prone pup, now rolling on his burly back in complete submission, pink belly exposed to the sunlight.

Marli closed her eyes and wiped the perspiration from her upper lip with the back of her trembling hand.

"I've got to go get Puerto," she whispered in simultaneous exhaustion and exhilaration.

"I know," Tammy responded, as she also caught her breath. "Puerto and Ben both need you," she added, looking down at their latest rescue effort, his bony tail whipping a hole in the soft grass, rosy tongue flapping like a loose shock strap on a sailboat.

"Maybe I can catch a plane tonight. No, no, too soon," Marli said. "Maybe tomorrow."

The other students had ventured back inside the community center to restart their aerobics. Marli and Tammy stood alone in the middle of the sprawling lush lawn, the sun directly overhead darting from one cloud to the next.

"Marli. I really do have to tell you something before you leave again."

Tammy's voice became serious, more serious than Marli could remember coming from her carefree friend.

"What is it? You sound so somber."

"I don't even know how to say this. But I just have to say it now or I never will."

"What? Just say it."

"I am the one who sent the text message about Franklin's death."

Marli took two steps back.

"No, don't back away. I'm trying to be honest. It was the coward's way out, but I was too scared to tell you in person."

"What are you talking about? Why would you do that?"

"Because I was so tired of keeping this secret. Of deceiving you. You're my best friend. You need . . . you deserve . . . to know."

"Know what? Tell me!"

"Nick killed Franklin."

Chapter Twenty-Five

"Tammy," Marli said, lowering her voice and looking directly into the eyes of her best friend. "What are you talking about? What do you mean Nick killed Franklin?"

"It's true. Franklin didn't fall off a ladder. Nick pushed him. Accidently pushed him. Franklin fell and hit his head."

"No. I don't believe you."

"It's true. Why would I make this up?"

"I don't know why! Why would Nick push Franklin? Why are you telling me this now?"

"I told you," Tammy said, tears swelling up in her eyes. "I couldn't keep it in any longer. I was going to tell you in Mexico, but everything was so wonderful. Like it used to be. When we were single and free. Like the old days." Tammy reached out to take Marli's hand.

"No, don't touch me! How could you keep this from me? How do you know this?"

"Nick told me. He called me when it happened. He panicked. He didn't know what to do. He was scared. I told him to call the police. I don't know what he did after we hung up, only that he finally called the police. That's all I know."

"Why didn't you tell me before? Why didn't you tell the police?"

"I don't know! I panicked, too! Nick didn't mean to hurt Franklin. It was an accident. I didn't want Nick to go to jail."

"Why not? You hate Nick!"

"I don't hate Nick," Tammy said in her calmest voice. "I love him."

Marli turned and started walking toward the parking lot, her head spinning. She could barely navigate the uneven turf, trying desperately to focus on each of her steps for fear of falling even further.

"Where are you going?" Tammy cried out, fully aware that Marli would not respond. Back in the community center, Tammy grabbed her purse and ran to the front of the building. Fumbling for her cell phone, she swiped open the screen and rapidly texted Nick: *Marli knows*.

"Is it true?" Marli screamed, pushing through Nick's office door at Reviva Pharmaceuticals, still wearing her workout clothes, her ponytail now a loose mess around the nape of her neck.

"Marli, what are you doing here?" Nick responded, somewhat startled as he rose from his office chair. "What's the matter?"

"Did you kill Franklin?" Marli asked.

"What? Shhhhh! What are you talking about?" Nick quickly sidestepped his soon-to-be ex-wife and shut the office door before his coworkers could hear the commotion.

"Did you kill Franklin? Answer me!" Marli shouted,

lurching at Nick and clutching the front of his tailored shirt with both fists.

"Get a hold of yourself," Nick said calmly, grabbing Marli's wrists and pushing her away.

"I can't believe you kept this from me. How could you do it? All my grief. All my pain. How could you?"

"All your pain?!" Nick snapped back. "How do you think I feel? I killed my son!"

Marli froze. How could this be happening?

"It was an accident, Marli. You have to believe me," Nick continued, lowering his voice to a reasonable level. "I went to see him at his apartment. I wanted to explain what happened between Tammy and me. That it was all a mistake."

Marli's eyes widened. She stepped back again, catching herself against Nick's office wall.

"You didn't know? I thought you knew. I thought Tammy told you."

"Told me what?"

Nick hesitated. "That Tammy and I were—are sometimes lovers. That Franklin walked in on us at our holiday party, the day before he died."

Marli felt the room begin to spin and sway. The walls seemed to cave in around her. It was all she could do to stay conscious.

"But Franklin was so angry. I couldn't reason with him. He wouldn't stop yelling at me. He called me disgusting. He said he wanted me to die! He said he was going to tell you. I grabbed him. I wanted him to stop screaming at me. He twisted out of my arms and lost his balance. And he fell. I couldn't stop him. I tried to grab him. But I couldn't catch him. Then I saw the blood. At first, just a trickle down the side of his head. Then more. And more. It just kept pooling on the floor. And he just lay there. He wouldn't move. He wouldn't move!" Nick fell back into a chair, shaking to near convulsions.

"He was dead, Marli! He was dead!"

"I don't understand!" Marli shook through her anguish and disbelief. "How can this be?! Why didn't you tell the police?"

"I didn't know what to do. I was afraid. I called Tammy. She told me to make it look like Franklin had fallen on his own, and I had just found him like that. Dead. She told me to look for a stepladder and place it by the Christmas tree like Franklin had fallen from it while hanging ornaments. So I did. I found a ladder in the closet. And placed it between Franklin and the tree. And then I called 911."

"Tammy told you to do all that?"

"Yes."

"And you . . . you and Tammy are lovers?"

"It started a long time ago. Long before Franklin died. But after Franklin's death, we were both so sick. So distraught. We stopped seeing each other. She hated me. I hated me! But you were so distant. So angry all the time. The grief was too much for me. That's when I started seeing Lisa. But that didn't last long after we returned home from Mexico. When you got that anonymous text message about Franklin's death, I knew it had to be Tammy. She was the only one who knew the truth. So I confronted her when she got back from Mexico. And we realized that we still loved each other. Neither one of us meant to hurt you. That's it, Marli. That's all of it."

This can't be happening. Nick killed Franklin. Nick loves Tammy. Tammy loves Nick!

Marli began to hyperventilate, her fast, abrupt breaths stripping her body of oxygen. Her head was spinning as she searched the room for a place to fall, for someone to catch her.

“Marli, are you alright?” Nick asked, coming from around his desk and reaching out to her. His eyes were wide and wet, his face flushed.

“I’m fine, I’m fine,” Marli managed to whisper, her arms outstretched, stopping Nick from coming closer. She backed away from him until her body hit the office wall, its cool, hard surface offering the support she needed to sink into the carpet and find her breath. “Please don’t come any closer.”

“Marli, please forgive me,” Nick said, his voice shaking.

“Forgive you for killing Franklin or screwing my best friend?”

“Both. Forgive me for both. I never meant to hurt you. All I’ve hurt is myself.”

“And our son!”

“I never meant to hurt Franklin. I live with my mistakes every minute of every day.”

Marli sat collapsed on the office floor, her legs pulled tight to her chest, and tried to grasp the scope of her world at that moment. She looked past Nick, hovering over her. She had to think rationally. She could not let her emotions, her heartache, her shock overwhelm her. Her marriage was over. Her best friend had betrayed her. Her mother was dead. Her son was dead.

How much more could she handle?

Then she thought of Ben and Puerto—and realized she could handle anything.

“Save it, Nick,” she said, pulling herself up off the floor and regaining her composure. “Listen carefully. This is what’s going to happen. I’m not an expert, but I know that providing false information to a police officer is a crime. And staging a fake death?! My bet is you would face a fairly hefty fine. Maybe even go to prison.”

Nick began to stutter, but Marli cut him off.

"But I am not going to call the police. It's over, it's behind us. I believe you when you say it was an accident. I know you loved Franklin. But in exchange for me not calling the police and telling them about your lies and coverup, you are going to relinquish all rights to our house and my retirement savings. You will not get a dime. And I don't care where you go or what you do, as long as you leave me alone."

She opened the office door and turned one last time to Nick.

"It's time for me to start thinking about myself—to start thinking about the rest of *my* life."

Time to start over with a better man—and a better dog—than Nick.

She closed the office door behind her.

Chapter Twenty-Six

"Ben! Ben, are you in there?" Marli shouted through the fly-specked window of Ben's veterinary clinic. She twisted the knob back and forth as she pushed on the stubborn front door that refused to open.

"Hola, señorita. Can I help you?" A hunched-over older man holding a straw broom approached Marli from the neighboring grocery and sundries market.

"Sí. Do you know where Dr. Rosado is?" Marli asked, wrapping her renegade curls into a tight ponytail with a stretchy hairband. "The door is locked."

"No, I'm sorry. I have not seen Dr. Rosado for several days. Is he all right?"

"I don't know. I hope so."

Marli's next stop was Ben's home in central Puerto Escondido, but again she was greeted with silence when she pounded on his front door.

"OK, Ben Rosado. Where are you and what have you done with my dog?" she asked out loud in frustration. The cab driver waited patiently at the curb, drumming his fingers on the steering wheel to the rhythm of a Mexican radio station.

"Can we just drive around?" Marli asked as she slid back into the taxicab.

"Sí. It is up to you. You just tell me when to stop."

"I will know it when I see it. It is a vacant lot. With a chain-link fence." Marli knew it was unlikely that Ben would be at the site of what he hoped would be his future animal shelter and spay clinic, but she had nowhere else to turn.

"OK, senorita. I hope we find what you are looking for."

The taxi rolled past one empty plot of land after another. Marli strained to remember something special about the address, anything that would help the cab driver find the weed-filled field and maybe, hopefully, Ben and Puerto.

"Do you want me to continue driving, senorita?" the agreeable cabbie said after about forty-five minutes of circling the paved streets.

"No. Can you take me to Hotel Santa Fe? That's where I'm staying."

Marli slumped back into the cracked vinyl seat and draped her bare arm out the passenger side window. The warm wind twisted up under her shirt sleeve. The ten-hour flight from San Jose to Oaxaca was catching up to her. She closed her eyes and let the humid breeze brush the loose strands of hair out of her face. Emotionally and physically exhausted, she could easily sleep the entire way to the hotel.

Without warning, a hard brake by the taxi driver forced Marli to jolt forward.

The cabbie shouted out his window at the driver of a speeding sedan as it shot through the stop sign.

"Wait!" Marli cried, spotting a rusty red Chevy truck in the parking lot out her window. "Where are we? What is this place?"

"This is the Agencia Municipal de Puerto Escondido. The local government office."

"Can you wait again, por favor?" Marli said as she exited the cab without giving the driver a chance to respond.

Marli negotiated several other vehicles radiating heat from the scorching asphalt as she approached the long, adobe-white, single-story building. A series of arches, each framed in bright-orange paint, fronted the structure. Ben exited through the swinging glass door, past a businessman in a crumpled gray suit, sweat seeping through the back of his jacket. Puerto and Escondido, waiting patiently on the walkway, wagged their long thin tails in unison at the sight of their human caretaker.

"Ben!" Marli called out.

"Marli?" Shock and surprise gripped Ben from within. "What are you doing here?"

Puerto sprang from the cement, his front two paws landing on Marli's thighs, almost knocking her to the ground. She kneeled down and embraced her dog, dropping to his level so she could adequately return the unrestrained affection.

"Someone needs a bath!" she laughed.

"So, you're back?" Ben asked.

"Yup. I'm back."

"Has it been thirty days? Are you back to get Puerto?"

"Today makes thirty, Ben. Thirty days exactly. But I'm not back to get Puerto. I'm back to stay."

The heat hovered over Puerto Escondido's central cemetery. Ben took Marli's hand and guided her through the quiet graveyard, passing the elegantly adorned, house-like crypts until they arrived at Lucy's. Puerto stayed close to Marli, never straying more than a few feet from her left or right, while Escondido trailed behind Ben.

Ben stopped when they came to a creamsicle-colored crypt. He kneeled in front of the altar and brushed away the dried leaves that always accumulated.

"This is beautiful," Marli said. "They're all so lovely . . . the decorations."

"Families offer gifts to help their loved ones in the afterlife," Ben said, replacing the faded, orange marigolds with fresh blossoms. He removed the lid to a tin of Mexican wedding cookies and placed the container by the entrance of the small home. "It's tradition. A nice way to remember. Candles light the way for the spirits. Photos are to remember and honor the deceased. People leave toys and sweets for children who have died. I bring marigolds and Mexican wedding cookies to honor Lucy. I don't really believe in all this stuff, but they were her favorites, and it can't hurt."

"It's good you have a place to come, to visit and talk to Lucy," Marli said. "One day, if you go back to San Jose with me, I'll take you to Franklin's grave."

"Lucy would have liked you," Ben said softly.

"I'm glad. I think Franklin would have liked you, too, a lot more than he liked his father."

"Let's sit." Ben escorted Marli to a nearby bench under the canopy of an evergreen Guayacán tree, its branches enveloped with purple-blue flowers providing an umbrella of much-needed shade.

"I missed you," Ben said. "I realize now that I should have called. I convinced myself that you just wanted a clean break. No hard goodbyes. And maybe you thought Puerto was better off here with me. But I was wrong."

Puerto circled three times in front of the bench and laid down with his head resting on Marli's feet. Escondido sniffed the ground before hopping onto the bench, forcing Ben to move closer to Marli to make room for the big mutt.

"I missed you, too. I missed Puerto," Marli said.

"I still can't believe Jenna erased all your messages, all your phone calls to me," Ben said. "But we don't have to worry about her any longer. She's out of my life now."

Puerto thumped his long, black tail against the short-trimmed grass as his greeting to a passing family on their way to a loved one's grave.

"Ben," Marli said, "being a mom was the most important thing in the world to me. That gave meaning to my life. But now, with Franklin gone, I want to do something more than picking out the right window coverings, which was basically my existence with Nick. I know I have my writing job. But it's not enough. Puerto changed my life. You changed my life. I want to help you do what you do best—help homeless animals."

Marli paused to organize the rest of her thoughts, to unfurl her words into something that made sense.

"Ben, do you want me here?" Marli asked. "I don't have to stay with you. I can get my own place. A place for me and Puerto. I'll get a job. My mom left me money, plus I will get the proceeds from the sale of my house after the divorce settlement. It will be enough to start your spay and neuter clinic. I want to do this—for you, for me. There is nothing left for me in California. I'm ready to begin a new life. And I would like it to be with you and Puerto. No pressure. No commitment. Just take it one day at a time. What do you think? If you think it's too soon—too soon for us, I will be on the next plane out of here."

Pushing away a stray wisp of hair from her face, Ben gently kissed her.

"How is that for an answer," he said.

Acknowledgments

This journey could not have happened without the support of my incredible husband, Mark Rakich. His encouragement and belief in my writing gave me the courage and momentum to turn almost 68,000 words into a story I have been wanting to tell for a lifetime.

Thank you to She Writes Press for giving me the thumbs up to move forward with my quest to be a novelist. My copy editor, Lorraine Fico-White, helped me move from journalist to novelist—shedding my long-engrained news writing styles and techniques to create a fiction book with no "head hopping." My project manager, Shannon Green, kept the production process flowing and me on track.

Thanks to Barrett Briske for her assistance securing permission to use the lyrics to "Have You Been to Jail for Justice?" sung by Peter, Paul and Mary, whose music stood for peace and equality. I had the pleasure of meeting Peter Yarrow in his lifelong quest for social justice. Not long before my publication date, Peter passed away. He and Mary Travers are dearly missed.

My dear friend, Manda Ness, always believed that I would one day publish. She has promised to accompany me on my book tour. I will hold her to that.

Many locations along the Mexican coast are important nesting sites for sea turtles. The National Mexican Turtle Center plays a crucial role in conservation through controlled nesting areas, specialized care and rehabilitation, and education to increase public awareness of the importance of protecting these magnificent animals. Please learn more at tortugasmazunte.org.

For the past fifteen years, my husband and I have rescued, fostered, and found loving families for nearly one hundred dogs and countless cats and kittens in our community. Our city, our state, and our country have a long way to go before we stop killing companion animals because our shelters are overcrowded and there are not enough homes. But the United States is a far cry from other countries where millions of stray dogs and cats fend for themselves, left on the streets to endure hunger, sickness, and injury until they die alone.

I acknowledge those animals—and hope for the day when kindness and compassion extend to all creatures.

Please spay and neuter.

About the Author

Cathryn Rakich has been a writer and editor for thirty-plus years, working in the news and nonprofit world. She currently writes a monthly column on animals and animal welfare for a local magazine and holds a bachelor's degree in journalism from Sacramento State University. In the thirty years she has volunteered for local animal rescue groups and shelters, she has fostered more than a hundred homeless pets. Cathryn lives in Sacramento, California, with her husband, four rescue dogs, and four rescue cats.

Looking for your next great read?

We can help!

Visit www.shewritespress.com/next-read
or scan the QR code below for a list
of our recommended titles.